THE
MOCKINGBIRDS

THE
MOCKINGBIRDS

Daisy Whitney

LB

LITTLE, BROWN AND COMPANY
New York · Boston

Little, Brown and Company

Hachette Book Group
237 Park Avenue, New York, NY 10017
Visit our website at www.lb-teens.com

Little, Brown and Company is a division of Hachette Book Group, Inc.
The Little, Brown name and logo are trademarks of Hachette Book Group, Inc.

First Edition: November 2010

The characters and events portrayed in this book are fictitious. Any similarity to real persons, living or dead, is coincidental and not intended by the author.

Library of Congress Cataloging-in-Publication Data
Whitney, Daisy.
   The Mockingbirds / Daisy Whitney. — 1st ed.
      p. cm.
   Summary: When Alex, a junior at an elite preparatory school, realizes that she may have been the victim of date rape, she confides in her roommates and sister, who convince her to seek help from a secret society, the Mockingbirds.
   ISBN 978-0-316-09053-7
   [1. Date rape—Fiction. 2. Secret societies—Fiction. 3. Justice—Fiction.
4. Boarding schools—Fiction. 5. Schools—Fiction. 6. Sisters—Fiction.] I. Title.
   PZ7.W6142Moc 2010   [Fic]—dc22   2009051257
10 9 8 7 6 5 4 3
RRD-C
Printed in the United States of America

For my husband, Jeff…
You have the wiliest mind,
the best sense of humor,
and my heart for always.
That, and you found the dog….

THE
MOCKINGBIRDS

Chapter One
FIRST TIME

Three things I know this second: I have morning breath, I'm naked, and I'm waking up next to a boy I don't know.

And there's a fourth thing now. It's ridiculously bright in my room. I drape my forearm over my eyes, blocking out the morning sun beating in through my windows, when it hits me—a fifth thing.

These are not my windows.

Which means this is not my bed.

My head pounds as I turn to look at this boy whose name I don't remember. He's still asleep, his chest moving up and down in time to an invisible metronome. I scan his features, his nose, his lips, searching for something, any-thing that rings a bell. A clue to connect me to him. But remembering last night is like looking through frosted glass. I see nothing. But I can hear one word, loud and clear.

Leave.

The word repeats in my head.

Leave.

It's beating louder, commanding me to get out of this bed, to get out of this room.

Get out. Get out. Get out.

My heart hammers and my head hurts and there's this taste in my mouth, this dry, parched taste, this heavy taste of a night I don't remember with...I squeeze my eyes shut. This can't be this hard. What's his name?

Remember, Goddamn it, remember.

Carver.

His name is Carver.

Deep breath. There, no need to panic, no need to be all crazy-dramatic. I've got his name. Another breath. The rest will come back to me. It will all make sense, so much sense I'll be laughing about it any second. I won't be able to *stop* laughing, because I'm sure there's some perfectly reasonable explanation.

As I look at the matted bedsheets twisting around this boy and me, snaking across his naked waist, curling around my exposed chest, a draft rushes through the room, bringing a fresh chill with it. That must be it. It's chilly...it's cold...it's January. Maybe it was snowing—we went sledding, I took a spill, changed out of my ice-cold clothes, and then crashed here in Carver's room.

No, it's *Carter.*

Definitely Carter.

I'm naked in bed with a boy and I can't even get his name right.

This boy, this bed, this room, me—we are like clumsy fingers on the piano, crashing across the wrong keys, and over the jarring music I hear that one word again.

Leave.

I slide closer to the edge of this too-small twin bed and dangle my naked feet until they touch the standard-issue Themis Academy carpeting—a Persian rug. His is crimson and tan with interlocking diamonds. I don't want to see a carpet like this again. Ever. I stand up slowly so the bed won't creak.

Then I grab my clothes from the floor, collecting underwear, jeans, tank top, purple sweater, pink socks, and black boots, all scattered on the diamonds of the carpet. I'm cold without them, freezing even, and I'd really like to cover up my breasts. I spot my bra in the indentation of a cheap red pleather beanbag. My adorable, cute, black-and-white polka-dot bra thrown carelessly onto the worst piece of furniture ever invented.

He threw my bra.

The room tilts, like I'm on one of those fun-house walkways, angling back and forth. Only it's not fun, because fun houses never are.

They're distorted.

I snatch my bra, pulling it close to me, and get dressed

quickly. As I yank up my socks, I notice a trash can teeming with Diet Coke cans. Carter doesn't even recycle? *Way to pick a winner, Alex.* Then I freeze, seeing something worse, far worse. Two condom wrappers on top of his garbage, each one ripped down the middle, each one empty.

I close my eyes. I must be seeing things. It's the morning, it's hazy, the sun is far too bright.

But when I open my eyes the wrappers are still here, Carter's still here, I'm still here. And nothing adds up the way I want it to. I zip up my boots in a flash, obeying the voice in my head shouting *Leave now!* Carter's still sleeping, his mouth hanging open unattractively. Small lines of white crust have formed on the corners of his lips. His blond hair is sticking up in all kinds of directions.

I step gingerly across the carpet, spying a small black bag near the closet door that looks as if it holds shaving lotion and stuff boys use. I don't want to open it and know what else is in there—tweezers? Do boys use tweezers? I don't want to know what they'd tweeze—but I hate the way my mouth tastes right now, because it tastes like last night. I grab my coat, then crouch down by the black bag and slowly undo the zipper, tooth by metal tooth. I hold my breath, look back at Carter. He shifts, flips to his other side.

Don't wake up. Don't wake up. Don't wake up.

I reach a hand into the bag, feel around for a tube of toothpaste. I pull it out, uncap it, squirt some onto my index finger. I scrub it across my teeth, erasing the sour taste, erasing the evidence, and drop the tube into the bag, the cap falling next to it. And at that moment Carter wakes up.

"Hey...," he says, not even groggily. He's just awake, plain and simple.

"Hey," I mumble. I don't usually mumble. No one is a mumbler at Themis Academy.

He rubs his chin with the palm of his hand.

A hand that touched me.

I wonder if I thought he was good-looking last night. In the morning he's not. He has white-blond hair, a sharp nose, pale eyes. Maybe he was funny is all I can think. Maybe he made me laugh. Maybe he's a riot and I laughed so hard my sides hurt. I place my right hand on my waist, hunting for the physical evidence.

He raises an eyebrow, almost winks at me. Something about the gesture reminds me of a politician. "So, did you have a good time last night?"

Let's see: I'm tiptoeing across your room, praying you won't wake up, can barely remember your name. Yeah, I had an epic night, just fantastic. Care to tell me what transpired between, say, midnight and, oh, ten minutes ago? Wait, don't bother. Let's just pretend this never happened and we'll never mention it again. Cool?

He leans back on the bed, rests his head on the pillow. "Want to go again?"

I narrow my eyes at him, crush my lips together, shake my head quickly. He thinks I'm easy.

"I have to study," I answer, taking a step backward toward the door.

"On a Saturday morning?"

Everyone at Themis studies on Saturdays, yes, even on Saturday mornings.

I nod. Another step.

"But term just started two days ago."

"Crazy teachers giving out homework already," I say, managing two steps this time. *What, you don't have homework yet? Are you in the slow track?* I want to say.

But he's not in the slow track. There is no slow track here. I wonder if Carter is in any of my classes.... Then I do the math. A junior class of two hundred, the odds are this won't be the last I see of him.

If I were a conductor, I would wave the baton and make all this vanish.

"Know what you mean," he says. "Spanish teacher assigned some massive essay already. I haven't started it yet."

That's one class where I'll be spared. I take French. *Dieu merci.*

"I gotta go."

"Okay, well, I'll call you," he says, making some sort of stupid phone-to-the-head gesture. Then he practically jumps out of bed. I jerk my head away because he's still naked and I don't want to know what he looks like naked. Out of the corner of my eye, I notice him reach for his boxers. He pulls them on as I wrap my palm around the doorknob, gripping it tightly.

I desperately want to leave, but I need to know for sure. "So, uh, I have to ask." I stop, barely able to choke out the words. "Did we...?" I can't bring myself to say them.

He smiles, looking as if he would beat his chest with his fists if he were maybe one species less evolved.

"Yeah, twice. After we saw the band. It was great." He looks triumphant.

But I feel like I just tasted tinfoil by mistake, the awful accidental taste that makes you want to spit it out. I pull the door open and do the one thing I should have done last night.

Leave.

Because you're supposed to remember your first time.

Chapter Two
MAKE-BELIEVE

There's this trick I have on the piano. When I reach a section of music that totally trips up my fingers and mangles my confidence, I call on the experts. I put the score away, close my eyes, and imagine I'm in Carnegie Hall. There's no audience, I'm not even onstage. I'm sitting in the first row next to Beethoven, Mozart, and Gershwin. It's just the four of us. I tell them the problem. Then I wait patiently for their guidance. They've never failed me before.

As I slip out the back stairwell, I present them with today's quandary, only this one is of the nonmusical variety. *What we have, gentlemen, is a girl who can't remember her first time. What we also have is a boy who says he had sex with her twice.*

Please piece together what happened in a way that makes sense to the girl.

I listen in silence as they ponder, waiting for their answer.

But today they say nothing.

It figures—they're men, after all. Besides, Beethoven's deaf anyway.

It's up to me to piece this together and I know nothing.

Nothing. I turn the word over a few times. *Nothing.*

Maybe *nothing* happened. Maybe it was all just an honest mistake, just a misunderstanding. Yes, that's what my composers meant to say. They meant to tell me Carter messed up when he said we did it. Carter goofed. Carter's the one who can't remember jack.

I walk faster across the eerily quiet maintenance lot, arms wrapped tightly around me, and say my new mantra—*nothing happened*—as I scan the grounds. I'm ready to dash behind a bush if I have to, dive into a foxhole, because my mission now is to return unseen. I'll go the long way: cross the maintenance lot, pass the track field, then cut onto the quad as if I were *leaving* my dorm, not returning to it. I will not be caught. I will not have anyone think I'm doing the walk of shame. Besides, I *can't* be doing the walk of shame, because *nothing happened.*

The more I repeat it, the more I'll believe it.

Nothing happened, I say as I pass the Dumpsters, then the shed.

I reach the edge of the track field next and see the first trap—a flock of girls running laps, clad only in skintight Lycra leggings and body-hugging jackets, carving out endless circles.

Their backs are to me for now, so I shift gears to power-walk—actual running would draw too much attention. I can't tell who's who from here, but I'm betting fellow juniors Anna Marie, Shoba, Caroline, and Natalie are out there. If I can traverse this back path around the field before they turn the corner, they won't see me.

Of course, they *are* runners and I'm merely a musician, so they're curving around the track before I'm even halfway along the edge of the field. I pull my coat collar up, cast my eyes down, and stuff my hands into my pockets, where I find sunglasses. I cover my eyes with them and now I'm just some press-shy teenage celebrity trying to avoid the paparazzi.

The track girls are focused, feet smacking the dirt, arms hinging in perfect synchronicity at their sides. Then one of them breaks away, bursting ahead like a Thoroughbred on the final turn. I'm almost at the edge of the field, ready to make a break for the quad, when I realize it's Natalie, shooting out like an Olympic sprinter.

Natalie, who's built like Serena Williams. Natalie, who slaughters track records in the spring, who smashes lacrosse sticks in the fall, who could crush me with her thigh muscle alone, even though I'm no pip-squeak. I'm five-seven. But she's over six feet and, really, what would I defend myself with? My long, slender fingers?

Her legs are a blur. She'll spot me any second and my plan will be shot. Kinda like my reputation. She'll see me, throw her head back, and grin cruelly because she'll have a tasty piece of gossip. She'll tell her friends and they'll all blab about me in the caf when they go eat their whole-wheat pasta and bananas and broccoli. And she'll tell her boyfriend, that senior Kevin Ward.

Because there's nothing better to talk about than who's into whom, who's doing whom, and who screwed whom. And in my case, all the circumstantial evidence—the time of day, my messy hair, my day-old clothes—screams that I'm someone worth talking about.

But I'm not. I swear I'm not. I picture banging my fist fiercely against a table before a judge, a jury of my fellow students, insisting nothing happened, insisting I wasn't even with Carter last night. I briefly consider the possibilities of playing possum, just dropping down into a ball, lying completely still on the cold ground. But then I come up with a better plan, a perfect plan. Forget the *nothing happened* one. Because I'll tell a new story; I'll reinvent last night.

Where was I last night? Funny you should ask. When I went backstage to meet the band—yes, they invited me backstage because they heard I rule the keys—we hung out, chilled to some music, then jammed together, me on keyboards all night long. I just left the club now. I know, wild times. But good clean fun.

Now that's a tale worth spreading. I should start the rumor myself.

"Hey, Alex!" Natalie's voice calls out. "Nice clothes from last night."

There's no jamming with the band, no all-night music, just me in my boots and bedhead, and the whole girls' track team now knows I didn't sleep in my room last night.

I want to yell back, "You know nothing!"

But she obviously knows something. She was there. At the club.

And I'm the one who knows nothing. I'm the one who has nothing to say as I watch my quiet prep school existence seep out the door like an overflowing sink, the water trickling out, slowly creeping up on everything in its path, ruining books, furniture, rugs, and last of all my privacy, my little corner of the world here as the piano girl.

Water damage is the worst, they say.

Natalie streaks on by, ahead of the pack. Her teammates are focused on catching her. They don't see me as I finally slip away from the field. But they'll know soon enough; that's how it goes with sports teams.

Sports.

I remember now—Carter plays something. He'd had practice for something last night before I met him. He mentioned this. I wonder if I tuned it out because my brain did its best impression of a sieve or because I detest sports. The great thing about Themis Academy is it's not one of those you-must-do-sports-or-else schools. You're not even required to play an organized sport.

I reach the main campus and survey the sprawling quad.

It's deserted. The lawn, cracked and hard now, but lush and green in the spring, is peppered with trees and framed by old buildings—classrooms, dorms, and the cafeteria too, a building built in 1912. Themis was founded a year later by members of the Progressive Party, ironic because Themis is hands-off in the only way that matters.

The school looks like a mini college campus, with old brick structures, Victorian buildings, and Colonial-style mansions converted into halls of learning. Even McGregor Hall's redbrick façade is laced with ivy that curls around the edges of the white windowpanes.

In front of McGregor Hall is a big bulletin board with flyers. I glance at them as I walk by. Casting call for *The Merry Wives of Windsor* (to be performed in front of the Faculty Club in a patented Themis special performance for teachers). Tryout for Coed Crew. But of course . . . everything is equal here. Then a notice for the Vegetarian Dinner Club, complete with cheese and crackers and carrots every night.

I see one more.

Join the Mockingbirds! Stand up, sing out! We're scouting new singers, so run, run, run on your way to our New Nine, where you can learn a simple trick . . .

Then there's a drawing of a bird on the corner, his watchful eye staring back at me.

It's code—all code—because the Mockingbirds aren't an a cappella singing group, as they pretend to be. And they most definitely are *not* having auditions for singers. No, the Mockingbirds are something much bigger and much quieter too, and it's tryout time for them, as it is at the start of every term.

The Mockingbirds are the law.

I leave the bulletin board in my wake and walk briskly to my nearby dorm, Taft-Hay Hall, a redbrick building three stories tall. I make a beeline for the arched doorway, but there's Mr. Christie, my history teacher and advisor, striding across the quad, looking as purposeful as I do. He has this crazy long-legged step, chin up, chest out, his reddish beard and mustache almost leading the way.

"Good morning, Alex. How are you?" he says, his voice deep.

"I'm fine, Mr. Christie," I say as he nears me.

"You're up early on a Saturday."

"Yeah, I think I'm developing insomnia," I say, trying the ruse on for size. There's got to be one lie I can tell that'll fool someone. "I've been up for hours," I add when he nods sympathetically.

He looks at me, all concerned. As if he knows the cure for insomnia. Like he's a trained insomnia exorcist and he can tell me just what to do.

"A cup of chamomile tea before bed might do just the trick," he says.

Right. That'll fix everything, and while we're at it, do you have anything that'll help me remember losing it with a guy I don't even know?

"I'll be sure to try that next time," I say, sounding all chipper and cheery.

He's pleased, like he just did his good deed for the day and helped a student in need, and he can now go on his merry way.

I should be glad Mr. Christie didn't notice, didn't put two and two together, didn't ask any more probing questions. Or maybe he'd already heard the story that I was up all night jamming with the band. It's a cool story, he thinks, and I am his advisee, so he doesn't report me.

Then I laugh silently to myself as I pound up the stairs into Taft-Hay Hall, my boots clicking on the stone steps. Because of course he believed me. The teachers, the headmistress, all the freaking administration, they never think we're up to anything. They think we never skirt the rules here at perfect, progressive, prestigious Themis Academy.

We're above the law, that's why we came here.

Right...

Chapter Three
AN EDUCATED GUESS

I don't go to my room. I go downstairs to the basement. At the bottom of the stairs there's a bin for lost-and-found, an enormous mound of hats, scarves, watches. Nothing ever gets found here. No one wants the stuff that's been lost. But I need to see the bin right now bacause it reminds me of a night I *can* remember.

One night last year I dared my boyfriend at the time, Daniel, to try to assemble a whole outfit from the lost-and-found bin. He rose to the challenge, digging all the way to the bottom of the bin, where he found a pair of red plaid pants likely from the seventies. Then he unearthed a canary-yellow cardigan, a mismatched pair of Dr. Martens—one black, one green, two sizes apart—and a tattered baby blue mesh cap that was trendy once upon a time.

"No wonder that's here," I said. Then he pulled me close and kissed me. It wasn't our first kiss. We'd been together for three months then. But it was memorable—one of those kisses you couldn't stop if you tried. I wanted to kiss him all night long.

So I run an experiment. I close my eyes and swap out the leading man. Daniel's dark blond hair becomes Carter's pale, almost white hair. Daniel's shoulders turn into Carter's. Daniel's lips, his cheeks, his hands, they all belong to Carter now. And I'm kissing Carter like I kissed Daniel. I squeeze my eyes shut tighter, forcing Carter to fit, forcing this kiss to become Carter's. But the puzzle pieces won't fit. I don't remember kissing Carter like this. I don't remember pulling him close to me, wanting it, wanting him.

But even though I was crazy about Daniel—he was the cellist here, and the way he held that instrument between his knees, the way he played it like he was caressing it, would make any self-respecting piano girl go weak in the knees—I didn't sleep with him. We didn't go all the way that night at the lost-and-found bin. We didn't any of the times we hung out in the summer.

We came close, very close, several times. Something always held me back, though. Daniel and I were connected in so many ways, two musicians after all. But except for the night in someone else's plaid pants and yellow sweater, he always took himself a bit too seriously. And the thing that really gets me, that makes my stomach turn in all sorts of good knots, is someone who can make me laugh.

17

All I can figure is Carter must have been really fucking funny.

Then I flash on something: a fuzzy muted memory of laughing with someone else back at the club, well before I wound up in Carter's room. Last night a whole group of us went to see Artful Rage, my absolute favorite band. They were playing in town, and juniors finally get Friday Night Out privileges the second half of the school year. My roommate's boyfriend, Sandeep, smuggled vodka into the club. I remember having a drink or two and then...

Maybe I met Carter there, maybe Sandeep introduced us. Or maybe Daniel's a dick for going away to college two years before me. He's at Dartmouth now, and we didn't even pretend to do the whole I'll-still-see-you-on-weekends thing because the last thing a college guy wants is a high school girlfriend tagging along. But if he were here, I would have been with him last night and not Carter.

I open my eyes and glare at the lost-and-found bin for a minute. I have this sudden, intense desire to topple it, to spill all these unclaimed, unwanted clothes in a huge messy pile. I put my hands on the edge and push, but it probably weighs more than a hundred pounds so I can't flip it over. I grab a handful of scarves and shirts and toss them on the floor, leaving a red scarf on top of the pile, like litter.

I head upstairs to my room.

T.S. is wide awake when I unlock the door. She's brushing her short blond hair, sitting on the edge of her already-made bed. She's dressed in her soccer uniform. I notice

Maia's bed; it's made too and her bathroom stuff is gone. She must be in the shower.

Then there's my bed and it's also made.

Only difference is I never unmade it last night.

I hate my made bed right now. I wish the comforter were tangled up in the sheets, wish it were proof I'd slept *here* all night long, like both my roommates did.

I brace myself for the inevitable inquisition from T.S., but instead a devilish smile fills her face. "Look what the cat dragged in!" she says.

I bet she'd been bubbling over, just waiting to use her cat-dragged-in line, and that's distracting her from asking other questions, like *Why are you coming home at seven thirty in the morning when you've never done that before and tell me everything, absolutely everything?!*

But the mere thought of cradling my pillow, tucking my feet under me, and sharing with my best friend every single detail of my first time makes me queasy. *Oh my God! Can you believe it? I had sex for the first time, with a guy I don't even know! And I don't remember it! Wow!*

After holding out on Daniel for six months, I threw it all away on a guy I met one random night. There must be something seriously wrong with me, like a defective computer where the hard drive crashes. This unit no longer works properly, sir. Please repair it and make it normal again.

I lie down on my bed with a pink-, orange-, and purple-patterned bedspread and place my hands beneath my head,

19

pulling my messy brown hair, badly in need of a brushing, into a mock ponytail. There's silence for a minute and I picture a tennis ball sputtering away, rolling to a standstill at the edge of the court.

"So...," T.S. says, raising an eyebrow. "Did you have a good time last night? I heard you had a blast after you started Circle of Death."

When she says those words, a memory races up.

"Nine of Diamonds!" Carter shouts, then brandishes the playing card for the group to see. There's a bunch of us crowded around a coffee table. "Rhyme time!" He strokes his chin, as if in deep contemplation. "Coral, C-O-R-A-L."

Then voices chime in. "Oral." "Floral." "Laurel." "Moral." "Quarrel."

"Damn," I say loudly. "That was my word."

Carter leans in close. "Guess you'll need another rhyme."

I look at the ceiling for a second, thinking, trying to pull another word into my brain. "I got it! Choral! Like Beethoven's Ninth Symphony, the Choral *Symphony?"*

"Nice try," Carter says. He gives me a look, kind of sweet, almost a wink there too. "But I don't think homonyms count in Circle of Death, and coral was my word."

I slam my palm on the table.

"Drink, drink, drink, drink," they all say in unison.

Sandeep takes his cue and fills my red tumbler with orange juice and a splash of vodka.

I take it, drink it down in one gulp — I am tough, I am

cool, I am invincible. Vodka doesn't burn my throat, I'm not even drunk, I'm totally sober. I'm back from winter break, we finally have Friday Night Out privileges, I just saw Artful Rage rock out in their live awesomeness tonight, and I am still on a mad music high. So I lean closer to Carter, my leg brushing up against his, my thigh near his thigh.

"The Ninth Symphony is my favorite piece of music ever written. I love Beethoven," I say to Carter. Or maybe it's a slur. "He's my boyfriend." Then I laugh, like a drunk person.

A thin coat of slime, muck covers me. I *flirted* with him. I came on to him. I wanted this to happen.

"Are you okay?" T.S. asks. "You just kind of spaced out there for a second."

"I'm fine," I say quickly, then ask, "you weren't there for Circle of Death?"

"I left after the concert. I had to work on my blog and get to bed by ten thirty," T.S. says. "Don't you remember?" she adds quizzically.

"That you're religious about going to bed early when you have practice with the Williamson girls' team? Yeah, that's been etched on my brain since freshman year."

"The Williamson *women's* team," she corrects, because evidently the second you graduate from high school and move on to college you're deemed a woman, no longer a girl. Anyway, the Themis *girls'* soccer team practices with the nearby Williamson *women's* team every other Saturday in the winter to help each team keep up their skills in the off-season. "But what I meant was, don't you remember starting the game?"

I ignore her question. "So, where did we play the game, oh-roommate-who-knows-all?"

"Sandeep told me you started the game in the common room over at his dorm."

Even though Sandeep is T.S.'s boyfriend, she doesn't use that word. She calls him her "relevant other." He calls her his "lady friend." They think their nicknames are cute and countercultural. Not surprising for someone who refuses to use, let alone acknowledge, her full name. She tells people *T.S.* stands for *Thalia Svetlana* because it sounds so ridiculous. She's been saying this ever since our freshman year, when we were first paired up as roommates. She says it seriously too, so everyone believes her and instantly gets why she'd go by *T.S.* instead.

"Hmm…"

"Hmm, what?" she asks. She stops stretching and sits down next to me, her regular routine suddenly taking a backseat.

"Hmm, nothing."

"So what happened with Carter?"

I sit up straight, ramrod straight. "You *know* him?"

"I don't know him. But he plays water polo."

Water polo boys are cocky assholes. Slick, showy, insincere, bred to be bankers. They're like junior frat boys.

"He's a wing," she adds. I give her a blank look. "That's the position he plays."

"Right. How could I forget how you know the roster for every single Themis sport?"

"It's one of my many adorable talents. Anyway, Sandeep said you went back to his room. That's where you were last night, right? In his room, fooling around?"

She assumes that's all I did. She knows me, knows I never slept with Daniel, knows I would never sleep with someone I just met. She figures Carter and I just made out.

I wish we just made out.

Nothing happened, my brain says quietly. But my head roars, protesting my game of make-believe again. I can feel this vein on my forehead pulsing harder now, practically popping out. I hate that vein. It's so ugly and it's so prominent when I get excited or riled up about something. I sometimes even notice it in photographs. I lie back down on the bed, press my fingers hard against my forehead, trying to forcibly push the headache out. I never get headaches, but now there's a jackhammer on my skull.

"That's where you were last night, right?" she repeats. "That's what Sandeep told me after you left." She says it like a statement, but it's more of a question. She's waiting for the answer, her green eyes boring a hole into me.

"Alex..." Her voice is low this time, nervous.

"Yes, I was there last night."

I was there with Carter and those two condoms. The proof. The evidence that doesn't lie. Carter used two condoms last night and thought it was great. He used two condoms with me last night. *With me.* There is no pretending, there is no *nothing happened.* We didn't just make out. We did *it* and I can't undo it. I can't even block it out because I've been tagged now by Natalie, marked for the rumor mill.

I should have just slept with Daniel. Then at least my first time would have mattered.

"You had me worried. I was picturing you wandering the streets or something."

Wandering the streets would have been wholly preferable. Hell, being homeless would be better right now. I can see myself sitting cross-legged on a sidewalk, hunched over beneath an awning, my psychedelic comforter wrapped around my shoulders. Passersby toss me dimes, nickels, sometimes a quarter. It's a rough life, but at least no one knows me.

"So do you like him? I saw you guys chatting at the concert, but then I left."

"What did you blog about last night?" I ask, changing the subject as I fix my eyes on the exposed brick wall in front of me. The other three walls are cream-colored, conducive to studying, Themis says. I glance down at our carpet. It's thicker than Carter's and has a floral pattern in peach and beige. I take some small comfort in this.

She shakes her head. "Nope. I want to know if you like him. Are you going to see him again? Are you going to go out with him?"

I picture Carter's crusty white mouth, his sharp nose. I picture my simulated kiss downstairs by the lost-and-found bin. My stomach twists. "No."

"Why not?" she asks.

I say nothing.

"What, did he smell or something?" she presses on.

I shake my head. "I just don't want to see him again."

"That's a bummer," she says. "You didn't have a good time with him?"

"I have *no idea* what kind of time I had with him."

I didn't mean to say that out loud. I don't want her to know I was so drunk, or so stupid, or so out of it, or so something that I can't remember. T.S. doesn't get smashed, she doesn't lose control. She sets rules for herself, then adheres to them. It's the athlete in her. She's rigorous and disciplined about everything. I'm only regimented about music.

"No idea?" T.S. asks. She pulls away from me a bit, making room for what I just said.

"No idea," she repeats. "What do you mean *no idea*?"

I shrug.

"Are you saying you don't remember?" she asks.

I flip over on my belly; the right side of my face is against my pillow. Immediately, her hand is on my shoulder. T.S. tries to right me, but I resist, staying facedown.

"Do you remember any of it?" she asks.

"Not really," I say, muffled into the bed.

"Alex, not remembering a night with someone isn't good."

More silence.

"You kissed him, right? You made out with him, but

that's all, right?" T.S. asks anxiously, like she's leading the witness, like she wants me to say *yes*.

Yes, I'm dying to say. *Yes,* that's all.

But I can't say that, so I shrug faintly.

"Look at me," she commands.

I place the pillow over my head this time, my face now pressed into the bedspread. T.S. won't stop though. She tugs at the pillow. I'm no match for her. She's strong, so she pries it off me.

"Alex, you're not three. Cut the crap and look at me."

I turn back over, facing her. Something in her voice reminds me of the time I learned her real name last semester. It was a Saturday morning in October and she had woken me up. "I'm late," she whispered. "How late?" I asked. "I was supposed to get my period yesterday. I'm totally freaking out because I was stupid. We did it without a condom once. Just once," she said. Her shoulders were shaking and she twisted a strand of her hair tighter and tighter. "I'll go get you a test," I said. I didn't have any weekend points then to go off-campus, but I didn't care. I ran to the nearest drugstore a mile away, bought her a test, and held her hand when she peed on the stick. She covered her eyes and made me look at it first. "Negative!" I told her. Then she said, "My name's not Thalia Svetlana. It's Tammy Stacy, but don't ever call me that."

I never have.

"Did you have sex with him?" she asks again.

I picture the condom wrappers.

"Yes."

"Wow, you had sex for the first time," she says, nodding slowly.

I say nothing.

"And you don't remember it," she states heavily.

"Evidently not."

"That's...," she begins, and then her voice trails off.

"That's what?" I ask.

"That's" — she tries again — "odd." Then she shakes her head.

"Odd?"

She doesn't answer. She just looks at her watch. "You know," she begins, going for a kind of casual tone, "our game doesn't start until ten thirty. Why don't we see if Casey wants to come visit?"

Casey is my sister. She's a junior at Williamson so we were never at Themis at the same time. She was a big-time soccer star when she was here, and now she's a big-time soccer star at Williamson, so she and T.S. know each other pretty well. The weird thing is Casey took a few years off from playing, stopped right in the middle of the season in her senior year at Themis. Maybe she got bored with it for a spell, but she started soccer again, came roaring back last semester at Williamson, better than ever.

Now T.S. sees my sister way more than I do during the school year. They discuss plays and strategies, since T.S. will be captain of the team next year. She wants to take Themis to nationals and then land a soccer scholarship for

college, even though she doesn't need one. (If football players can get a free ride, she damn well wants one too.)

"Casey," she says quietly into the phone. "Can you come
over?"

I could be wrong, but I don't think T.S. is calling Casey
right now for the secret to landing the game-scoring goal
each time she hits the field.

Chapter Four
BLACKOUT

"We never just hang out with Casey before your games," I say as T.S. pulls on sweatpants over her soccer shorts.

"Change your clothes," she instructs, reaching for a pullover fleece next. "You can't go out in the same clothes you wore last night."

"Why are we going out? I thought Casey was coming here."

"She is. But we're not meeting here. We're meeting in the Captains' Room."

"What the hell is the Captains' Room?"

She gives me a look like I'm stupid. "In the athletic complex. For team captains. She still has her captain's key."

"From four years ago?"

"When you get a captain's key, you keep it for life."

"Where's your key, since you're captain next year?"

"I get it in a ceremony at the end of the year."

"Of course. Anyway, why don't we just meet here?"

"Captains' Room is quiet. Plus it's reserved for soccer right now, so no one else can use it."

"But she's not the Themis soccer captain."

"She *was* a captain. She supersedes current captains if she wants use of the Captains' Room."

"Yet another thing about jocks that makes no sense," I say as I toss last night's tainted wardrobe into my laundry bag and pull on my robe. "I'm going to shower first," I say, and walk to the bathroom.

I turn the water all the way up, hotter than usual. The near-boiling water stings my skin, but I don't step away. I stand under the showerhead, close my eyes, and picture the reddish-pink splotches that must be forming on my skin. I lift my face to the hot stream, letting the water pelt my face. Then I turn around, feeling the burn of the heat on my hair, my back, my legs. Several rounds of shampoo and soap later, I am done and I am red.

I return to our room, pull on fresh clothes, and administer the fastest blow-dry I can manage as T.S. fidgets, eager to be on our way. I twist my mostly dry hair in a ponytail and pull on a cap. One look in the mirror tells me I resemble something close to a lobster, but that's far better than the way I looked before.

"C'mon. Let's go before the hallways get crowded and everyone wants to chat," she says.

"I really don't want to run into Carter. He could be at the athletic complex."

"There's no water polo practice today."

"So? He could be like you, practicing on off days."

"One, if he were like me, I'd know him better. Two, the pool is in a separate building, so let's go," she says, opening the door.

"I don't want to see Natalie. She was at the track field earlier. She saw me walking back to my room and obviously knows something is up. She was all snarky and *nice clothes, Alex.*"

"Natalie Moretti?" T.S. scoffs, shutting the door behind us.

"Yeah, the Amazon."

"She's just a track girl. So what?"

"You disparage other female athletes now?" I ask as we head down the back stairwell, though T.S. sometimes does. She has her own caste system for all the athletes, all the teams. Don't get her started on it; she can go on all day and night.

"Well, track is just sheer speed. Soccer, that takes speed and skill and finesse."

Like I said...

"Speaking of soccer," I begin, "let's get back to why we're meeting my sister. Why did you call her? Why is she coming? Why are we meeting in secret?"

"We're not meeting in secret," T.S. insists as she pushes open the back door and a blast of cold air hits us.

"I would have to say meeting in the Captains' Room is pretty secretive. What's the deal, T.S.?" I'm half-tempted to use her real name, but a promise is a promise.

"There's no deal," she says crisply.

"Then why is this so urgent?"

"Let's talk about other stuff right now," T.S. says as we walk across the quad to the gymnasium. "Like our spring project. I think I know what I'm going to do mine on."

I relent, knowing I've lost this battle. "What are you going to do yours on?" I ask as we pass McGregor Hall.

"Stereotypes. I did a blog post on it. I even talked to Casey about it last night."

"About your blog?"

"About doing my spring project on stereotypes. Whether there is any truth to them. When we can lean on them, when we can't."

"And your conclusion?"

"I think they're based on something. They start with something that maybe is a kernel of truth or was a kernel of truth at some point. Then they take on lives of their own."

I picture a stereotype rising up out of bed, stretching its arms, arching its back, becoming bigger than itself, like a growth, a wart.

"Like your stereotypes about track girls. So what does Casey think? Is there something to them?" I ask as my hands grow colder and I push them into my pockets, wishing I'd brought gloves.

T.S. shakes her head. "Nope, she says stereotypes are wrong. She says they lead to irreparable harm. I say they are based in truth and we need to understand the truth, but sometimes break through them. So I choose to *respectfully* disagree with Casey."

"Aren't we all just so polite," I remark.

"What are you going to do yours on?" she asks me, as if she doesn't already know.

"You know! We've talked about it before."

"I was teasing. I know you've been planning it since you started freshman year," T.S. says.

She's right. I have been planning to do my project on Beethoven's Ninth Symphony, the love of my freaking life. "Ode to Joy," the most famous part from the fourth movement, is the first piece of music I ever learned to play. That music is a part of me and I'm sure I would die without it. I would play it on an accordion, on a cheap little recorder, if those were the only options. I would whistle it if all instruments on earth were smashed.

The great irony is Beethoven slapped all pianists in the face with the Ninth Symphony. There's not even a part for the piano in it. Trumpets, oboes, they get their glory days in the greatest symphony ever written, but not piano. But then along came the Hungarian composer Franz Liszt, who transcribed Beethoven's work for piano. I have a crush on Franz Liszt for that alone. So naturally I'll do my spring project on the Ninth Symphony. But as we near the gymnasium, I feel something like dirt in my mouth thinking of the notes in "Ode to Joy." Because suddenly the song, *my song*, reminds me of Carter. I can hear it playing in his room.

"You like this song, don't you?"

"Hmm...?" I ask sleepily.

"You said earlier it's your favorite piece of music ever written. I have it on my iPod—you know, from the Die Hard *sound track. I want to play it for you."*

I don't say anything, just lean against the wall, then I'm sinking down. I hear it, the first note, E.

I can taste more dirt now, picturing his Al Green moves, his pickup-artist tricks, trying to get laid using my German composer. And it worked. I guess I'm that easy. One snippet of Beethoven and I'm spread out on a bed for the first time. Thanks, Ludwig. You're a pal.

T.S. pulls open the door to the athletic complex and I lower my head, not wanting to see Natalie or any of the other track girls.

"You're with me," T.S. says calmly. "Don't worry about Natalie or anyone."

"What, am I your bitch or something? They don't touch another jock's property?" I ask as a girl with socks up to her knees ducks into the nearby locker room.

"Athletes' code," T.S. says with a wink. "Besides, she knows I could kick her ass."

"Yeah right."

We walk down a long hallway past coaches' offices and supply closets and metal shelves of basketballs. At the end is a door bearing what looks like a coat of arms—a navy blue shield, in the middle an illustration of a ball and a unisex face looking proudly in the distance. I shake my head, bemused at such a display. The endowment for the athletic department must be pretty sizable. There's a crisp sheet of paper taped under the shield with today's schedule for the room with times and teams marked off.

T.S. raps twice, then says, "Forward.here."

The door opens, as if by magic, but on the other side is my sister.

Casey looks just like me. There's no mistaking we're sisters. We could almost be twins. She has brown hair like me, straight, but not silky straight, more like thick-hair straight. The kind you can twist around and pin up in a pile on your head. Her brown eyes are just regular brown, not chocolate, not caramel, not coffee-colored—just brown, like mine. She's in her soccer clothes, but as usual she blow-dried her hair this morning for a half hour and looks as if she just stepped out of a salon.

"Hey, Alex. How are you doing?" she says to me, putting a hand on my back and leading me into the lair of the captains emeriti.

I shrug off her hand. "I'd be better without the cloak and dagger," I say, looking around. The room is tiny, the size of a small office. But there are three chairs, a coffee machine, several mugs, a sink, a microwave, a half-pint fridge, a basket with shiny red apples, a tray with tea bags, and a series of cubbies along one wall, containing cleats, composition books, uniforms, and changes of clothes. The walls are covered in plaques, awards, framed photos of teams.

"Besides," I add pointedly, "why would I not be okay?"

Casey doesn't answer. She crosses three feet or so to a high-backed leather chair. She doesn't sit down, just rests her hand on the back of the chair. T.S. stands too, as if she's waiting for a sign. I bet it's some other part of the captains' code. Do not sit until the captain sits. But I don't need an invitation. I can pick my own chair in the captains' inner sanctum, so I plop down in the chair next to Casey, pulling it a few inches away from hers, giving myself some distance.

"You think we can get some coffee here, or are these cups just for show?" I ask.

"We don't have a Frappuccino maker," Casey says playfully. "I'll make you tea."

"Just something strong, please," I say.

Casey turns on the faucet, fills three mugs with water, and hands them to T.S., who puts them in the microwave. When the tea's ready T.S. hands me mine first, then squeezes my shoulder gently. I don't want to be touched, so I shirk away.

T.S. gives Casey a knowing look, like that's how they expected me to react. Casey takes a sip of her tea, then sets her mug down on a small round end table.

"So what happened last night?" she asks, in the same tone she'd use to inquire if there was any ice cream left in the freezer.

"What happened?" I repeat.

She tries again. "Yeah, what happened last night?"

"Why are you asking me?"

"I'm your sister."

"And that has something to do with last night how?"

"It's cool. We can talk about something else. Did you see that girl in the hall with the knee sock? Total fashion faux—"

I cut her off. "Why are you two acting like this, like you have some weird secret you won't even talk to me about?" It feels as if ants are all over me and I scratch my calf, like they're crawling up it.

"There's no secret," Casey says.

I fold my arms against my chest.

Casey takes another drink, T.S. follows suit, and all three of us remain quiet. Then Casey makes her move.

"So, what was the deal with that guy?" she asks.

"That's why I'm here? To tell you both about my first time?" I look to T.S. and kind of want to spit at her right now. "Thanks, T.S. I really appreciate you dragging me to the *Captains' Room* for this. Next time why don't you just take me to the caf so we can do it in front of the whole school? Everyone's going to know soon enough anyway."

"Alex, it's not like that," T.S. says.

I hold up a hand, my palm to her, and shake my head as I stand, move to the sink, and put my mug down next to it. I don't look at them, just place my hands on the edge of the slim counter, grabbing it, pressing hard with my fingers, sending all the tension, all the bubbling anger in my body into my hands. I could break this counter, I imagine, split it in two and watch it splinter under my hands. When I turn around, something inside me snaps.

"You want to know what happened? You guys really want to know? Fine. I'll tell you. Here's what happened. I met a guy, I had some drinks"—I direct this at T.S.—"that your *boyfriend* supplied. And then I had sex. Twice, evidently. So it was a stupid hookup. So I'm a slut. So what? Have I embarrassed you? Have I left some taint on your Captains' Room?"

I stare hard at Casey now, who has conducted her fair share of experimentation in college. She has dated short guys, tall guys, chubby guys, jocks, nerds, blacks, Asians, Republicans, actors, even a couple of bisexuals, not to mention a girl here and there. "You've hooked up way more times than I have," I continue, pointing a finger at her. I know all about her conquests. She'd told me the good, bad, and ugly during our summers in New Haven when we sat outside on coffee shop benches, drank our frothy concoctions, and played catch-up. "You've had sex with more people than I could count. So I don't know why you're acting as if it's a big deal, like we have to sit down and have tea and whisper and pet my head like I'm a freaking wounded bird you found on the side of the road."

I reach roughly for my mug, take a deep pull, like it's whiskey in a flask, and then I bang my mug down. "I'm going," I declare.

Casey stands up, places her hand on the countertop near

me, her right palm flat on the Formica. It's some kind of therapist gesture, and I can't stand it. I back away, against the wall, feeling the hard edges of the plaques digging into my spine.

"Leave. Me. Alone," I say.

"No."

"I mean it. Back away."

But I can't move, because I'm boxed in by Casey, who looks me in the eyes and speaks softly, "I don't give a shit how many guys you hook up with as long as you use a condom. What I care about is whether you said yes. That's the only thing that matters."

She leaves it there—*that's the only thing that matters*—hanging in midair, suspended, light as a feather. I close my eyes, press my thumb and middle fingers against my nose. The ants are gone, but my headache resurfaces, traveling around my body now, setting up camp in my neck, then my shoulders, before sprinting down into my legs, my feet, my toes. My whole body is racked, every muscle tense, every bone on edge.

I hear Casey's voice again. "Alex, did you say yes? Did you say yes when you had sex with Carter? Either time?"

Yes, yes, yes. No, no, no.

I don't know.

I don't know the things about last night that matter. I don't know what words were said or not said. I push my fingers harder against the bridge of my nose, like I'm directing all the dormant memories there, commanding them like a sorcerer to break free of their shackles, come out of hiding and reveal everything.

I say the words to myself.

Yes.

No.

Weighing them, one against the other on scales, hoping one scale will tip in favor of the other, making everything clear.

Yes, no, yes, no.

One or the other.

I try desperately to remember, reaching deep into the recesses of last night to recall the one most important word—*yes*. But it won't surface. All I can see are the band, the drinks, the card game, a kiss, then "Ode to Joy." Then black, blank nothingness. Nothing at all. Then waking up.

"I don't know," I whisper as I open my eyes. The tightness in my body subsides and now I feel like a rag doll, wrung dry.

"You don't know," Casey repeats.

"I don't know. I don't remember," I say, my voice shaking for the first time. "I don't remember anything," I say again as my throat tightens.

Fat silence fills the room and I look at Casey next to me, at T.S., who perches on the edge of her chair.

"When a girl doesn't remember what happened there's usually a reason," Casey says.

"What, was I drugged?" I ask nervously because that would explain everything. If Carter gave me one of those drugs...

"I doubt it, but you did drink a lot," T.S. says. "Sandeep called me last night after you left with Carter. He told me you had three drinks at the card game. Plus, you skipped dinner. You said you were too excited about seeing Artful Rage to eat. You were bouncing off the walls all day about Friday Night Out privileges. You're skinny, Alex. Three drinks on an empty stomach, that'll knock someone your size out."

Knock someone my size out. The words, they ring in my ears.

Knock. Out. Knock. Out.

I picture myself as a boxer, bruised and battered, chin bloody, eyes swollen. I try to do that little toe bounce thing boxers do, but I can't. I'm too worn out. I'm woozy, thoughts swimming aimlessly around my head. And that's when it happens. My opponent slams his gloved fist into my chest, then my cheek, then my head. I'm knocked out.

"Knocked out?" I ask quietly, imagining Boxer Alex slumped down in the corner of the ring, clinging to the ropes, head hanging low.

"Alex, I think the reason you don't remember having sex with Carter is you were passed out," T.S. says.

"Like a blackout or something?"

"You could have blacked out. And while you were blacked out you could have been totally into him and having the time of your life or whatever," Casey offers. "But even if that was the case, even if you blacked out, you were not in a condition to be having sex at all. So maybe it went

41

like this: you made out, you went back to his room. He probably goes to the bathroom to brush his teeth or pee or whatever. So you sit down on the bed to steady yourself. Then it hits you. The room is spinning and you're wasted. Your head meets the pillow. Boom. You're asleep, passed out, whatever you want to call it."

"So if I was asleep we didn't have sex, then?" I offer sort of feebly, hoping that's what happened, clinging to a faint, fuzzy memory of slumber.

"I don't know what happened, Alex," Casey continues. "Only you do and he does. And you'll know for sure when you remember more. But I'm just saying something doesn't sound right. It sounds as if he had sex with you while you were sleeping. Alex, it sounds like he raped you."

Chapter Five
DETECTIVE WORK

The four-letter word has been lobbed.

Like a bomb waiting to go off, it ticks, ticks, ticks. Louder, a siren screaming closer, a wail starting to surround me. It pierces my eardrums and the word rattles in my skull. It's a buzzing now, like construction on a New York street and you can't hear yourself talk or even think. Finally the bomb explodes, blasting the four letters apart, shredding them to pieces, leaving behind silence, cold silence, and...

"What's it called that a bomb leaves behind?" I direct the question to Casey.

"I don't know," she says.

"Residue," T.S. offers quickly.

"It's not residue," I insist. "What's the word for it? It's not collateral damage. It's not residue. What is it?"

"Shrapnel. It's shrapnel," T.S. says.

"Yes!" I say, snapping two fingers. "Shrapnel. That's what I was thinking of."

Then I clasp my palms together and say, "What should we do now? It's too early for lunch." Before they can answer, I smack my forehead with my palm. "Oh, I forgot! You guys have your game! You should get to your game, right? I don't want to hold you up. Maybe I'll even come to it for once. Cheer you. But who should I root for?"

Casey stands up and puts her hands firmly on my shoulders. "Alex," she says, cutting me off. I look down at the floor. "Alex," she says again. I start counting the number of lines in the floorboards. "Alex," she says one more time. A knot rises up in my throat. I swallow, but it's still there.

"How did this happen to me?" I whisper.

She pulls me close. I close my eyes, collapse into her, my arms limp at my side. We stay like that for a minute, an hour, maybe all day. Then Casey says, "Alex, I know it doesn't make it better, but it happens to a lot of girls."

I untangle myself from my sister, collect my voice, and say, "No. I really don't understand how this happened."

"What do you mean?"

"I mean, how did this happen?" I direct this question to T.S. "You were there. How did this happen? How did this happen to *me*?"

"I was there at the concert, but I left before the drinking game started. I don't know how drunk you were." I wince when she says that. I barely drink. I don't even like the taste of alcohol. I'm the girl at parties who doesn't care about booze. How did I become the girl who got that drunk? T.S. continues, "You should talk to Sandeep. He was there until you left."

I recoil. "I don't want to talk to him. I don't want everyone knowing my business."

"Sandeep was there the whole time. He knows you left with Carter. He knows you spent the night—" She stops, corrects herself. "He knows you wound up in Carter's room. He won't judge. You know he's not like that. He would never judge you."

I look away, focusing on a framed photo of a golden blond boy holding a lacrosse stick and smiling wide, way too chipper for my taste.

I turn back to Casey and T.S. "Isn't it entirely possible we just had bad sex, like it was just a mistake? You know, I slept with him and I just…" I grasp for the words. "Isn't it possible I just—I don't know—blocked it out?"

"Alex, there is a *reason* you don't remember. I don't think you were ever in a position to say yes. And I also think you need to do your best to figure out what happened. For your own peace of mind," Casey says.

I close my eyes, sigh heavily. "Sandeep. Natalie Moretti. The whole girls' track team. We might as well hire a skywriter at this rate."

But I also know I'll go to Sandeep. This is like homework and I have never backed down from an assignment.

"Let's find out how messed up I was," I say.

"I'm going with you," T.S. says. "I'm going to skip the game."

"You never skip games."

"Well, I am today," T.S. says.

"And listen, Alex," Casey begins. "You have options. You could go to the police."

I whip around. "Are you joking?" I ask, but I don't wait for her to answer. "Because I would *never* go to the police. Not for something like this."

"Why not?" Casey asks.

"Because then Mom and Dad would know, and they'd have a collective meltdown that would burn a hole in the solar system. Not to mention they wouldn't approve of that whole underage drinking thing. And there's that little fact of my having to recount the whole experience to the cops, who would insist on a rape kit like on TV, and I can't imagine anything I'd want to do less than that."

"Then, what about the Mockingbirds? They can help you."

"You want me to be a poster child or something?"

"I want what's right."

"The Mockingbirds are your project, not mine," I say.

Casey holds up her hands. "It's totally up to you. You don't have to go to the Mockingbirds. If you want to move on, pretend this never happened—"

Yes, God, yes.

"—Then I respect that," she adds. "It's your choice."

But was it really *my choice*? Was it ever my choice last night? Did I choose? Could I choose?

I have to know.

I tip my chin to the door. "Let's get out of here."

Casey locks the door behind us and we walk silently down the long hallway. There's no banter this time, no joking like on the way here. We leave the athletic complex and T.S. texts Sandeep as Casey unlocks her bike. Casey says she'll call later, come by later too. Then she rides off, and T.S. and I head for Brooks Hall.

It looks like a miniature castle with little turrets, curved windows, and a big set of stone steps leading up to its dark brown double wood doors. I know this much—Carter lives in a different dorm than Sandeep. This is a small victory for me today, both the memory and the luck.

Once inside, T.S. knocks on Sandeep's door. He opens it, flashes T.S. a smile, and gives her a kiss on the lips. My stomach curls and I look away because I'm not a public kisser. Daniel and I made out in the basement, the music hall, the deserted stacks on the third floor of Pryor Library. Never in the quad, never in the caf, and never in front of friends. But evidently I was quite a public kisser last night. I was exactly the person I'm not.

"Hey, guys," Martin says, giving us a quick nod. He's Sandeep's roommate and he's busy stuffing a biology textbook the size of an encyclopedia set into his backpack. He was at the concert last night. He saw me drinking; he probably knows I left with Carter. I focus on the window at the end of the room so I don't have to meet his eyes. "I'm heading over to Pryor," Martin adds. He'll soon be eye-deep in that textbook. Martin is insanely driven to be a biologist. Everyone at Themis is insanely driven about something.

"Did you know a recent study found that the western scrub-jay can plan for the future?" Martin says randomly, perhaps the biggest non sequitur I've heard in my life.

"Where do you come up with this stuff, Martin?" T.S. asks.

"Google News," he says as if the answer were obvious. "Yeah, these birds stored food in different rooms for the next day and they could remember what food they stored, when they stored it, and where they stored it, even when the other birds were watching."

"Was that a hard test for the birds, Martin? Being able to remember shit when their buddies were watching?" Sandeep teases.

"It gives new meaning to the term *birdbrain*, doesn't it?" Martin says with a glint in his eyes as he hoists his book-laden backpack onto his shoulder. "There's a lot going on in those tiny little heads."

Despite myself I laugh a little, then notice T.S. and Sandeep both are rolling their eyes. "See, Alex thought it was funny," Martin points out.

"I did," I manage to say. The least I can do is talk like a normal person, react like a normal person. I'm not going to be that person who goes mute, who writes on Post-it Notes because she can't deal.

"Get out of here," T.S. says playfully.

"Someday, when the world is run by ornithologists, you won't be so quick to dispatch me."

He leaves and I sit down at Martin's vacated desk chair. T.S. makes herself comfortable, sitting cross-legged on Sandeep's bed. The room is sparse, like most boys' rooms, though Sandeep has managed to slather his half of the walls with felt pennants for the Baltimore Orioles. He's from Maryland and possesses an unholy zeal for the home team. Signs of Martin's personality and his slavish devotion to science are more meager. The only evidence lies in a dartboard above his desk. On the bull's-eye he's written *Nobel Prize*.

"This is weird," I blurt out.

Sandeep sits down next to T.S. I look away from them, from him mostly. I don't want to meet his eyes. I don't want to have that moment where I know and he knows and we both know I was easy and drunk and stupid. But Sandeep was the last one standing. He was there the whole time, there until I left with Carter.

Sandeep was sober. He doesn't drink. He just supplies. I think he likes supplying because it makes him cool, but he likes not drinking because it preserves his brain cells. He plans to be a hand surgeon, the best hand surgeon there has ever been. So he doesn't want to risk losing even one particle of gray matter to booze, he has said.

I steel myself for what I'll learn, then begin. "So what

happened last night? The details are kind of fuzzy to me and I want to know the good, the bad, and the ugly."

Sandeep's a good guy and a good-looking guy. His skin is brown and his eyes are light green and he has close-cropped and, I'm told, very soft black hair. It's his eyes, though, that melted T.S. They're pretty much unnervingly beautiful. He doesn't know about the pregnancy scare. T.S. got her period that afternoon and never told him she'd taken a test; she never told anyone but me.

"Well, you know we went to Artful Rage, right?"

I roll my eyes. "Yeah, I remember that. We met in the quad—Martin, you, me, T.S., Maia, Cleo, Julie from down the hall, and Julie's boyfriend, Sam, from town." I motion with my hands for him to speed up because I know what happened next. We made up songs about our new Friday Night Out privileges as we walked the mile or so to Salem Jim's. They stamped our hands with the no-drinking sign— a baby bottle, so emasculating—and we went inside. The band played, we sang and screamed and made our voices go hoarse. Then things got fuzzier.

"Is Artful Rage where...," I stop, take a breath. "Where we met Carter?"

Sandeep nods. "He was with another group from the school, the water polo guys."

"What were we doing even talking to water polo guys?" I ask. "We never hang out with them."

"Everyone was kind of talking to everyone," Sandeep recounts. "All the juniors were psyched about finally having

Friday Night Out privileges, so it was one of those nights, you know. About twenty-two people from Themis at the concert."

"My, aren't we precise," T.S. says to Sandeep.

He raises his eyebrows at her as if his precision is no big deal. Because to him, it isn't a big deal.

"I remember the band," I offer.

Sandeep nods. "Yeah, they were pretty good. I don't think you were totally smashed until later on."

I don't like the way he says that, even though it's true. I don't like being the girl who was totally smashed, or even just "tipsy" or "buzzed." I should be more like Sandeep and T.S., more in control. I'll just drink grape soda from now on.

"Anyway, so everyone starts talking to each other and—"

"Wait, wait, wait!" T.S. interjects, waving her hand frantically. "That's when I said just because we don't usually like water polo boys doesn't mean we shouldn't talk to them." She says this excitedly at first, then clasps a hand to her mouth and her eyes go wide. "Alex, I'm so sorry. It's my fault."

I give her a look. "What are you talking about?"

"I told you to talk to him."

"Actually, you said it to everyone, to the group, not to Alex," Sandeep corrects.

She ignores him, keeps her eyes on me. "Alex, I'm sorry."

"T.S., that is the most ridiculous thing you've ever said

in your entire life, or at the least the entire part of your life I've known you. So I'm just going to pretend you didn't say it, since obviously it has no bearing whatsoever."

I turn back to Sandeep. "So we're all going kumbaya and talking at the show. I remember that mostly. Then the show ends...."

"Right, then we all came back to the common room here. And you'd had one shot at the concert."

He says it so clinically, so medically; he's not judging me, just giving his residents the report on his patient, teaching them how to do rounds. I see him wearing dark blue surgeon scrubs, a cap for his hair. He still has hair when he's thirty-five, I decide, and practicing medicine at some leading hospital. He doesn't even have to look at the patient's chart. He knows it all by heart, everything about the patient.

"So I poured some more for everyone," he says, rattling off names next. "T.S. and Maia had already left, Martin was long gone after the concert, so it was Cleo, Julie, Sam, Carter."

I put my head in my hands. Cleo, Julie, Sam, and Carter. Natalie, the track team, and on and on and on...

"And then you suggested Circle of Death," Sandeep says.

"How much more did I drink?" I ask, looking up again.

"You had two and a half more shots with your orange juice."

T.S. raises her eyebrows. "Two and a half?"

"Yes. She didn't finish the third shot."

He doesn't falter as he informs his charges. The residents seize their notebooks and write this down in their doctorly scrawls, *two and a half more shots,* translating the amount perfectly into milliliters or cc or whatever doctor language they write in.

"Three and a half total is a lot of vodka on an empty stomach," T.S. says sympathetically. "It would be hard for anyone to remember what happened."

"You weigh about one hundred and ten pounds," Sandeep instructs. "So three and a half drinks in three hours would make your blood alcohol content point zero eight. Which is considered legally drunk. At your size, on an empty stomach, you're dealing with slowed reaction times, emotional swings, impaired judgment."

Impaired judgment.

There it is again, a word, a phrase, hanging in the middle of the room, having legs, arms, and a life form of its own. Just like when Casey said, "That's the only thing that matters," back in the Captains' Room an hour or so ago.

"And he kissed you, in front of everyone," Sandeep adds.

Because I would never kiss a water polo boy, I would never make the first move, I would never get it on with a soon-to-be frat boy. He started it, he started it all.

"And you guys were kind of going at it on the couch, making out, but the game kept going on and then Carter just pulls you up and leads you out of there."

Out of there. To the place where I can't rely on anyone

else's account, anyone else's unassailable recollection. Just my own splotchy one.

"Thank you." I stand up.

"Where are you going?" T.S. asks.

"Back," I say.

"I'll come with you."

"No, you don't have to."

"I want to. We want to." She speaks for him as if she's his representative or something. Maybe she is, because he rises and the three of us head out together, down the hall, down the stairs, and out into the cold and far-too-sunny January day. They walk me all the way back to Taft-Hay Hall.

"You going to be okay?" T.S. asks.

"I want to take a nap."

"Call me if you need anything. We'll talk more later, okay? Promise?"

I nod, head inside, up the stairs, and back into my room. Maia's here, listening to The Clash, drinking afternoon tea and reading a book.

"Good afternoon. And in case you're wondering, I've decided to forgive you for dashing off this morning without giving me the goods," Maia says, half chiding, but she never really sounds annoyed. I suspect that's because of the British accent. Maia's parents are from Singapore, but they have lived in London her whole life, so she's this amazing mix of Asian and British. She's wearing her sleek black hair in a high ponytail, as she does most days. She has that kind of gorgeous long hair that would probably stop traffic if she wore it down. Maybe she wears it up as a courtesy, as traffic accident prevention. The hair, the accent—she was given the gifts that only make her better at what she was born to do: debate.

"Thanks, but there aren't any goods," I say, then kick off my Vans into the closet.

She waves a hand in the air dismissively, her other hand holding a mug of Earl Grey, which she drinks pretty much every afternoon. You can take the girl out of Britain....

"I bet you told T.S. what you did last night," she says quietly.

Any other day the words would be a sharp knife. Because they're true. We might look like a threesome, but we're really a pair plus one. Maia and I were matched up last year in English lit to give a presentation we called Great Sidekicks in Literary History. We chose Falstaff from *Henry V*, Jim from *Huck Finn,* and Watson from *Sherlock Holmes.* Then Maia tossed in the Nurse from *Romeo and Juliet* and launched into her very own soliloquy on how English literature scholars should expand the definition of a sidekick to include the very impressive *curriculum vitae* of several female supporting characters. She was brilliant and the whole class gave her a standing ovation.

"You are a goddess of words," I told her afterward. "Like Zeus or something."

"Athena," Maia corrected. She stopped, reconsidered. "Scratch that. I'm Wonder Woman. She doesn't even need a sidekick."

"Want to go to lunch with me, Wonder Woman?" I asked.

She said yes and we became fast friends. Then Maia's roommate got kicked out at the end of last year. It was our very own Themis scandal since the only thing that gets you kicked out is failing, and her roommate was so addicted to painkillers she spent most of her days too loopy to finish a sentence, let alone a homework assignment. So we asked Maia to room with us junior year. The three of us are super close, but T.S. is still the one I turn to first.

"So listen to this," Maia says, quickly moving to a new topic. "Mr. Baumann already wants the whole debate team to do one of the patented Themis performances for the Faculty Club. Can you believe it? We'll be doing a parliamentary debate on the pros and cons of the foreign policy of the current White House administration when the club meets again."

"First *Merry Wives*, then foreign policy," I say, grateful there's one person who doesn't want to talk about last night.

"It's pointless too. I mean, it doesn't count toward the debate circuit," she adds, referring to the national debate tournaments held every year. "But they say it's practice, good practice, for the circuit." She pumps a fist in the air, imitating her debate advisor. "You know it's just for show though."

"Totally for show."

"I swear, Alex, someday I'm going to write a bloody exposé on this weird fetish, practically an obsession, Themis has for its students. The teachers constantly want us to perform."

Themis fancies itself as some sort of Utopia, drawing the best and the brightest, and the school loves to trot us out in these bizarre sort of private performances for the faculty — debate, music, acting. It's the faculty's reward for teaching here or something, puppet shows by the students themselves.

"Hey, do you happen to know Hadley Blaine?" Maia asks.

I shake my head. "Why?"

"He mentioned your name today at the Debate Club meeting."

"Why would he mention my name?"

Maia shrugs. "I don't know. I overheard him talking to another guy there."

"Who?"

"Henry Rowland. They're both swimmers."

"What'd they say?"

"Don't know. I asked them to be quiet because I had to start the meeting."

"Oh," I say. Then I see a flash of red.

I point to Maia's neck. "What's that?"

"What's what?"

"On your neck."

"Oh, it's my new scarf. Isn't it delicious? I went to the basement to get my clothes out of the dryer, and there it was on the floor, next to the lost-and-found bin. I thought it was vaguely ironic to wear something from the lost-and-found bin."

"Take it off."

"What?"

"Take it off, Maia."

"Why? I think it's kind of cool, don't you, in a retro kind of way?"

"No. Just please take it off."

"It's just a scarf, Alex. Are you okay?" she asks. "You're kind of freaking me out here."

No, I'm not okay. Because it's not just a scarf. It's a reminder that Carter was nothing like Daniel at the lost-and-found bin.

"I'm sorry, Maia. I have this crazy headache and I just need to sleep."

And without looking at her, I slide into my bed, under the covers, where I should have been last night.

Chapter Six

WHILE I WAS SLEEPING

I don't run into Carter the rest of the weekend, but I know I won't be lucky enough to avoid him altogether. So on Monday morning I survey English class cautiously. I peer over my left shoulder, then my right. I don't see his white-blond hair, so I breathe. He's not in English, not in French. I tell myself it's entirely possible I could have zero shared classes with him. Of course, it's also entirely possible I could fly to Jupiter tomorrow.

Themis isn't one of those so-small-it's-claustrophobic schools, but it's not massive either. There are about two hundred students in each year. It's hard to know everyone, but it's easy to know *most* students.

"Who are you looking for?" someone whispers.

I turn to see my good friend and music buddy Jones Miner, who's sitting behind me. His light brown hair falls in his face. He keeps his hair shoulder-length, rock-star length, he says. I've known him since we were freshmen because he plays violin. We play together often, in orchestra, in quartets, in two-on-one practices with the music teacher, and of course in puppet show performances for the Faculty Club, like this one we have to do next month—a Mozart sonata. Because, well, we're really the two best musicians the school has.

Funny thing is, Jones would rather be playing electric guitar. His parents don't want him to, so he compromised, or really, tricked them. He scored a ticket out of the house for four years, where he can play guitar in his room all he wants.

"No one," I whisper back as Julie walks into the classroom. She lives down the hall from me and she is going to save the world someday, I'm sure of it. She started a group here called Change Agents, so she's always heading up this or that fund-raising drive or volunteer project. We'll chit-chat in the common room or while we brush our teeth at night and she'll often suggest I come help out on her latest feed-the-homeless efforts.

She was there *that night,* and when I see her walk past my desk, I look the other way because I can't help but wonder what she saw, if she thinks I asked for it. My chest tightens and I half-expect her to say something cruel, even though Julie doesn't have a mean bone in her body. Instead, she just gives me a wave before she sits down.

Then a runner darts into the room. The runner never says a word; he just waits for an attendance slip from our teacher, Ms. Peck. Runners help out in the office by collecting attendance slips from each class. This would be a menial task at many other schools. But thanks to the point system here, their job is actually pretty important. Themis awards attendance points you can cash in for off campus privileges, sort of like a weekend pass but to the movies or the coffee shop. Points are key if you ever want a real social life, if you ever want to have a real date. The rewards get better with each passing year. Freshmen can use points to have lunch off campus once a month, sophomores once a week. Juniors can cash them in for three lunches per week, including weekends. Plus, you can use points in the second half of junior year for Friday Night Out privileges. Seniors can come and go as they please for lunch and can leave campus Friday and Saturday nights. Of course, you can also lose points if you skip class or don't show up for your extracurricular activities.

Ms. Peck hands the paper to the runner, who dashes out, then clears her throat, peering at us over the top of her tortoiseshell glasses with lenses the size of Frisbees. "Good Monday morning to you all," she says. She still has a slight Texan accent—she's from there—but she rarely slips up with *y'all*. That wouldn't really go over well at Themis.

"Good morning, Ms. Peck," we say in unison. All the female teachers here are referred to as *Ms.* whether they're married or not. With this policy, the administration thinks the faculty's marital status is off the table, a non-topic of discussion for the students. As if we all don't already know exactly which teachers are married, divorced, single, cheating, in marriage counseling, or dating. We know everything that goes on here and we always will.

The consequence of that is someone probably knows about me. Natalie knows where I was Friday night *and* Saturday morning. Then I remember her boyfriend, Kevin, is a water polo player, like Carter. I slump down in my chair, the reality hitting me. I'm sure she's told the whole track team she saw me doing what she thinks was the walk of shame from Carter's room. And Kevin has probably told the water polo team.

I shake my head, shake the thought away like a leaf that has fallen in my hair. The leaf falls to the ground, and I picture myself stepping on it. The brown, crackling leaf turns to rubble under my foot. I kind of wish it were Natalie under my foot.

"This semester, as you may well know," Ms. Peck continues, tucking her dishwater blond pageboy-cut hair behind her ears, "is dedicated to Shakespeare. We're going to read a play a week. So that's five acts per play, one act per night for all you math wizzes out there." She thinks she's funny. She even adds her own comic pause as if we're all just about to cue up our laugh track right now. But we don't give her the satisfaction. "And since term is sixteen weeks with one week for finals, you can expect to have read"—she pauses *again,* the shameless ham—"four squared plays by Shakespeare."

Thanks for the math. We suck at math here at Themis so your arithmetic prowess helps immensely.

She marches over to the blackboard, her comedy routine having fallen flat, and reaches for a piece of chalk. "And as part of our Shakespeare immersion this term, you each are going to write a modern adaptation of one of Shakespeare's plays, and you can expect that to be at least forty pages."

Now she pauses for dramatic effect because that is dramatic. I would groan, all fifteen of us would groan right now if we weren't masters of restraint. You take your assignments like a man here. Ms. Peck looks a tad defeated. I bet the sadist in her—the sadist in every teacher—was hoping for some resistance, some squirming in our chairs at least.

"I have already assigned a different play to each student. I will go through the list now."

She turns to the blackboard and begins scratching out names of plays, then a slash mark, then the name of a student.

Emily gets *Romeo and Juliet.* I scoff silently. That's the easiest one to adapt. You don't even have to read it to rewrite it.

Brent lands *Hamlet.* Same deal. No-brainer.

Julie snags *Othello.* Jealousy, piece of cake.

I wonder vaguely if Ms. Peck is playing favorites, if she likes that trio of students best. She doles out the next round, *Henry V, Richard III, Antony and Cleopatra*. My name's not next to any of those so I dodge a bullet, though Jones winds up with *Antony and Cleopatra*. Then she sidesteps to the obscure, actually assigning *Troilus and Cressida* and *Titus Andronicus* for this project, to Henry and Elyse, respectively. Ms. Peck must have a wicked bone to pick with them!

Then I'm next, and my task, it turns out, is to adapt *The Tempest*.

I know nothing about *The Tempest*.

When she writes my name, Henry turns around and gives me a look, more like a leer, as if he had a dirty dream about me last night or something. *Henry Rowland*. He was one of the guys who mentioned my name in Maia's Debate Club meeting. Natalie Moretti isn't the only person talking about me behind my back. Henry Rowland is too. It's like there's a sandwich board on me; the front says *I'm Easy, Just Ask Carter*. But the back would say *He's Wrong, People. He's Totally Completely Wrong*. I look down at my books, not wanting to meet Henry's eyes. Fifty minutes later the bell rings and I gather my books, keeping my eyes averted.

"Hey, Alex. It was fun hanging with you Friday night," Julie says, tapping my desk. "You know, I'm organizing a new project to mentor underprivileged grade-schoolers here in Providence. Would love to talk to you about it sometime."

"Great. Totally. Count me in," I say as I grab my backpack, relieved she has no interest in discussing Friday night.

"I'll catch up with you soon, then," Julie says, and leaves.

"So, you think there's any way I could work in a little guitar solo into *Antony and Cleopatra*?" Jones asks.

"That would totally rock," I say, and wait for Jones so we can walk out together. I don't want to be alone if I run into Carter, so I'm making Jones my secret buffer, my safety net.

"Pretty crazy assignment, don't you think?" he asks as we walk down the hall and file out onto the quad. I wrap my scarf around my neck and pull on gloves, wishing I could go all Audrey Hepburn and place the scarf over my head, then don a pair of massive brown sunglasses. No one would recognize me. No one could stare at me.

"Yeah," I say. "But they're all like that. It's like a battle to give the most bizarre, complicated, unusual, cutting-edge assignment."

"I know," he says, shaking his head. "I bet they have contests."

"They probably place bets on who has the best students. They think we're perfect in every possible way."

"Perfect grades, perfect attendance, perfect performance," he says. "Hey, I gotta run. I have Spanish now."

My face feels hot for a second. He's probably in the same Spanish class with Carter. I look away; even hearing the name of the class Carter might be in embarrasses me.

"See ya," I say, and then scoot off to Taft-Hay Hall. I have an open period so I might as well do a little research on *The Tempest*. I sprint up the three flights of stairs to my room and slam the door behind me. I peel off my gloves, coat, and scarf, sit down at my desk, flip open my computer, and fire up a browser window. I'm a good student. I don't procrastinate and I do my homework on time, but for some reason I feel insanely compelled to look up *The Tempest* this very second.

I find its Wikipedia entry.

A sorcerer who's a duke, sent to an island with his daughter, banished there by his own brother...

Okay, I can do that....A modern-day hipster magician who wears pencil-thin skinny jeans gets duped by his brother, some kind of power monger–type who wants to be the sole heir to the family's skateboarding business....

I read more.

A storm, a ship run aground...

Instead of a storm, our hero shuts down Internet access for a day, the brother's business grinds to a halt.... Yes, that works.

I read more of the play's synopsis until I see something on Wikipedia that I can't not see.

Following Caliban's attempted rape of Miranda...

I read that line again. There must be a mistake; I'm seeing things, inventing things. Wikipedia could be wrong, so I Google other *Tempest* synopses. I look up Shakespeare scholars and the backstory is still the same: Attempted rape, attempted rape, attempted rape.

I don't really believe in signs, but I do kind of believe in karma and the universe and stuff like that. Is this the universe telling me something? Like there's a reason Ms. Peck gave me this play? Like this play was *meant* to be assigned to me?

I look down at the floor, contemplating. It's then that I see a red sheet of paper on the carpet. I pick it up. It's that bird again. The same flyer I saw before.

Join the Mockingbirds! Stand up, sing out! We're scouting new singers, so run, run, run on your way to our New Nine, where you can learn a simple trick....

There's a note on this one from T.S. In her curlicue writing—she still uses a heart on top of each little *i*—it reads: *Think about it.*

I fold it into quarters and put it in my back pocket.

Think about it, she says. She's not telling me to think about trying out for the Mockingbirds' New Nine. She's telling me to think about *going* to the Mockingbirds. Asking for their help.

I think about the words—*learn a simple trick*—and where they come from.

"First of all, if you can learn a simple trick, Scout, you'll get along better with all kinds of folks."

They're from *To Kill a Mockingbird*, naturally, since that's where the Mockingbirds get their name. We read it in freshman English. Our teacher gave us this crazy assignment where we had to take the first half of the book and compare the characters and their challenges back in the

1930s to modern day. It was supposed to make the book more relevant, but it still seemed kind of dated to me. The only part I liked was the trial.

The trial.

It's like a train just slammed into me. Because the trial was about a rape. Only in *To Kill a Mockingbird* he didn't do it. Tom Robinson was unjustly accused of rape. I crumple down onto my bed, a flash of doubt coursing through me. What if Carter is my Tom Robinson? What if I'm the one who's wrong?

I twist around so I can look out the window. All the way on the other side of the quad is the white door that leads into Richardson Hall, Carter's dorm. I stare hard at the door, as if it offers answers, secrets. Then a boy walks up the steps, not Carter, just someone else, and opens the door.

We didn't go in that door. We went in a back door and then...

The room looks bigger than mine. A lot bigger. And he has a single. I wonder how he got a single. At least I think it's a single. The room feels tilted, or maybe that's just the fact that my shoulders are kind of swaying back and forth right now.

"I'm going to use the bathroom for a sec. Be right back," *he says, and the door shuts softly behind him. I hear "Ode to Joy" crashing through the speakers.*

I nod. At least I think I do. I think I move my head. My feet feel funny, kind of loose on the ground, and I'm already sinking down. So I decide to lie down. The bed's so far away. I don't think I can make it. So I just sink down onto the crimson and tan diamonds. Better. But what would be even better is full horizontality. I somehow manage to take off my coat, leave it on the floor, make my way to the bed, and collapse into sleep.

The door closes, and the boy is inside Richardson Hall. Inside the building where Carter fucked me while I was sleeping.

Chapter Seven
BEGGING FOR IT

Lunchtime.

Part of me feels like I'm walking into the lion's den. Another part of me knows I can't become the freak who eats in her room just to avoid other students. Besides, maybe there's nothing to be worried about, I reason as I walk into the cafeteria with Maia and T.S. Maybe no one's really talking about me. Maybe they already gossiped over the weekend and they're on to someone else.

"I saw your note back in the room," I say to T.S. Her short blond hair hits her cheeks.

"And?" she asks.

"What note?" Maia interrupts.

"Nothing," I say quickly.

"Oh no, you don't," Maia says firmly as we drop our

bags at our usual spot, a wooden table near the edge of the cafeteria. Martin and Sandeep are already seated. "What's going on?" Maia asks.

I head over to the food line, grab an apple, then make my way to the salad bar. As I spoon lettuce onto my plate, someone starts talking to me. It's Kevin Ward. My stomach drops.

"Hi, Alex," he says. He has light brown hair, wavy, and cool brown eyes. I picture him playing water polo as I dunk him, press his head underwater for a very long time so he can't talk to me. When he rises to the surface, his hair is flat and wet, his eyes are red, and he's gasping for air at the side of the pool.

"Hi." I add garbanzo beans to my plate.

"How was your weekend?" he says, a grin on his face. He's never asked me anything before. We don't chat at the salad bar. We don't chat anywhere.

"Fine."

He raises an eyebrow. "Modest," he says softly.

"Excuse me?" I ask.

"I heard it was better than fine," he says, then winks at me. He leans in close to me. "I can go more than twice. If you're up for it, I could go five, six times."

Then he heads to the table with the other water polo boys. Just as he sits down, he's joined by Carter. Kevin high-fives Carter, then tips his forehead back toward me. Carter looks over from across the cafeteria, doesn't say anything, just mouths something to me, something like "go again?"

My hands shake; my plate of lettuce and garbanzo beans threatens to spill onto the white tiled floor. Carter has seen me at my worst, my most vulnerable, and now he's telling his friends. I was a virgin—I'd still be a virgin if it weren't for what he did to me while I was passed out. I walk quickly to the table, place my plate down, and say to Martin and Sandeep, "I'm going to skip lunch. This salad looks gross."

I grab my backpack and rush out. As I push the doors open, Natalie saunters in, towering over me. "Hey, Alex, where are your shades today? They were a nice touch." Then she leans her head back and laughs as she brushes past me. I notice she even has muscles in her neck.

I mutter under my breath, "You better get a leash for your boyfriend, Natalie. He sounds like the type who strays."

But she's already gone and I'd never have the guts to dish right back to her. I'm nothing, helpless. I couldn't say no to Carter, I can't even talk back to Natalie. I reach the quad, then stop for a second, considering where to go. My room, music hall, my next class that doesn't start for forty-five minutes? Somewhere, anywhere but here. Maybe the school office to withdraw?

I'll say I'm sorry, I'm not cut out for Themis. I'll call my parents, tell them I'd rather be in a public school in New Haven and please can I come live at home again? I'll go straight to my house when the school bell rings each day, practice piano in the living room, never go out, never see anyone except my parents. Maybe I'll even ask my mom to homeschool me, and even that will be better than being surrounded by all these people, everywhere, climbing all over me, stepping on me, talking about me, thinking they know me.

T.S. bursts through the doors with Maia next to her. "What happened back there?" Maia asks.

I look at T.S., who knows what happened Friday night. I look at Maia, who doesn't. "I slept with Carter on the water polo team and he told Kevin Ward," I tell Maia. "And Natalie Moretti told the whole track team."

"Bastard," Maia says, though it hardly sounds like a swear from her. "You want me to go take care of him for you? I can undress them with my words, with my vicious rhetoric," she says. Then she holds her hands up and flexes her fingers like a cat, her long nails painted dark blue. "Or my claws."

I momentarily savor the thought of Maia cracking Carter's head, then Kevin's, then Natalie's. Then T.S. jumps in.

"You didn't sleep with him. He raped you," T.S. says, her green eyes deadly serious.

Maia's dark brown eyes go wide in shock. She takes a deep breath. "Alex, my God! Are you okay?"

I don't answer. I look back at T.S. "Are you sure? I mean, totally sure?" I ask, because this thing is like whiplash. Doubt, certainty, doubt, certainty. It changes from one second to the next.

"You were too drunk to give consent, Alex," T.S. says.

"You were not able to say yes. He's not supposed to have sex with you under those conditions. I knew as soon as you told me what happened, I knew you weren't in a state of mind to have sex with anyone. Then Sandeep just confirmed it beyond a shadow of a doubt when he told us how *much* you drank."

Maia cracks her knuckles. She's ready for a fight. "Guys, just say the word. Seriously," she says. A group of freshmen girls walking to the cafeteria glance over at us. Maia stares them down. They look away instantly.

"No, don't do that," I say.

"You could go to the police, then. You could tell them what happened and press charges," Maia offers up.

"No way am I going to the cops. No way in hell! I'm not pressing charges or going to court or involving my parents or the authorities."

"You don't have to," T.S. says. "There's another way."

I know what she wants me to do.

"You could go to the Mockingbirds," she says.

"Shh...I don't want anyone to hear," I say.

"Well?" T.S. asks. "Do you want to?"

"I don't *want* to do anything," I say, because I want this to go away. I don't want to be the poster child for date rape.

"And what about the next time he says something about you?" T.S. asks. "What about the next time he tells his friends he thinks you're an easy lay? What about when he tells other boys he banged you twice the first time he met you?"

I grit my teeth, kind of grinding them against each other. I press harder, so it feels as if my teeth might split. I picture little bits of white sawdust spreading around in my mouth, a molar shearing off, like a glacier calving in the Arctic.

"Maybe he won't," I say softly, looking for a quiet way out, a secret back door I can slip through. I'm just a quiet mouse and I disappear into the woods.

"I bet he already has," T.S. says.

"Maybe he just told Kevin," I offer pathetically, my voice quavering. I suck the tightness in my throat back in. "Maybe they're best friends. I mean, I told you, T.S. And I told Maia now. And Natalie knows because she saw me and goes out with Kevin. Maybe it's just the three of them who know. That's not bad, right?"

Maia takes over. "Let's say for the sake of argument that he just told Kevin. And Natalie, oh-silent-quiet Natalie, hasn't told a soul either. Would that change what happened Friday night?"

"That has nothing to do with this."

T.S. raises an eyebrow. "So him raping you has nothing to do with whether you go to the Mockingbirds? It has everything to do with it."

"Don't use that word."

"Let's see, then, if he just told one person," Maia suggests. "I doubt it, considering that Hadley and Henry were talking about you at Debate on Saturday, and they're on the swim team. They're friends with all the water polo players. Let's find out how far the bastard is spreading lies or not. I know the swimmers. And Hadley Blaine is dying to become my second-in-command in the Debate Club, so I can get pretty much anything out of him."

She wheels around and heads back into the cafeteria. I stare at T.S. "What's she doing?"

T.S. shakes her head. "I don't know, but she moves pretty fast."

"Yeah."

"I mean, she went from not knowing to interrogating in about ten seconds. The mob should recruit her. She'd be the muscle," T.S. says, trying her best to keep the mood light. But I can't laugh right now. I sink down to the ground, sitting on the cold grass. I pick a few pieces out of the lawn. T.S. sits next to me.

"Listen," she says softly. "I just think you need to stand up for yourself."

"You act as if I'm a victim, like I've always been some kind of victim."

"I don't think you've always been the victim. But you're one now, and I think you should do something about it."

"Are the Mockingbirds really going to solve this?" I ask.

"You know their track record as well as I do," T.S. says as Maia returns, joining us on the ground. She huffs a few times, almost like she's blowing out smoke before she can talk. She's fuming, and the nail on her middle finger is broken, jagged. There's a tiny bit of blood on her finger.

I point to it, wide-eyed. "What happened?"

She takes one more breath, then adjusts her ponytail.

"The whole team knows. Both teams, actually. Swim team, water polo team."

I drop my head into my hands.

She continues. "I sat down next to Hadley and asked him if he'd want to help me with the prep work for the next debate, and he practically panted in excitement. Then a bunch of guys at the table laughed, and I leaned close to Hadley and said, 'What's so funny to your mates?' And he said, 'Carter's entertaining his teammates with his weekend activities report.'"

I grind my teeth again, and I swear I crush one of my own canines into dust in my mouth.

"So I tell Hadley to be at practice two hours early to help, and he starts telling me about how he'll do this and that, but I just pretended to listen and instead focused on what Carter was saying. Carter didn't realize I was listening to him instead of Hadley. And that's when I dug my nails into the table because it was all I could do not to gouge Carter's eyes out. This one ripped off"—Maia stops, holds up the finger with the torn nail—"when he told them that you were"—she pauses, collects herself—"*begging* for it."

I jump up. "That's a lie!"

I won't let him have the last word.

I turn to T.S. "Take me to the Mockingbirds."

Chapter Eight
QUARTERS

Physics that afternoon is worse than lunch because Carter is in my class. The vein in my forehead beats so hard I'm afraid everyone can hear it. I'm convinced it's going to burst, explode in a shower of blood in class, and everyone will turn around and say, "For a good time, call Alex."

But Carter doesn't notice me, and we're all taking furious notes anyway while Mr. Waldman goes on about the Meissner effect, magnetic fields, and superconductors. The only saving grace is we have assigned seating. Carter sits in the front row and I'm all the way in the back next to Martin. I spend the entire class thinking *don't turn around, don't turn around, don't turn around* as I invent new ways to use Martin as a potential shield if Carter so much as moves a muscle in my direction.

I know Martin well enough. I remember seeing his face a lot last year because he was a runner in some of my classes. But I didn't meet him officially until T.S. and Sandeep started dating after spring break sophomore year. Pretty soon, we all were sharing a table in the caf, and since T.S. and Sandeep live in their own little bubble most of the time, Martin and I talk to each other more than to them. Martin's goofy, like with the birdbrain thing, but also very driven. He's tall with kind of shaggy brown hair, slightly a bit mussed up, and brown eyes that have tiny flecks of green in them. He's wearing a long-sleeve T-shirt and a wristband or something. He leans in, whispers so low I can barely hear, "You know, you can levitate stuff with the Meissner effect."

I give a silent laugh, then whisper super quietly, "Maybe you can, but I definitely can't."

"I'll show you sometime. You know, since I'm a science geek and all," he says as if it's an insider's secret, his being a science geek. Then I notice Martin reach into his front jeans pocket. He swipes out his cell phone surreptitiously so Mr. Waldman doesn't notice. He flicks open the screen, then closes it shut just as quickly as he opened it. His shoulders tense; he rests his forehead in his hands for a moment. I'm about to ask if he's okay when he moves his hand down the spiral-bound paper, writing at the bottom of the page in neat, blocky letters: *I WILL SEE YOU AT EIGHT.*

I furrow my brow. *WHY?* I write back in my notebook.

He answers: *I AM ON BOARD OF MOCKING-BIRDS.*

"Oh." It slips out softly from my mouth, but Mr. Waldman doesn't notice. He's busy drawing a magnet on the board, the bald spot on the back of his head glaring out at us. It never occurred to me Martin would be involved. It never occurred to me *who* would be involved. Politics, issues, and stuff that doesn't involve dead composers have never been my thing, so I've barely given a second thought to who was in the Mockingbirds. The irony is I *should* know more about the Mockingbirds than most students.

My sister started it when she was a senior here. I didn't know it at the time, since I was only in eighth grade and living at home in New Haven. But she had told me about them a week before I left for Themis. She was busy packing for her first year of college, and I was practicing a complicated Liszt piece on the piano, planning to impress my music teacher the second I set foot on campus.

Casey popped downstairs and sat next to me on the bench, a rare public appearance for her. She'd spent most of the summer in a bad funk, holed up in her room and barely interacting with another human being.

"There's something you need to know about Themis," she said. "You have to watch your back because the teachers and administration won't do it for you."

"What's that supposed to mean?"

Casey told me about a group of seniors from the National

Honor Society who got bored one year and started a blog called "The Dishonorables." It was an attack on students who weren't part of the group. The administration heard about it and did nothing.

"Why would they?" I asked, a little underwhelmed by the whole thing. "It was just a stupid blog. People say dumb stuff on the Internet all the time."

"It wasn't just saying 'dumb stuff' on the Internet. It was relentless insults and taunts and bullying. And one of the girls was so messed up from it—from the name-calling— she left Themis and..."

"And nobody cared then?"

"Other than her, no. That's my point, Alex. Students shouldn't have to deal with that," she said, getting that look in her eyes like she was on a mission, like she was about to suit up and play soccer. "Themis totally ignores everything because the very idea of bullying destroys their notion of who Themis students are—of who they're educating to be future leaders of the world and all that stuff. They let it happen," she said, shaking her head in disgust. "So I decided to do something about it."

That something was the Mockingbirds.

Then she handed me the book—*To Kill a Mockingbird*—and told me to read it. "If *stuff* happens while you're at Themis, just know you have options."

She left the room, and I returned to Liszt because it all sounded kind of melodramatic to me. Then I started at

Themis, and I didn't really think about the Mockingbirds for the next two and a half years, except to use the copy of the book Casey gave me in my freshman lit class.

Now I'm thinking I might need to crack open that book again.

I look at Martin the Mockingbird as he writes one more note: *BRING QUARTERS.*

♦ ♦ ♦

Boo Radley's been leaving gifts for Scout and Jem as I bite into my apple. I turn the page, and now there are two pennies in the knothole of the tree next to their house. I take another bite, there's twine; then another, there are two soap figures; another, then the knothole's covered in concrete.

Which seems quite *unjust* to me, I decide as I toss the apple core into the trash.

Maia brought the apple back for me because I wasn't about to set foot in the cafeteria again. She has her headphones on. She blasts them whenever she's studying, so I can tell she's listening to Roxy Music now. Maia has a thing for British bands from the last century.

"Maia!" I shout. She's tapping her foot and she's hunched over a book on her desk, so she doesn't hear me. I take a piece of paper, crumple it up, and throw it at her. I hit her shoulder. She looks up, pulls the headphones off.

"Might there be a more civilized way to get my attention?"

"Did you know Martin was in the Mockingbirds?" I ask.

"Martin Summers," she says. "Of course. He's on the board, along with Amy Nichols and Ilana Ahearn."

"How do you know?"

"Because I like to know these sorts of things," Maia says playfully.

"I don't even know who those other people are and I definitely didn't know Martin was on it. He told me in physics today." I add, "Do you think everyone knows who's in the Mockingbirds?"

"Some students know. It's not supposed to be a secret entirely. That's partly how they have influence. But I don't think they broadcast the names. It's designed to be somewhat clandestine. And you know me—I like to know the things that not everybody else knows. Even if you asked T.S., she couldn't tell you the names of the others. She barely even knew Martin was on it, and she sees him more than we do."

"Maia...do you think *he* knows everything already? Martin, I mean."

"I honestly don't know," she says. "But why are you so worried about Martin?"

I shrug. "It's just I pictured strangers or something, students I don't really know. It all seemed very abstract and removed when we talked about it earlier today and totally like some bizarre Internet prank when Casey told me about it before I came here. But now it's real and *I'm* going there.

And there'll be students with names and faces and there'll be Martin too, someone I do know."

"It might make it easier, right?"

"I guess. We'll see...."

Then T.S. returns, opens the door with a flourish, and taps her watch. She's been gone most of the day, soccer practice after class (they still practice in the off-season, which delights T.S. to no end), then dinner, then visiting with Sandeep.

"We can't be late," she says.

"I wasn't going to be late," I say.

"Never said you were. All I'm saying is let's be on time."

"No, girls. Let's be early!" Maia declares joyously, hopping up from her desk.

"What is this, a party?" I ask.

Maia looks momentarily dejected. "I'm not invited?"

"I just didn't think about it."

Maia rolls her eyes. "Typical."

"Don't go there now," T.S. says sharply to Maia. "This is about Alex, not you."

Maia holds up her hands. "I believe I'm allowed to have an opinion and my opinion is I'm just as invested in this as you are, T.S. And I am equally committed to Alex."

"Guys," I say. "I want you both there."

"Besides," Maia says, giving us both a sly look, "I did do my fair share of recon. It's no surprise, really. You know, James Bond is my countryman."

With that, the tension seeps out of the room and T.S.

says, "Maybe you can go sniff out some laundry for us then, Ms. Bond."

"What do we need laundry for?" Maia asks.

"If you were really a top secret spy, you would know. Since you're not, grab your laundry. Both of you."

We do as we're told, snagging our laundry bags from the closet. T.S. extracts a roll of quarters from the pocket of her shorts. "I have mine."

I pat my back pocket, where I stuffed three dollars in quarters after Martin's tip. "Me too."

Maia dashes to her desk and grabs a handful of quarters, then we follow T.S. down the hall, laundry bags in tow, like a couple of hobos.

"This is really glam. Mind telling us what laundry has to do with the you-know-whats?" I ask.

T.S. shakes her head. "You guys are the worst secret agents ever. You cannot put clues together."

"You know, Maia, you should do your spring project on James Bond," I say in a faux British accent and even force a smile, because I don't want to be the dark and silent "date rape girl." I can still laugh, like I did at Martin's birdbrain joke. I can still be funny—or at least try to be.

"That's a fantastic idea," Maia says. She skips once, then turns around and walks backward so she can face us and talk. "You know, I could actually do something on the symbolism of the Bond Girl."

"Okay, I'll take the bait," T.S. says as she pushes

open the door to the stairwell. "What does the Bond Girl symbolize?"

"Independence. Because she's usually smart, rich, and self-employed, meaning she doesn't work for the government."

I open the front door of the dorm as I ask, "So it's better to be a Bond Girl than to be James Bond?" I like that we're not talking about me or the Mockingbirds or the four-letter word, so I'm happy to keep steering the conversation to the trivial.

T.S. shakes her head, points down the stairs. "Do you do laundry outside, dork?"

"Are we really doing laundry?" I ask.

T.S. nods.

"I thought it was just a cover."

Maia returns to my question. "It's totally better to be the Bond Girl. You should never work for the government."

"So, if you think about it, the Bond Girl really defies the idea of the Bond Girl *stereotype*," I say, catching T.S.'s attention with the last word.

"As the reigning expert on stereotypes I'd have to say the Bond Girl both embraces them and defies them," T.S. says.

"You're both wrong. She *rises* above them," Maia counters as T.S. opens the door to the basement level of the dorm. Someone's cleaned up the mess I made of the lost-and-found bin.

"Okay, can we take a break from the Bond Girl debate so you can tell us where the hell we're going?" I ask.

T.S. flips her short California Girl hair and tips her chin down the hall. "The laundry room."

"Right, yeah, figured that one out, T.S.," I say. "I mean, why are we going to the laundry room?"

"The Mockingbirds."

"I know that! But why *there*?" I ask.

"You'll see," she says.

"Do you know Martin's in it?" I ask.

"I'd heard he was in it," she says.

"Why does everyone know these things and I don't?"

"Like I told you before, not *everyone* knows," Maia says.

But I still feel like an idiot. Maybe I don't pay enough attention to what's going on around me. Maybe if I paid more attention, I wouldn't have been...I stop in my tracks, place a palm against the cold concrete wall. I still can't say the four-letter word, even to myself, even silently.

"You okay?" T.S. asks. I'm still holding on to the wall.

"I'm fine," I manage to say, and then keep walking.

"Anyway, as for Martin, yes I knew he was involved, but it's not as if we really talk about it. The case they heard last semester involved a bunch of freshmen anyway, no one we knew. Theater students, I think."

"Don't you think it's weird? That he's on it?"

T.S. looks at me. "Not really. Martin's always been, I don't know, above the fray."

I think about that for a moment: *above the fray*. Then the sound of a whirring dryer grows louder as my laundry bag bumps against my lower back. We continue our march down the linoleum floor and I can now hear more than one dryer going, tumbling in harmony, tossing clothes in end-less circles. The double doors to the laundry room are wide open. There's a sign on one of them, just a sheet of white paper with words in all caps in blue ballpoint pen: *THE KNOTHOLE.*

Clever. Very clever.

Chapter Nine

ATTICUS AND BOO ROLLED INTO ONE

I hear a voice asking, "What movie introduced audiences to a Mogwai named Gizmo?"

The question comes from a girl sitting cross-legged on a beat-up old mustard-colored couch all the way in the back of the laundry room. Her black hair is super-short, spiky almost, and she wears tight black jeans, black Converse high-tops, and a long-sleeve gray shirt. At first I think the question is for us, like a trick question, or a secret code or something. We have to answer it correctly or we can't pass through. Maybe we'll even fall through a trapdoor planted just a few feet in front of us. Then someone answers, a disembodied voice coming from the ground below us.

"Dude, *Gremlins,*" a familiar voice says.

"Nice," the short-haired girl says. Then to us, "Hey, want to play Trivial Pursuit?"

"Sure," T.S. says.

We walk past three rows of dryers and washers—one to our left, one to our right, and one on the far right wall. A boy and another girl pop up from the floor. The boy is Martin.

"Hey, Alex," he says. He has a gentle look in his eyes, caring even. Then he nods casually to Maia and T.S., acknowledging them.

"Hi," I say, still a little nervous to see him here, to even be here at all.

"Hey there," the other girl says. She's tall, dark-skinned with long braided hair and deep brown eyes. She's curvy too, big breasts and wide hips and wears a blue tank top and a long gray skirt. I've never met her before. "I'm Ilana," she says, offering a hand. I shake and notice her skin is toasty, as if she's been sitting next to a fire. Must be the dryers. They're all on high.

"Alex," I say.

The three of them shake hands with T.S. and Maia next, which must be some sort of Mockingbirds gentlemanly—or gentlewomanly, as Maia would say—protocol. Then the short-haired girl stands. I've never had any classes with her either. "I'm Amy. Thanks for reaching out. You're our first this term. Martin told us you guys all know each other. Cool."

Cool? Is that cool? But if she says so, fine, it's *cool*.

"Do you want to start your laundry and then sit down?" Amy asks next.

It's less of a question, more of a directive. Maia, T.S., and I file over to the washing machines. I wonder if we're just supposed to dry the clothes. I turn around, "Just dry?" I ask.

Amy, Ilana, and Martin all laugh, as if on cue. "You can wash your clothes," Amy says. "We're not into weird shit like making you dry clothes before you wash them."

I nod, then stuff the clothes in a machine, add soap, and punch the quarters in. Maia and T.S. do the same and we return to the couch area.

"Sit next to me," Amy says to me, patting the spot next to her on the couch. I do as I'm told. Ilana takes a chair this time, a mismatched partner to the couch. The chair looks as if it was born red but too many pizza stains over the years have turned it the color of grease. The pizza stains remind me I'm still hungry—that dinner would have been nice. T.S. sits on the other side of Amy, while Maia takes a spot on the floor next to Martin. There's a Trivial Pursuit game there with orange, purple, and blue pies on various spots on the board. They all have a few wedges in them already.

"You can be on my team," Amy says to me, and hands me a die. Ilana nods to T.S. and Martin to Maia.

I roll, wondering what this could possibly have to do with why we're here. But before the red dotted cube even lands Amy begins, "The game is for show, in case you were wondering. The laundry is for show too."

I nod, then land a six. "You move," Amy instructs. "Orange pie."

I move the orange pie to a music space. But Martin doesn't take out a card. Instead he says, "My parents tortured me with this game growing up. They made me play eighties Trivial Pursuit every Friday, so I took their board game over break and am determined to beat them at it just to prove you don't have to have lived through that decade to win the game."

He's just Martin, trying to be funny, to poke fun at himself too. It's not so weird he's here, after all.

"So rather than tell us about some British hair band, the first order of business is actually for me to let you know everything you say here is completely confidential," Amy says. Her voice is sweet, innocent sounding, despite the gravity behind the words. "Everything you say here stays here until you decide if you want to take it to the next step."

"What's the next step exactly?" I ask.

"Don't worry. We'll get there. For now, I want you to understand who we are, what we do, and why we exist. I have no doubt you know about our founding, right?"

"Just kind of sketchy details," I say, rattling off the little bit Casey had shared the week before I started at Themis, including the part about it being a justice system for the students, by the students.

Amy nods. "Exactly. We're Boo Radley and Atticus Finch all rolled into one. And our mission is to make things right. We investigate and try crimes committed by students against their fellow students."

Ilana jumps in. "We have to," she says, her voice strong,

passionate. "The administration thinks because Themis is this liberal, progressive school, nothing bad could happen here. There's no hate speech, no bullying here. How could there be? It's Themis. We're too good for that." She scoffs, then keeps going. "So they have their training programs every year about being politically correct and right and wrong and they think that's enough. They think being *enlightened* is enough, that we'd never do anything wrong because we're here and because they had Diversity Day for us."

When we were freshmen, we all went through an "Awareness Day." We learned about being good citizens, about bullying, about drug and alcohol addiction. We learned about suicide prevention too. The year before I got here, a Themis girl killed herself. It was all sort of hush-hush. No one talked about the specifics much, but the school made sure to talk about warning signs at Diversity Day.

So because the school had passed on its modern wisdom, nothing could go wrong. We've been trained to be good, because we *are* good. Everything is wonderful. No one gets punished—no student ever gets punished other than losing an attendance point here and there—because the administration thinks we're perfect. Because if we weren't, it would reflect badly on them. Just don't flunk a class though!

Maia can't resist jumping in. "That's completely what happened with my roommate, Kelly, last year. There was never any acknowledgment of her problem with prescription drugs. They didn't ask what was wrong or look into what her issues might be. Instead, she was just the girl who failed, so she's the girl who couldn't come back."

"They can't accept we're not perfect. We're teenagers, we're awful sometimes," Amy adds.

"That's why your sister started the Mockingbirds," Martin continues, and it occurs to me these three people—two strangers, one friend—probably know more about Casey's motives than I know. Maybe there's even a Mockingbirds history book somewhere, full of rules and laws and all the violations ever brought before them. Martin adds, "Because the school has given us no choice but to police ourselves."

Amy takes over now. "So what happened to you, Alex?" she asks, her clear blue eyes fixed on me.

I swallow hard. How am I supposed to tell them what happened? I can't even say the word to myself, let alone out loud. I close my eyes and wish Casey were here to speak for me. But instead the voice I hear belongs to T.S.

"Alex went out with a group of us Friday night and we were drinking and she got really drunk and wound up back in this guy's room, Carter Hutchinson's room. And she passed out. And he had sex with her twice," T.S. says, her voice threatening to break, but staying strong as the anger cements. She has her own anger over this, just like I have my shame.

I open my eyes and look away from them all. I watch the clothes, wet and clean in the washing machines. The dirt removed, they're new again. Like I can be, if I let them help me.

"I'm sorry, Alex," Amy says. Ilana and Martin murmur their condolences too.

I wipe away something wet on my cheek and look back at everyone. I shrug my shoulders, ready to move on. I don't need a public mourning—however well-intentioned—for what I've lost. "What now?" I ask.

"You mean what can we do?" Amy asks me.

"Yeah, what can you do?"

"Do you remember two years ago when Paul Oko stopped playing football?" Amy asks.

"He was the quarterback, right?" I say. Paul Oko was a star athlete, the pretty boy of the school, the golden child. One day, he simply stopped playing quarterback. I had never been to a Themis football game, but you didn't have to follow football to know about his exodus from the team. Especially because he *chose* to quit. I was a freshman but I still heard murmurs that there was more to it. He didn't just lose interest in his favorite sport.

Maia dives back in, always eager to contribute. "Right, it was totally out of the blue. One night in the cafeteria he just stood up and said 'I can't play football anymore. I'm quitting the team.'"

"Do you know *why* he quit?" Amy asks, looking to Maia now to see if she knows the answer.

But Maia always knows the answer. "Of course. He was the one who kept calling the receiver a faggot. Every day at practice Paul kept saying he didn't want to pass to a queer," Maia recalls. For a second Maia reminds me of T.S. with her encyclopedic knowledge of sports, but there's a key difference between them. T.S. allocates brain space for sports, plays, and strategy, Maia for people.

Amy nods. "The receiver came to us. Classic hate speech case."

"You're the reason he quit?" I ask, looking at Amy, Ilana, Martin. "I mean, that was the Mockingbirds? You can do that?"

"Just like we heard the case of the Dishonorables. We call them by the name they called their victims," Amy says with a snort. "Anyway, they all were leaders of the Honor Society. President, VP, secretary, and treasurer. Proof that power corrupts, right? Anyway, the Mockingbirds heard that case three years ago, when Casey was a senior. We heard Paul's case two years ago. Heard them both right here in this laundry room, and the council ruled in both cases. Seniors were guilty, Paul Oko was guilty."

"Are you the council?" I ask.

Amy shakes her head. "No, we're just the board of governors. We run the group, but we don't decide guilt or innocence. The council does, and it consists of nine students we appoint each term. The New Nine, so to speak. We're interviewing candidates now, so our tryout flyers are around campus. They come up through our system," she says, and I wonder what she means by *system,* but I don't ask. "Then we'll settle on the nine. And then when it's time for a case, three are randomly chosen a few days before to hear the case and render a verdict. That way the council can't really

be manipulated or bribed for a specific case. It keeps everything honest and it works."

"The council just hears the cases," Ilana adds in her
smooth voice. "In a perfect world—in the world Themis
thinks we have—there'd be no cases. But there are never
no cases. There are always too many cases. There's always
someone doing something wrong."

"So when Paul was found guilty, you made him resign
from the team?" I ask.

"We don't make people do anything," Amy says. "But
he knew what he was getting into."

Martin steps in to explain. "If you consent to a hearing
one way or the other, as the accused or the plaintiff, you
agree to the consequences," he says.

"And those are?"

"The thing you love most is taken away," Amy says.
"That's the punishment. That's the justice we can dole out.
Paul quit, as you know. And before our time, the four students on the Honor Society stepped down too. They
had to."

I let that sink in for a minute, the idea—no, the reality—
that underground justice is alive and well at Themis Academy. That students mete out punishments. That other
students adhere to them. "But what if the other person
doesn't agree to that? I mean, how do you enforce it?"
I ask.

The trace of an impish grin forms on Amy's pert face.
"We don't usually have to enforce it. Most students agree

to the code, because the code is for them. We're here for each other. So it's not usually a problem."

Ilana leans her head to one side, then the other, stretching her neck, as she adds, "But just in case, we make sure students are, how shall we say, *compelled* to appear before the hearing and agree to the terms."

"You don't beat them up, do you?" Maia asks aggressively. "Because that would go against the whole purpose of the group, you know? You're supposed to be 'doing good.'"

Ilana and Amy exchange smiles. "I like that you brought your bulldog, Alex."

"English bulldog," Maia adds, never content to let someone else get the last word.

"Martin, do you want to explain?" Amy asks.

Martin leans closer to us, his brown hair falling into his eyes. He pushes his hair back, then is dead serious. "We're not violent and we don't bully. That would go against what we stand for. We're here to be good, to do good, and to make a difference. And we have nonviolent ways of helping students in need, like you."

Ilana jumps in. "We helped some freshmen last semester," she says. "All sorts of absurd backstabbing going on amongst the young thespian community. But we got it sorted out."

They're masked avengers, Robin Hood or Spider-Man, caped crusaders fighting for truth, justice, the American way.

"So...," Amy says, breaking the silence. "If we take your case on—"

"You don't take on every case?" I ask, interrupting her and silently taking in the possibility that, after all this, I might be stuck dealing with this alone.

Amy shakes her head. "Nope. We vet them first. We have to make sure it's a case we can handle fairly."

I wonder how they'll be sure when I can't even remember everything. I hate that I was that drunk. I hate that I became someone who can't remember, whose defense rests on having been in a completely unremembering state of mind.

"...So as I was saying, if we try this case, it would be the first date rape case for the Mockingbirds, Alex. We're still relatively new and the code of conduct is evolving. And because of our mission—we want to be fair and just—we'll need to revise the code of conduct to include date rape. The original code was just written broadly, that's all. So we want to cover all our bases. And then we'll have to vote on it."

"The three of you?" T.S. asks.

Ilana chuckles. "No, not us," she says. "You don't seem to get it. The three of us are only here to make sure the Mockingbirds exist. The Mockingbirds are really all of us, all the students. *We* don't matter. *You* matter. The students matter. The students will vote on the revisions. The code is for the students. Everything we do is for the students, for each other."

"We'll meet separately to prepare and then let you know when the vote is," Amy says. Then she looks to me and almost drops her hand on my leg. I can sense it would be in a friendly way, a caring way, but she stops, guessing that physical contact isn't my thing right now. This understanding, this awareness, flickers through her blue eyes in an instant and it's as if she possesses a sort of heightened sensitivity. "But don't worry about it, Alex. It's a formality. It'll pass. The administration might not get it, but most students know it's not something we want happening here."

"And if it passes?" I ask quietly.

"Then, assuming we accept your case, you have the option to have a hearing before the council, like a mock trial, only it's real and has real consequences. But we're getting ahead of ourselves, Alex."

I picture Carter here in this room in a mock witness stand, being grilled by prosecutors, forced to defend his defenseless behavior, all of it, the date rape and the ugly rumors. I picture having to listen, to recount what happened for him, for the council. I don't want to do that, not at all. But then I picture a semester of vicious whispers and nasty lies in the cafeteria and the halls of the school—a semester of being "Easy Alex."

"So does anyone want to finish this?" Martin asks, cupping the die in his right palm, his fingers wrapped over it. He tosses it onto the board and moves two spots when he rolls a deuce. "Wild card," he says. Then he looks to Amy and she to me.

"And now," she says, "you're going to need to tell us your account of what happened that night so we can decide if we want to take your case on—if it's the type of case where we can be fair and be good."

So I begin the story....

Chapter Ten
SMASHING E

I have this dream sometimes, only it's not really a dream. I'm awake and imagining. And in the waking dream, I'm in the cramped lavatory of an airplane. I wash my hands with the liquid soap, smelling faintly of lemongrass, or at least what the manufacturer thinks is lemongrass, but it's really just some industrial substitute scent. The skin on my hands is dry and flaky afterward, but that happens on airplanes. They suck the moisture out of you.

Anyway, I turn to the door and push the lock to the side. I try to unlock the door, but I can't. I keep pushing, jamming harder to slide the lock over, but the door never opens and I'm stuck there in the airplane bathroom, surrounded by stale air and industrial soap scents, and my face grows hotter and my fear grows higher and all I want is out, out, out.

I always thought if I were raped I would feel that way. Or maybe that way magnified times ten, twenty, one hundred. I've thought about rape before. I pictured it happening to me. A dark alley, some rough guy I don't know who's five times my size grabs me and forces me to my knees, a knife to my throat. Sometimes I'd picture it happening in my house while everyone was asleep. He'd come in through my window and hover above me. I'd be startled awake, pinned down in my own bed, everything I know that's right in the world ripped out of my chest.

That is rape.

I know rape is something else too. It's just I always thought of it in a very specific way—with a very specific kind of attacker—not in a way I'd have to defend, not in a way where I'd have to preface everything with "I was drunk, really drunk."

And that's what I'm saying as I tell the story of *that night* to Ilana, Amy, Martin, and really to T.S. and Maia in detail for the first time. I tell them I was really, really drunk, knowing they'll decide if my story is good enough—or really, bad enough—for them to take me on.

I finish and Amy immediately says they'll take the case. Somehow I passed the first test. In some weird way, it's reassuring. Her speed in deciding to take me on is more evidence that what happened that night wasn't right.

103

The three of them pack up Trivial Pursuit while the three of us grab our laundry.

"So the next step is we're going to take a vote with the students to revise the code," Amy tells me before we leave. "And then you can decide if you want to move forward."

I nod and Amy says she'll be in touch soon. We leave and when we hit the landing of the stairwell that leads both outdoors and upstairs, I say to Maia and T.S., "Guys, I need to go practice. Can you take my laundry back up?"

"Sure," T.S. says, reaching for my bag. "You okay?"

"I'm fine."

"Do you think you want to take it to a hearing?" T.S. asks gently.

I do, but I don't. I don't, but I do.

All I want right now is to be as far away from this as I possibly can. So I shrug, pull on a sweatshirt from my now clean and dry laundry, and then leave for the music hall. It's cold out so I wrap my arms around myself and put my head down. I look at the stone pathway, the patches of dead grass next to it, the light from the quad's old-fashioned street-lamps bouncing off the trees, and I don't notice I'm about to walk into someone. "Oh," I say, my heart beating faster, my mind praying it's not Carter. But when I look up I see Martin.

"Hey," he says.

"How'd you get here so fast?" I ask, taking a step back.

"I had a feeling you'd be going to the music hall."

"How'd you know?"

"Because everyone knows you're the star piano player."

"But how did you know I was going there tonight?" I cross my arms. Because now he seems like Mockingbird Martin, not Martin Martin.

"I saw you leave. I was walking back to my dorm and I saw you walking across the quad and I didn't want you to walk by yourself."

"I'm okay," I insist.

"I know you're okay. I know you're tough."

"Tough? How do you know I'm tough?"

"You have to be tough to stand up for what's right," he says.

"Is that what I'm doing?"

He nods firmly and the look in his eyes is clear, resolute. "Yes, God, yes."

I look at the ground.

"Hey," he says softly. "I'm sorry you went through it. I'm sorry it happened. And I know it wasn't easy to tell your friends or to tell us or to tell me, the only guy there tonight, even though I was at the concert."

"Wait. Does that mean they can't take my case on? Is it a conflict of interest you being there earlier that night?"

He shakes his head quickly. "No. It won't have any impact. I told Amy before the meeting."

"Oh," I say, figuring his telling Amy must be another part of the Mockingbirds be-on-the-up-and-up protocol.

"Anyway, I hope you don't feel weird or anything around me. Because you shouldn't."

What, is he reading my mind? "How did you know I felt that way?" I ask.

He gives a half-smile. His eyes, they light up again, even in the darkness. I think it's the green flecks. I wish I had green flecks in my eyes. Mine are just brown.

"I sensed it so I wanted to say it. And because we're friends already. That's why I want to walk you to the music hall. May I?"

It occurs to me he's asking to be nice, to do the right thing, because he's the type of guy who sees a girl alone at night and doesn't hit on her, doesn't leer, doesn't try anything but simply asks if he can walk her to where she's going. He's the opposite of Carter. He's above the fray.

"So how are those birdbrains?" I ask as we start walking.

He smiles, holds up his index finger, then lowers his voice. "Mark my words, Alex. Someday jays will take over the world. They will be our masters, our leaders, and we will bow down before them."

I imagine a blue jay in the Oval Office wearing a tiny gray suit, a red-and-blue-striped tie around his neck. His feathery head is tucked down; he pores over a policy position his defense secretary—a cardinal—slipped onto his desk earlier this morning. The jay reaches for a fountain pen, his wing stretching out to grab the heavy silver pen, and a servant pops in, a person, a human, carrying a tray of tea and cookies—wait, make that worms—and hands it to the presidential bird. I laugh, both at the scene in my mind and Martin, for planting the seed. I like how he can go from serious and real to silly and fun in a heartbeat, and to know what's needed in that same heartbeat too.

"I will consider myself forewarned, then, of the inevitable blue jay coup."

"Actually, they're scrub-jays. Anyway, just don't tell anyone about my conspiracy theories, okay? They might think I'm crazy," he says, then circles his index finger near his ear, the universal gesture for loony.

"Your scrub-jay secret is safe with me," I say playfully, but then I don't feel so playful anymore because I think about *my* secret, only it's not a secret anymore. He knows, T.S. knows, Maia knows, the Mockingbirds know. If I go through with a mock trial, more people will know. *Everyone* will know.

"Thank you, Martin," I say when I reach the door to the music hall. It'll be unlocked. It's always unlocked. That's the Themis way. But I don't invite him in, nor does he ask to go in.

"So, I'm just going to hang out over there," he says, pointing to a thick oak tree twenty, thirty feet away, its branches bare for the winter. "I'm going to sit down on the grass and finish conjugating French verbs in the pluperfect tense or something, and when you're done, you'll pretend you just ran into me for the first time tonight, that I wasn't waiting for you, and then I'll walk you back."

"But it's freezing out," I say.

"And I have a coat," he says, pointing to his fleece pullover.

"You don't have to wait for me," I say.

"I know," he adds.

"You don't have to," I say again.

"But I'd like to. I'll just be over there, okay?"

I nod and walk into the music hall. It's dark and quiet and all mine and I don't turn on the light because I don't want to draw anyone's attention to my being here except Martin. Besides, I can play without lights. I push everything else out of my mind. Amy, Ilana, Paul Oko, the receiver, the dishonored seniors, the theater backstabbers, my sister the crusader, my apple for dinner, *that night,* even Martin sitting under the tree on the cold, hard ground. They all are vapor to me now. I settle in at the piano, my sanctuary, thinking this is home; this is me. This is what I do. This is the me before, during, and after *that night.*

I have a Mozart performance with Jones coming up soon, Sonata for Violin and Piano no. 35. I close my eyes and practice my part. The first movement I know well. The second I know expertly. The third I know, but it can be better. I make mental Post-its to review with my music teacher. When I'm done, I feel centered, relaxed, connected. I feel as if I could play all night and not grow tired. So I go back to my standby, to "Ode to Joy."

As my middle finger presses down on E, I hear it playing *that night* and I'm back in time.

"Mmm…," a voice whispers near my ear. Or in my mouth. I'm not really sure. It's probably in my mouth, I

reason. Because his tongue is there too. His tongue is pressed into my mouth, touching my tongue. I've never liked deep kissing. I like lip kissing, sweet kisses, soft lips like Daniel's, not tongues with minds of their own. "Let's go back to my room," he says.

Something sounds very reasonable about that idea. It sounds like a plan, a well thought-out plan. He stands up and reaches for my hand. I stumble a bit when I stand, so he holds my hand tighter, then leads me out of the room, down the hall, and to the back stairs.

"It's late, so we have to be careful," he says.

"Right. Careful," I agree, holding tight to the railing as I walk down the stairs.

Then we're outside behind Richardson Hall. At least I think it's Richardson Hall. Anyway, it's dark, and it's night, and the air is clear, and for a second my head is clear. I breathe deeply, breathing in the clear air. And when I do, I know I don't want to go to his room. I don't want to go at all. I want to go to my bed and crash forever.

"Um, I'm going to go back to my room," I manage. The words are sticky in my throat. It doesn't seem like he hears them.

"Carter, I want to go back," I say louder.

But he still doesn't respond. Instead, he holds my hand tighter, gripping it hard, and my knuckles feel like putty under his big hands. I feel like a dog on a leash, pulling her head back, resisting, but the owner pulls forward, insisting.

The dog doesn't win. The dog never wins. The owner drags him along. I wish I could bark. Or bite.

"You'll like my room," he says, ignoring my request. "I have 'Ode to Joy.'"

I play faster, harder, like "Ode to Joy" is a phone I want to throw against the wall. I play it like my mom just told me I'm grounded for a month and I'm so mad at her I take the phone and throw it against the wall in my bedroom. And the battery pops out and the phone goes dead. And my mom says she'll take it out of my allowance, the money for a new phone, because this one can't be fixed. But I don't care because it felt good to throw it, felt good to break it.

It feels so good to play hard and calloused and fierce because now I'm angry, angry at things that happened while I was sleeping. And I'm angry at Beethoven. Because now my music is infected. Because my last great escape is tainted. It's one thing for a memory to rear its head when T.S. just happens to mention Beethoven's name, like she did on the way to the Captains' Room. But it's another thing entirely for Carter to invade my piano, my music, my home.

I slam the cover over the keys; the notes sound a faint cry as they're tucked in violently for the night. But that's not enough for me right now. It's not enough at all. Nothing is mine anymore. I have nothing separate from *that night.*

I lift the lid again, clench my jaw, and dare the first note—E—to fuck with me. I press it hard with my index finger.

Take that.

But the memories stay silent.

Afraid, are you, piano? Think I can't handle it? Let's do it again, then.

I jam harder on the E, pressing with a fury that borders on a hurricane.

Still nothing but the note.

Bring it on. Show me more. Show me all of that night.

I slam my hand on the piano, then I make a fist and smash it into the keys. I do it again and again and again. I can own this piano. I can teach this piano not to mess with me. The notes scream out, but I don't stop. They're crying now, begging for mercy, but I'm not through yet.

By the time I'm done, my hand stings, my bones hurt, and I'm actually panting. I step back, take a few calming breaths. My chest rises and falls. Then I look at the piano and I gasp because I swear the middle E is just a hair's breadth shorter than the keys next to it. I cover my mouth with my hand, astonished, embarrassed, ashamed at what I've done. I maimed the piano.

"I'm sorry. I'm so sorry," I say, my voice breaking, my throat burning. I sink down to my knees and I touch the damaged key, barely brushing it. It's tender and I don't want to hurt it any more.

I pull on my jacket, noticing there's now a dull throb starting in the back of my neck. I'm getting another headache. I don't know if Carter is giving me headaches or if I'm giving them to myself. But I deserve this one for what I did. I won't take an aspirin. I won't take a Tylenol. I will let this headache hurt me.

I leave the music hall and Martin's there, as he said he would be. He shuts his French book, puts his paper away, and stands up. I don't say anything at first. He doesn't either. He heard me, he must have heard me. He doesn't mention it.

"What happened to the freshmen last semester?" I ask as we walk.

"What happened?" he repeats.

"Yes. You heard their case, right?"

"It didn't go to trial," he says.

"So what happened?"

"They confessed. They took their punishment."

"I take it I won't be seeing these freshmen in the production of *Merry Wives of Windsor* this semester, then."

"You are correct in that assumption. Not *Merry Wives*, not anything."

"Good," I say. "They deserved it."

But I don't know if I'm talking about them or Carter or myself right now. Everything inside me is like a mangled mass of cars on the highway, and I'm waiting for the paramedics to come untangle them.

Chapter Eleven
PIANO INJUSTICE

"We need more scientists," Mr. Christie declares from the front of the classroom.

He's standing, but he places a foot on the seat of a chair. He kind of leans into the chair, placing his right hand on his right knee, in emphasis or something, as if this position makes him a more passionate lecturer. It can only mean he's about to dispense a new assignment, especially since it's the start of a new week—our second full week of classes.

He strokes his reddish beard, pushes his wire-rimmed glasses back up on his nose. He wears corduroy slacks, a button-down shirt, a shabby jacket. I wonder if he wishes he were at Williamson instead, if he'd rather be a college professor, but then I'm sure like all the others he thinks Themis is its own sort of heaven. Tenure awarded after just a few years, the wildest assignments you can dream up, and a whole army of students to sing and dance for you.

"Thomas Friedman says we need more scientists," Mr. Christie says, elaborating in his deep baritone. He pauses. He pauses a lot in his lectures. I bet when he writes his lectures he puts *pause here* in his notes. "Do we need more scientists?" he asks. "Is that what our world needs? As the world gets flatter and we run in place faster just to keep up, do you" — he pauses again, this time to point at all of us in the room — "agree?"

We don't know. We haven't read the book. But he's about to assign it to us.

Still rocking back and forth against his right leg, he says, "Tonight, I want you to begin reading *The World Is Flat: A Brief History of the Twenty-first Century*. And I want you to think about what we need most. You can agree or disagree with Mr. Friedman."

Of course. It's encouraged, in fact. We're not expected to agree with teachers or texts or the conventional wisdom. We are expected, however, to back up our dissent with facts and arguments and logic. Mr. Christie teaches history, but not the pilgrims and tea party kind. He teaches world affairs. He says he's concerned with what's happening today in the United States and in the world and how we got here. That's why he's not going to assign any textbooks this semester, he says. Instead, we will read modern works by modern writers on the modern world and come to modern conclusions, he says.

"Please read the first five chapters before the next class," Mr. Christie says. "For each chapter, I want you to write a ten-word statement on what each of you deems the most cogent point in that chapter—no more, no fewer than ten words. You need to be able to distill your thoughts and impressions succinctly and be prepared to present them in a lively discussion."

He pauses, paints a smile on his face. He looks pleased with himself, as if he can simply decide by fiat that the discussion will be *lively*. Make it so, Mr. Christie, make it so.

"Class dismissed."

I reach for my backpack and sling it over my shoulder, ready to leave with T.S., until Mr. Christie calls me over. He's my junior advisor. I walk to the front of the classroom as the other students file out. "Alex, let's chat for a minute," Mr. Christie says.

He still hasn't moved his leg off that chair. He rests his hand on his knee, as if he's a statue. Maybe there's glue on the bottom of his shoe. Maybe he realized it when he parked his foot up there and now he's too proud to admit it. Maybe he's going to ask me for a knife or an X-Acto blade to slide between the bottom of his shoe and this chair. But then he takes his foot off the chair and stands like a normal person. Well, as normal as any Themis teacher can be.

"Let's talk about your spring project," he says. Another deep pause. "What would you like to do? How would you like to make your mark on Themis Academy?"

I picture a dog, a naughty little beagle pup named Amelia, whizzing on the carpet, making her mark.

"This is kind of going to be a big surprise and all, but I thought I'd do something music-related."

He misses the sarcasm, just beams instead. His eyes are like saucers, as if I just said the most creative, delightful thing a student has ever uttered.

"Music-related! That's genius!"

Who would have thought the piano girl would do her project on music? It's mind-blowing!

"Tell me more, Alex."

I'm about to utter the name of my favorite symphony, then I stop. Because Beethoven betrayed me last week. And then I betrayed him with the way I played. How can I do my spring project on Beethoven after what we did to each other? He didn't even write a piano part in the Ninth Symphony, for God's sake. He wrote a million piano concertos but just happened to leave out *my* instrument from the greatest piece of music ever written. How's that for injustice?

Then I realize it's perfect. *Injustice.* It's the perfect subject because it suits me right now.

"I want to do my spring project on the injustice of Beethoven *not* writing a part for the piano in the Ninth Symphony. Did you realize that, Mr. Christie? He left the piano out. It's scored for the largest group of instruments of *any* Beethoven symphony and yet he left out the best instrument ever in the entire world," I say crisply. "He included

116

trumpets and horns and oboes and violins and even a bassoon of all things. There are vocals in it too. You can be a singer and sing 'Ode to Joy' in the Ninth Symphony. But what do we get? Nothing. Nothing at all."

Mr. Christie nods, several times. Then he narrows his boring brown teacher's eyes and assumes a thoughtful, contemplative look. "I think that's simply a brilliant idea, Alex."

He holds up his index finger, then places it against his mouth. "You can research scholars, music experts, interview great classical pianists...."

Blah, blah, blah. As if I don't know how to do research.

"But how ever will we have you perform it if there's not a piano part?" Mr. Christie asks, looking absolutely confounded.

My heart stops. Did Mr. Christie actually just say that? "Perform it? I can perform it? For the whole school?"

I tell myself not to show emotion in front of him, but my brain is pretty much popping all over with excitement.

"That's ideally the goal. A performance for the entire student body and the teachers. But how would you do it if there's no piano part?"

My eyes widen and I'm the only kid in class who knows the answer. "Liszt," I say, and in that moment I want to kiss the Hungarian composer. "Franz Liszt transcribed it for the piano. It was a daunting task, and it took him years. He almost stopped. But he soldiered on and he did it. And that's why he's my musical hero. That's the heart of my spring project."

117

For a moment I feel chills, good chills, thinking of Liszt, thinking of his dedication, his brilliance, his quest to turn all of Beethoven's symphonies into solo pieces for the piano Liszt loved as much as I do.

"I am totally behind this. But we will also have to get it approved, of course, by Miss Damata," he says, then quickly corrects his faux pas. "I meant *Ms.* Damata."

But she's already Miss Damata to me now. "Miss Damata? Who's that?" I ask.

"She's the new music teacher."

"I didn't know we had a new music teacher," I say. Elective classes like music start the second week of the term.

"Mr. Graser had a job offer in California over the holiday break," Mr. Christie says, referring to Themis's previous music teacher. "He accepted it, but never fear. Everything happens for a reason, for we were able to quickly secure Victoria Damata. She has taught at Juilliard."

"Juilliard?" I ask, practically salivating. She knows people. She knows the right people. She can help me get in. I will do whatever she wants. Juilliard has less than an eight percent acceptance rate, and if a former teacher from Juilliard just landed at my school I will do everything on this earth to get in her good graces, and she will write me the most amazing letter, and she will phone up all her contacts, and she will put in all sorts of good words for me, and in less than two years I will be in New York training under the greatest teachers the world has ever known.

"Yes, Juilliard. I do know how very much you want to go there."

I nod, unable to speak. I will curtsey when I meet Miss Damata. I will sweep her office, empty the trash, fetch her sheet music any time of day or night.

"Allow me to introduce you. Come with me."

Mr. Christie gestures to the door of his classroom and I walk out with him, then across the quad, where for the first time ever I'm grateful for his presence. Today, he's my Carter buffer. He opens the door to the music hall in some sort of ridiculously gallant gesture and there's *Ms.* Damata at the piano. Her blond hair is piled on top of her head; she wears a high-necked beige blouse, a pencil-thin green skirt. I flinch for a second, thinking she knows what I did to the piano that night last week.

But then she smiles, warm and kind, and I know she could never be mad at me for that. She would understand.

I adore her instantly.

Chapter Twelve
A WINK AND A NOD

Miss Damata is a rock star.

She's performed as a soloist with the Chicago Symphony Orchestra, London Symphony Orchestra, and New York Philharmonic. She won the Rachmaninoff Piano Competition. She plays in the Mostly Mozart Festivals in the summer. Oh, and she has a bachelor's degree in music from Juilliard too.

I know this because I haven't stopped asking her questions. She is gracious and warm; she answers everything I ask. I ply her with more questions. "Who is your favorite composer?" I ask.

"Schumann," she answers. "Anything by Schumann."

"I love Schumann too," I say. "Wait. Do you mean Clara or Robert?" I ask. Robert Schumann was the more famous of the married pair of pianists, but his wife, Clara, wrote beautiful piano pieces, concertos, even a piano trio.

"Clara," Miss Damata says.

"Me too!" I say, and my stomach growls. I place a hand on my belly, hoping she didn't hear. I haven't gone to the cafeteria since the run-in there last week with Carter and Kevin. I've been subsisting on pretzels and Clif Bars and whatever T.S. or Maia brings back for me. "Most people don't know about her work," I add. "But, then again, you're not most people. You're a star. You're a Juilliard grad! A Juilliard teacher."

She simply smiles and says "thank you," then continues. "Her work was very romantic. But she stopped composing after she turned thirty-six," Miss Damata says. Her voice is like powder, falling snow. "She even said, 'I once believed that I possessed creative talent, but I have given up this idea; a woman must not desire to compose—there has never yet been one able to do it. Should I expect to be the one?'"

"I've always thought it was terrible she felt that way. It was completely an *injustice* that she stopped composing," I add, dropping in my new favorite word as we bond more over Clara. "It's like we're the poorer for it."

"Especially because she was so genuinely talented. She wasn't just talented for a woman. She was talented period. She could hold a candle and then some to the men, and our field is dominated by men. The teachers, the students, the composers, the stars."

A twinge of guilt rushes through me because I have never given Clara a spot in my assembly of greats. I have never asked for her guidance when I needed musical help. I have turned only to men, and those men let me down after *that night*. I bet Clara wouldn't have let me down. I bet Clara would have had something to say. I glance down at the piano, at the key I abused. It looks fine—it's been playing fine for the last week—but I should say something.

"Miss Damata," I begin, "do you think the E sounds off, like maybe someone..." I trail off, leaving my unspoken question hanging there.

She plays a few bars from Liszt's Consolation no. 3; the notes are like a morning bird singing. "It sounds just the same as always to me."

I close my eyes and listen to her play, and the piece soothes me. I picture it smoothing out the keys, restoring them under her gentle touch to the way they were before.

"Do you know Schumann's March in E-flat Major?" Miss Damata asks.

I open my eyes. "Yes."

"Would you like to play it with me?" she says.

We play Clara Schumann's piano duet together and I feel the first ounce of unblemished joy I've felt since *that night*. When we're done Miss Damata tells me she's *delighted* to be teaching me this year. "You're everything Mr. Graser said you would be. We're going to have a great year," she says.

If I were a blusher, I would blush. Instead I ask, "Why would you come to Themis when you were at Juilliard, when you've performed on world stages? That's so much bigger than us."

"Juilliard is a wonderful place, Alex," she says. A strand of hair falls down out of her bun. She reaches for the blond pieces, tucks them behind her ear, and continues. "But I guess I'm not that different from Clara Schumann. I didn't think Manhattan was a good place to raise a family. I wanted a quieter life."

Maybe she has kids, but even so I swear I will never understand adults, even the cool ones like Miss Damata.

After we finish I take the long way to physics class, my boots crunching against the frozen ground as I go. Even though I'll have to see Carter *in* class, I refuse to run into him on the way *to* class. I can't give him a chance to try to talk to me, to try to touch me. So I have meticulously plotted out circuitous routes to all my classes. Maia did some detective work for me—I have a hunch Amy, Ilana, and Martin helped her out too over the last week—and we were able to reverse engineer Carter's entire schedule. She placed it on my desk the other night with a flourish.

"Ta-da," she said. "This is for when we can't be there to walk with you."

We mapped out how *not* to see him, down to the very second so I could still make it to classes on time. Now I take the long way everywhere, even though it's winter, even though it's freezing or snowing or sleeting or basically spitting up something wet and cold nearly every day in Providence.

Today, the ice is a minefield behind the music hall. I dodge one patch, but my left boot catches the next one the wrong way and before I know it, my feet are sliding out from under me and my ass collides with the cold, hard ground.

"Crap," I mutter as I push myself up, grabbing my backpack. I stand and my right cheek already hurts and I can tell I will have a gigantic bruise by the end of the day. I make it to physics, wishing I were the kind of student who could just ditch a class, but I'm not a ditcher. I've never missed a class. And I'm not going to miss one now, even with an ass bruise the size of Alaska, even though Carter will walk into class any second.

I slide into my seat and Martin gives me a quick look. I'd be lying if I said I didn't feel a little awkward around him now, but he's also the only reason I can survive physics.

"I still have to show you those levitation pics," he says, and I don't feel awkward anymore.

"I was worried you were holding out on me," I tease.

"Never," he says.

But before I can say something else, I freeze. Carter saunters in, unzips his jacket, stops for a second, gives me a look, then winks. I can see the tip of his tongue almost sticking out the side of his mouth, in what he must think is some vaguely seductive, sexy invitation. I feel my stomach coil like a spring, hard and tight. He turns back and keeps walking, sliding into his seat at the front.

Then Mr. Waldman enters the room, briskly, not even looking at us. When he reaches the podium, he peers out at the class, his bald head bobbing quickly, his eyes moving up and down each aisle, taking attendance. He writes something down on a piece of paper. Two seconds later a runner walks in and rushes up the aisle to Mr. Waldman, who holds the attendance slip in his outstretched hand. The student grabs it and heads out, but before he leaves I see him glance at Martin. Martin gives the student a nod, firm, precise. The runner gives him a quick one in return, then darts out.

I look to Martin, my curiosity piqued. Does he know all the runners back from when he was a runner? But he's reaching for a pencil, looking the other way. When class ends, Martin puts a hand gently on my back and guides me out of class. He's protecting me, getting me out of Carter's line of sight. We walk across the quad and pass the bulletin board in front of McGregor Hall, where flyers flap in the wind. Martin tips his chin toward the board, where there's a red notice with the bird staring at us.

The big bold letters are the words of Atticus Finch to his daughter, Scout.

You never really understand a person until you consider things from his point of view.

It's about playing fair.

That's why the Mockingbirds consider all views — all votes — in the revised time for our first concert.

Then there's a time and a date—one week from now. But the Mockingbirds won't be performing then. Instead, they'll be counting votes, adding up how many Themis students think date rape is a crime worthy of being deemed a violation of the only code of conduct that matters here.

Martin leans in to whisper. "Students have a full week to get their votes in. We think it's more than enough time. You'll find the ballot under your door tomorrow morning after first period."

Chapter Thirteen

THE START OF SOMETHING

The next day, I'm dying for English class to end. I look at the clock, willing it to tick closer to ten so I can sprint out of here and grab the piece of paper that's sure to be under my door.

Five more minutes.

Four more minutes.

Three more, two more, one more...

"And don't forget, I want to see your first scenes in your Shakespeare adaptations by the end of the week," Ms. Peck says.

The bell rings and I turn to Jones, my wingman. I want to tell him to run, sprint, fly with me. But I haven't told him the other stuff yet, the reason I'm dying to see what's under my door.

"How's our Mozart sonata coming along?" I ask as we leave the classroom.

"I need to practice more. I'm sure you know it cold."

"Of course."

"I'm sure you're going to kick my ass in it," he says.

"Maybe I should."

"Why can't they just let me play Clapton?" he half-moans.

"Why don't you do your spring project on Clapton and then you can?" I suggest as we walk across the quad. It's snowing lightly, but the flakes coming down are wet, watery snow. Still, a pair of brave jock boys play Frisbee in only jeans and T-shirts, as if they're proving how tough they are. I do a quick scan, eyes darting back and forth, checking for signs of Carter, Kevin, water polo players. They're nowhere to be seen. Still, I'm glad to have Jones next to me.

"Hey," he says. "Today's the day, right?"

My cheeks burn and I suddenly feel exposed. "How did you know?" I ask quietly.

"Know?" he replies casually. "Everyone knows. I mean, you vote, right?"

"Oh, you mean the vote?" I breathe again.

"What else would I mean?"

"To revise the code of conduct?" I ask eagerly, just to make sure he's talking about the vote in general, not me in particular.

"Obviously."

"So how are you going to vote?" I ask.

Jones stops and gives me a look. His hair falls onto his face and he brushes it back with his long fingers. "How am I going to vote? What do you think? Do you think I'm some kind of troglodyte?"

"Points for using an SAT word!"

"I rock in the SAT points department, and they're only two months away," he says triumphantly as we reach Taft-Hay Hall. "Still...," he says, his voice trailing off.

"Still what?"

"I still think it's strange that students try other students."

"You do?"

"Yeah, it's weird. It should be the school or students working with the school."

I give him a look. "Jones. You know what they're like."

"I know. I'm just saying it *should* be that way."

"But it's not," I say, willing myself not to get emotional, "and we don't have another choice."

"I just wish there was a better way."

"This *is* the better way," I insist.

Jones gives me a crooked smile. "You're drinking the Kool-Aid, aren't you?"

I should tell him. I should tell him what happened.

"Why are you so worked up about this, Alex?" he asks. "I thought you were all music all the time."

He's my friend and I should tell him. But there will be time enough for that later.

"I better go vote," I say, and then dash up the three

flights of stairs and into my room. I close the door tightly behind me, and there it is.

A white sheet of paper, but with the familiar bird trademark. I pick it up, take it to my desk, and sit down.

> **Sexual assault is against the standards to which Themis students hold themselves. Sexual assault is sexual contact (not just intercourse) where one of the parties has not given or cannot give active verbal consent, i.e., uttered a clear "yes" to the action. If a person does not say "no" that does not mean he or she said "yes." Silence does not equal consent. Silence could mean fear, confusion, inebriation. The only thing that means yes is yes. A lack of yes is a no.**

Somewhere in this school, somewhere in another dorm room, Carter could be reading this too. And if he is, is his mind churning, sick with the knowledge he did *this*? That he did what he's reading? Is he afraid I know that he did this? Is he afraid because this vote could give me the power to do something about it, the power to be someone other than that girl who's not eating dinner, not eating lunch?

My eyes narrow; they burn the white paper in front of me. A hole burns in it, I swear, all black and charred in the middle of the words *not say "no"* as I remember his tongue pushing into my mouth, his crusty lips the next morning, and above all, his unforgivable laziness in not recycling his Diet Coke.

Who doesn't recycle? I mean, really. Who doesn't recycle a soda can?

Someone who'd do *this*.

I pick up my pencil and make my mark on the paper hard, a coarse check mark next to YES.

As I write I push the pencil down so hard on the paper it splinters; the point of the pencil actually shears off. But then I look down and I see the pencil tip is still intact, so I must have just imagined it breaking or wanted it to break. I put the pencil down, fold up the paper, and look out the window. The snow's getting wetter, mushier.

I fold the paper in quarters, then eighths, then sixteenths, and bring it to the mailbox for the Mockingbirds in the student activities office, where they're listed as "The Mockingbirds/a cappella singing group." Then, since it's my free period, I head to the library to start my research on the injustice of the Ninth Symphony. The snow's wetter, almost rain now, and I've forgotten my umbrella, so I walk faster. When I get there I push my wet hair away from my face and head toward the computer catalog, eyeing a free computer at the end of the row. A student who has been sitting at another computer stands up, practically bumping into me.

It's Carter and I'm paralyzed. This is what I try to avoid; this is why I don't eat at the cafeteria anymore; this is why I take the long way to class; this is why I have wingmen.

"Hey," he says in his library voice. "What are you up to?"

I consider darting down the reference aisle, hiding inside the tall, heavy, dark blue books. I'll open the cover of a big, fat one; curl up inside; tuck myself into the pages; and close the cover, away from him and from me with him.

"So...," he says, letting the word hang out for a minute. I try not to look at him. I try to look disinterested, bored, busy, something. But I can still see him even when I try not to. His white-blond hair isn't water polo–boy wet right now. It's barely wet at all. I bet he has an umbrella. This strikes me as strange. A boy who'd rape a girl carries an umbrella. A boy who fucks sleeping girls totes an umbrella to protect himself from the possibility of rain, sleet, or snow.

"Why is it every time I see you, you look away?" he asks, taking another step closer. He reaches a hand toward me, as if he's about to touch a strand of my hair.

"Don't," I say, barely audible. He doesn't hear me but instinctively, I push my hair away from my face, pulling it back, holding on to it in a one-handed ponytail so he can't touch it. I imagine an invisible wall between us, me on my side, he on his where he can't reach me. From my side, I notice his sharp nose, his high cheekbones, his blue eyes. I don't remember his eyes. My eyes were closed. He's tall too, probably six feet. His shoulders are broad.

"I didn't know your last name, so I couldn't find you in the school directory. So I couldn't call you," he adds, his voice oily.

Liar, I want to say. You didn't want to call, you wanted to brag. That's what you did in front of your dumb friends, you liar. Besides, you could have found me easily. I'm not hard to find. No one is.

"Because all I want is to see you again. Don't you want to see me?"

How can he act this way, how can he talk normally to me? I look at him curiously, like a science experiment, at his blue eyes—slate blue, it turns out—and his strangely shaped nose, and I feel as if I'm floating above him, as if I'm a hospital patient flatlining. I separate from my body and hover above myself, dispassionately regarding the scene unfolding below me. I watch it play out, two people who shouldn't be talking to each other *are* talking to each other and it makes no sense, so all I can do is watch it from above in my hospital gown.

Did you vote? Did you vote to make nonconsensual sex, like you had with me, a punishable offense? Did you, Carter? Did you did you did you?

"Why?" I ask.

"Why?" he repeats, taken aback.

"Yes, why?"

Because you leer at me in physics, you lie about me to your friends. Why are you asking me out?

Then I remember why he's talking to me. He thinks I'm easy. He wants another screw he doesn't have to work for. My chest burns, red and itchy and hot, and my heart wants to jump out like a karate-chopping, machete-wielding sort of kamikaze fighter and smack, smack, smack him into dust, just a big puff of dust and black smoke and cartoon stars in the air until—poof. He's gone.

But he's right here still, and now he's smiling at me,

trying to look sweet, but I'm not fooled. He's a wolf. "So, you going to let me have your number this time?" he asks again. "Besides, my birthday's next month and it'd be a fun way to celebrate."

I'm not a piece of cake.

"I have to go." Then I turn around and leave. Forget the computer catalog, forget the research, forget the snow-turned-rain. I'll get wet, soaking wet. I'll run in the rain, anything to get away. I push open the library door, hit the slick concrete steps, and run. I run down the steps, little stabs of water hitting my cheeks. The sky is heavy, stuffed with dark clouds as I run across the quad, past McGregor Hall, and up the stone steps to my dorm, wanting to know, needing to know what had happened *before* I was wasted, before I passed out. I want to know why I'd talk to Carter, why I'd flirt with him, why I'd kiss someone like that. As I push open the oak door, my shoulder slams into someone.

"Sorry," I mutter.

"Hey, Alex!"

It's Julie.

"I've been wanting to catch up with you," she says, and then launches into her usual monologue on how good it makes you feel to help out underprivileged kids. Her blond ponytail bounces as she talks, and just like clockwork, like a door slamming shut, I'm back.

"Why does T.S. always make us do things we don't want

to do?" I lean in and ask Martin as Julie dances nearby, her blond ponytail bouncing as she moves.

Martin shrugs. T.S. has just informed us we need to make nice with the water polo boys so we can break free of stereotypes. "I think that's what your best friend's girlfriend is supposed to do. I think it's technically the definition."

I laugh, a half-tipsy, half-not laugh. "Like if I looked it up in the dictionary that's what I'd see?"

Martin nods sagely, but mock sagely. "Most definitely. I looked it up the other night." It's loud in here so he cups a hand over my ear as he talks to me. His hair tickles my cheek. It feels soft. His hair is light brown, a little on the shaggy side, but good shaggy. I have an impulse to reach up and touch his hair now that I've just discovered it feels nice on my skin.

The band plays louder. The sounds from the stage, the drummer, the guitarist, the Artful Rage singer with his crooning voice, pound against my chest.

"I wonder if the definition is the same for best friend. In my case, you know," I say, this time close to his ear.

"How was your winter break?" Martin says, abruptly changing the conversation.

"Uneventful," I say. "Yours?"

"Eventful. My girlfriend broke up with me," he offers. "She was from my hometown. She applied to Themis as a midyear transfer but didn't get in. So she went to some school in Virginia instead and said sayonara."

"Are you sad? Did you want her to come here?"

"I thought I'd be sadder, but the truth is I was kind of dreading the possibility of her coming to Themis."

"Well, it's a damn good thing she didn't get in, then."

"You're telling me."

"Why were you dreading it?"

"I just think we grew apart. I mean, it's hard when you don't go to the same school. I'd rather be with someone at the same school, you know?"

"Totally. I dated a senior end of last year. He went off to Dartmouth and we didn't even pretend to do that I'll-see-you-on-weekends thing."

"It's too hard to be with someone miles away, especially when...," he says, then his voice trails off.

There's a pause. The music fills it, but it seems like awkward silence. I'm a little buzzed—a highly unusual state for me—so I place both my hands back around Martin's ear again. My right hand on top, brushing against his hair, my left hand underneath, touching his cheek. "When what?" I ask. I'm whispering now, but he can still hear me.

He doesn't answer immediately. It's like he's thinking of how he meant to finish his sentence when he says with a chuckle, "When she called me a science geek when she broke up with me."

I crack up when he says that. I'm not sure why it's so funny, I just like that he's cool with who he is. So I say, "I think it's cool that you're a science geek."

"Yeah, I'm not afraid to fly my geek flag," he says, and he's looking straight at me. I realize his eyes are regular brown, like mine, but with hints of green that make them vibrant and soft at the same time.

"Maybe we should just date people from the same school," Martin says.

He's not buzzed like me. He sounds totally sober. I don't think he's even been drinking. And I like his suggestion. But before I can say anything, I realize I really have to pee. "I have to pee," I say, then head to the bathroom.

When I return to our group, Martin's not waiting for me. He's talking to Cleo. I'm bummed, but mostly annoyed because I was liking talking to him. I turn away from them, toward the stage, and practically step on the person standing next to me.

"Sorry," I say.

The boy I stepped on looks playful, mischievous, then he says, "My name is Carter and I play water polo."

He says it as if he's at an AA meeting, as if he's confessing. Then I realize, he kind of is. Because we're supposed to get over our water polo stereotypes, I've been told, I reach out a hand to shake his. He leans toward me. "I love this band."

"Me too," I say, and it comes out a little flirtatiously.

Then I hear the first note of my favorite Artful Rage song. "I love this song!" I shout, and grab Carter's arm, rushing to the stage with him.

"Does that sound like something you'd want to do?" Julie is asking me.

"What?"

"Do you want to help out?"

"I gotta go, Julie," I say, and take the stairs two at a time. I reach my floor, race down the hall, yank open my door, then slam it shut behind me and slump down against the inside of it.

It's like how the shaken snow in a snow globe falls quietly down, revealing the scene. There's Martin and me, he's telling me he's single, I'm telling him I like science geeks — *science geeks,* that's what he was hinting at that time in physics class. Then he's saying we should date people at the same school; *we* are at the same school. Then Carter's there and Martin's not and the music plays and suddenly Carter looks good.

I shake the snow globe again. The white flakes scatter, covering up the scene. But even though it flurries I can still see one thing clearly. I went back with the wrong guy.

Chapter Fourteen
DAMAGED GOODS

Martin Summers.

Martin the science geek.

Martin with his soft brown hair.

Martin, the guy I've known since our best friends started going out, the guy I talk to in the caf, the guy I sit next to in physics, the guy who believes in the Atticus Finch–Boo Radley brand of justice.

Martin the Mockingbird.

Martin and I were flirting *that night*. Martin and I were talking and flirting and touching each other just barely, just the tiniest bit like you do when you first start to like someone.

I stand up, look in the mirror on the back of my door, and see a girl with wet hair, wet clothes, wet shoes. A girl who had two choices *that night*. A girl who chose badly. If I hadn't talked to Carter, if I'd had the guts to keep talking to Martin, I might be having lunch in the cafeteria today and tomorrow and the next day. I might be using points to have Frappuccinos with Martin off campus. I might have gone four years without ever needing to know more about the Mockingbirds than I knew the day Casey told me about stuff going down.

I grab a towel, flip my head over, and dry my rain-soaked hair. Then I do something I've never done at Themis. I ditch my next class. It's French and Martin's in it and I don't know how to talk to him now. I'll lose points for missing class, but I don't care. I have nowhere to go, no one to go with. So I slip under my orange and purple bedspread and spend the next two hours finishing *To Kill a Mockingbird*.

◆ ◆ ◆

My absence at French does not go unnoticed. That afternoon while T.S. is punishing soccer balls and Maia is massaging words at Debate Club, there's a knock on my door.

"Who's there?" I ask.

"It's Martin."

"Just a sec," I call out, and quickly run a brush through my hair and fumble around on my desk to find my lip gloss. But as I'm making my lips shiny, I feel foolish. Martin can't possibly like me now that he knows I got drunk and stupid and went to Carter's room. I'm damaged goods, and whatever spark there might have been between us *that night* surely has been snuffed out. I drop the lip gloss on my desk and open the door.

"Hey there," he says.

"Hi," I say as he walks in.

"I brought you the French homework," he says, and reaches for a piece of paper from his back pocket. He hands it to me. "Ms. Dumas gave us a Rimbaud poem and we're supposed to write a response—in French and in rhyme—by Friday."

My jaw drops. "Shoot me. Just shoot me now."

"What? You mean you harbor no aspirations to be a French poet?" he says.

"None whatsoever," I say, and once again the mood lightens. I tell myself everything is cool because nothing happened between us and nothing will happen and that's totally fine because I shouldn't even be thinking about boys right now. I shouldn't even be contemplating any boys, especially not boys who look so good in those jeans.

"Do you want to work on it together?" I ask, and then suddenly wish I could take it back. He'll think I like him. He'll think I'm trying to start something again. He won't want to have anything to do with me beyond his civic duty as a Mockingbird.

"*J'aimerais vraiment ça,*" he says.

My face flushes and I look away for a second. I tell myself it's nothing, but I still like the way it sounds, the way he sounds. *I would like that very much.*

"Here?" he asks, and looks around.

I shake my head quickly. I'm not ready for a boy to be in my room.

"Let's go to the common room," I say, and we head down the hall and spend the next hour inventing fake French words that rhyme before we dive into the most wretched French homework known to studentkind.

When we're done he says goodbye. I say goodbye too, but what I really want to say is *I liked that very much*.

Chapter Fifteen

KANGAROO COURT

"Encore, encore!"

Mr. Christie calls out in his booming voice. He pops up from his high-backed leather chair and claps some more, glancing back and forth at his fellow teachers here in the Faculty Club. They include Miss Damata, Mr. Waldman, Ms. Peck, Ms. Dumas, the Spanish teacher Mr. Bandoro, and the headmistress, Ms. Vartan. Jones and I just finished our Mozart sonata and we rocked, we owned that sonata like nobody's business, but we're not doing an encore. They're lucky they got one piece of music.

"How about some Gershwin next time?" Mr. Christie suggests as he strides over to us at the front of the room.

With it high ceilings, wood-paneled walls, and a brilliant blue Turkish rug, the Faculty Club screams "Ivory tower."

It's an enclave for cloistered professors with tony leather couches and chairs, floor-to-ceiling bookshelves with leather-bound editions, a crackling fire in the fireplace keeping us all warm, and a table with chocolate-chip cookies and mugs of hot cocoa and marshmallows. Mr. Christie offers us each a hot chocolate. I shake my head. They can pull the strings and make us perform, but they can't make us drink kid drinks.

"I think Gershwin would be lovely," Ms. Peck adds, joining us.

"*Rhapsody in Blue* or *An American in Paris*?" Mr. Christie asks her earnestly.

"Maybe A Parisian Rhapsody or A Blue American," she offers, making a very bad joke. Mr. Christie guffaws nonetheless.

I stare hard at Jones, trying not to crack a smile. He nods his head subtly at the two of them and I know what he's thinking, the same thing I'm thinking—they're probably doing it on the side. Jones and I slip away from the two of them so they can make their googly eyes or whatever. We say hello to a few teachers, saying thanks and smiling, always smiling, when they say what a great job we did. Then I hear Mr. Waldman talking to the headmistress. "Perhaps next time we all could go see a water polo match. Wouldn't that be fun? We do have the best water polo players, don't you think?"

It's as if Carter's everywhere and I can't get away.

"Let's go," I say to Jones, and we head out of there. He

walks me back to my dorm, both of us battling the frigid January day as we pull our hats lower and our coats tighter. When I reach my dorm room, I turn the heat up and start to thaw. I hunker down and polish off my world affairs homework, then write another scene in *The Tempest*.

Maia's off at a debate tournament (she's already done her Faculty Club mock debate), and T.S. is at soccer practice—an indoor one today, she said, because it's just too damn cold outside even for soccer babes. Those were her words, not mine. As I finish the last line of Miranda's dialogue I realize how hungry I am. It's been a week since I voted, which means we should know the results any day, any minute. And another week since I went to the Mockingbirds in the first place. Two full weeks of eating scraps in my room. Maybe I should have had that hot chocolate, should have stuffed some cookies in my pocket. I grab my computer and turn on an episode of *Law and Order* to distract myself.

My stomach growls as the episode ends and T.S. bursts in.

"Dinner for you," she declares, and hands me a turkey sandwich on rye bread with cheese. "Chef's special."

"Thank God. I'm only slightly famished."

She strips out of her soccer clothes, grabs a towel and her shower supplies, then opens the door to leave. I take a big bite of the sandwich as she pokes her head back in. "Oh, I almost forgot. I just ran into Amy and she told me the vote to revise the code officially passed. So they can hear your case now if you want them to." She holds the door open with her free hand, the other hand holding the shower basket. "Do you want to?"

I think of Carter in the library, Carter in the cafeteria, Carter in physics, Carter—for all intents and purposes—in the Faculty Club. Still, I say nothing.

"Well, at least you have the option now," T.S. adds. "We should probably let Amy know this weekend."

"Okay."

"So how about we meet Casey on Saturday and then decide? We have plenty of points to go off campus for lunch."

"Do you guys have some sort of plan to get me to say yes or something?"

T.S. rolls her eyes as if the idea is crazy.

"I know you want me to do this, T.S.," I say. "That's why you called Amy, that's why you brought me to the meeting."

"I brought you there so you'd know you have options. I brought you there because you asked me to."

"Because you felt guilty," I say. "But you shouldn't."

"I'm not doing this out of guilt."

"You don't feel guilty anymore, do you? I don't want you to."

"You told me not to that day in Sandeep's room. So I'm not doing this out of guilt. I'm doing this because it's right."

"I know."

"And like I said all along, this is *your* choice."

There's that word again. *Choice.* Now that I have a choice, what do I choose: go quietly into the night or cause a scene?

"I'll go if we can go to Curry in a Hurry," I say. "Because you know I love chicken tandoori."

"You want chicken tandoori, we're there," T.S. says.

♦ ♦ ♦

Curry in a Hurry is Casey's favorite restaurant on Kentfield Street, a fast-food Indian eatery right on the edge of Williamson's campus. I have always liked coming here because it's removed from Themis. It's a whole other world teeming with college students with college concerns. I like the escape, especially today.

As we sit down with our food, a girl walks by wearing a teal blue coat that swings around her hips. "What a great coat," Casey says to us. Then she turns around to the girl, leans back, and calls out, "I love your coat." Casey's never been one to miss a fashion moment. Even today in the dead of winter, she's wearing her purple boots with three-inch heels.

The girl says thanks and then Casey digs into her saag paneer. After she takes a bite, she asks me, "So are they doing the thing with the runners?"

"What thing?" I ask.

"The Mockingbirds," she says, as if the answer were obvious.

"Yeah, I figured that much. I meant what thing with the runners?"

Casey laughs. "I forgot. You don't know anything about the way the Mockingbirds operate," she says.

"Yeah, because you never really wanted to share any of the details. Remember?"

I give her a look and don't say anything. Casey doesn't take the bait, just spears another cheese cube with her fork. We both stay silent for a minute or so. But T.S. isn't interested in our sisterly face-offs, so she jumps in.

"Most of the school runners are part of the Mockingbirds," T.S. explains, tucking her blond hair behind her ears.

"You've enlisted the runners in the group?" I say, raising an eyebrow.

Casey nods like a proud parent.

"How does that work? How does the administration not know?"

"Like I said, not all are part of the Mockingbirds. But that's our feeder system. Because the runner job is a volunteer, first-come, first-served kind of thing, the Mockingbirds highly encourage anyone who wants to become a full-fledged Mockingbird to volunteer to be a runner first," Casey says, explaining the inner workings as if she were still in the Mockingbirds.

"And then what happens?"

"Well, the runners are silent but powerful. When they get the attendance slips, they'll mark a certain student *not present* if we need them to be marked as not present."

"Even if they are present," I state, realizing that's why Martin exchanged a nod with the runner in physics last week, and a few more times since then. Then I realize Martin himself was once a runner and it makes sense now — that's how he got his start. The runners are like a proving ground. "But the teacher knows they were really there," I point out, going back to the attendance issue.

"Doesn't matter. The office records the points or detracts the points from the attendance slips. So when you get your point total each week, you don't know how they were tallied. It's skimming off the top. But we skim enough off so it gets harder and harder to cash in for off-campus privileges," Casey explains.

"That's pretty clever," I admit. "But what's the point?"

"Lets the students know we're serious."

"But do the students know it's the Mockingbirds who are doing it?"

"Not usually at first. But when we get closer to serving notice, it becomes clear, and they can start putting two and two together, and we want them to put two and two together, so they show up if they're called to a hearing."

"But the Mockingbirds are supposed to be good," I insist.

"Right," Casey says quickly. "We don't harass and we don't harm. We just like to show we're for real. We just make it clear we're not to be messed with."

"But what if I decide not to press charges? Then wouldn't it be unfair to have docked his points?"

"If you don't press charges, they'll give back all his points, and some extra too, and no one will have been the wiser," Casey explains.

"What if he's found not—" I stop, shuddering at the thought of Carter being found not guilty. Instead, I say, "What if the accused is judged innocent?"

"Then the accused is invited to serve on the Mockingbirds in an advisory capacity to help them better consider the rights of others who are accused," Casey says.

I nod, impressed with the checks and balances my sister built into the group.

"That's only happened once or twice, and it was for lesser crimes. Like a stealing case a couple years back," T.S. points out.

I turn to my best friend. "You seem to know everything. Are you secretly part of the Mockingbirds? Are you on the council or something and you haven't told me?"

"No," T.S. says. "It's just Casey and I have been talking recently about how the group works and stuff."

"Did you meet in dark parking lots or just send each other Morse code signals?"

"Duh. We talk about it over e-mail or after the soccer scrimmages, where I usually kick Themis's ass all over the field," Casey says.

"You wish," T.S. fires back.

I look at T.S. "But *why*? Why are you suddenly so interested in everything related to the Mockingbirds?"

"Because you're my best friend, dork."

I put my fork down. Even though I know which way I've been leaning, I don't want decisions made for me. "So have you guys already decided I'm pressing charges, then? I mean, what's the point in *my* deciding? You seem like you already have with all your meetings and conversations and tactics."

"I just want you to feel safe again, Alex," T.S. says. "Because judging from the way you're eating, you haven't felt safe in weeks. I know you're scared. You walk around campus avoiding him, taking the long way to class, not going to meals. Are you going to skip every meal this year to avoid him?"

"I don't know," I say, taking another bite of my chicken.

T.S. grows agitated. "Don't you want Themis to feel safe? My God, you were at the Faculty Club performing the other day, and now they're going to go see Carter play water polo. They don't have a clue. They can bring in the best teachers in the world, they can challenge our minds, they can send us off to Ivy League colleges. But they are powerless outside the classroom. They offer you hot chocolate and then plan the next puppet show."

While T.S. pauses to catch her breath, I look at my sister, her brown hair like mine, her brown eyes like mine. She's my almost-twin on the surface. But we're not the same. She's Susan B. Anthony; she's a rabble-rouser; she's standing up for the rights of the downtrodden. Me, I can barely even commit to one of Julie's weekend volunteer projects.

151

"Why did you start the Mockingbirds?" I ask pointedly.

She holds my gaze, doesn't look away. "Because I had to."

I scoff. "What does that mean? *You had to?*"

"Because I couldn't just stand by and watch students hurt each other."

"Right, I know that, Casey. But why *you*? What motivated you? Was it just seeing the seniors bully the other kids and that was enough? That was all it took? You said, 'whoa, I have to be the one to stop this'?"

I've never asked her these questions before. I've never dug into her reasons. They didn't matter. Now they do.

She takes a deep breath. "You know the girl who committed suicide right before you got to Themis?"

I nod. "I know of her. She's why we had the training day on warning signs."

"Well, she was being bullied."

"She was one of the kids the seniors were bullying?"

Casey shakes her head. "No, she wasn't part of that. But she was a senior too, same year as me. Same dorm. Same floor."

"You knew her?" I ask.

Casey nods, looks away for the briefest of seconds, then back at me. "I heard what was going on with her," Casey says. "I saw what it led to. I saw what can happen when things get out of control."

"That's why you started the Mockingbirds."

"I didn't want that to happen again. I didn't know at the

time what that kind of behavior could lead someone to do. To end her life. So when I saw the seniors bullying the kids who weren't in the Honor Society I couldn't just stand by and watch it happen again. I knew I had to do something. I had to give them options."

"Casey," I say softly, "I'm not going to end my life just because of what one stupid asshole did to me."

"I know, Alex. You're stronger than that, and you have options. So what do you want to do?" she asks. "Press charges?"

It's as if I'm on a cop show. A guy in a suit with a five o'clock shadow brings me to a room with a one-way mirror, shows me the lineup, and tells me to take my time. He waits patiently while I size up the suspects. *The one in the middle,* I say. *Him?* the cop asks. I nod, certain. *Book him,* the cop tells his associate.

I take another bite of my chicken. I'm almost finished with it and I'm still ravenous. I reach for a piece of Casey's naan bread. "This is my life. This is my junior year. I don't want the whole school knowing my business. Well, more than they already know," I say.

"The hearings are closed," Casey explains. "Just the council, the plaintiff, the accused, and the witnesses you call."

I give her a look. "You can call it closed all you want. And it can be closed. But you know as well as I do that everyone will know."

"Yes, everyone will probably know. But some people know already—they know Carter's story. Whose story do you want them to know? The one where you were 'begging for it'? Because that's what they're going to know. Or do you want people to know the truth, that he date-raped you? Because you can help other girls to stay away from him and protect themselves from other boys like him. You do this, be the first, and you make it harder for other boys this year, next year, years to come, to do this ever again. This is bigger than you."

All I want to do is go back to me, the *not* political me, the *not* legal me, the me I was when I could just play music, just go to the music hall and be with my piano and my notes and my composers and not be afraid to walk to class and not have to hide out during dinner and not to have to eat Clif Bars for sustenance. Because I am hungry, I am really hungry. I am so hungry I reach for more of Casey's bread and then I stab my fork into her saag paneer and I gobble that up and then I take a bite of T.S.'s lentils with yogurt dip.

And I hate being this hungry.

And I hate that I can't be me.

And I hate that I can't do anything anymore without the memories of Carter and that day and that night haunting me, following me everywhere I go.

And I want to go back to the way it was, the way *I* was.

The thing you love most is taken away. That's what happens if you're found guilty by the Mockingbirds—the thing you love most is taken away. For me, it already was. Beethoven's not mine anymore. But maybe if I do this, I can have his music back.

I swallow the last bite of lentils. It tastes good. Then I look at my sister and my best friend. "I'm in," I say.

Chapter Sixteen

SHOCK TREATMENT

A few days later, Amy visits me. "I heard you were hungry," she says as I open the door to my room.

"Sure," I say, gesturing for her to come in. She's wearing a thin gray turtleneck sweater and skinny jeans and carrying a casserole dish with potholders. A canvas bag is tucked under her arm. She tips her chin to my desk. "Desk for the dinner table?"

"Absolutely. The desk is the best table there is," I say, pushing my laptop aside to make room for the food. I wasn't expecting Amy tonight, but I'm not entirely surprised either. She places the blue-and-white casserole dish down, removes the top, then takes two plates, two forks, and a large serving spoon from her bag.

"Mind if I join you?"

"Of course not," I say.

"I made mac and cheese," she says, and I guess that makes Amy a rarity—one of the only Themis students to use the kitchens in the common rooms.

"I love mac and cheese."

"I made it from scratch. My mom has this awesome recipe," she says, and starts scooping big spoonfuls of gooey mac and cheese onto the plastic plates. "She uses a block of cheddar, a block of Monterey Jack, and a block of cream cheese."

"So this is probably similar to what Hollywood stars eat when working on their six-packs?" I joke, and point to my abs.

"Totally. Anyway, it's supergood and perfect for this time of year," Amy says, pulling out the chair from Maia's desk.

I glance at the food, and my mouth starts to water. My desire for it is almost sinful. "It looks delicious," I say, uttering a complete understatement. "Plus, it beats sandwiches."

I sit back down at my desk, where I had been sketching out the next scene in *The Tempest* before Amy appeared. Maia's practicing for a debate tournament. T.S. is studying—or something—in Sandeep's room. Amy hands me a plate and fork, then takes one for herself and settles in. I take a bite of the mac and cheese and it's amazing. I want to roll my eyes and moan, but I restrain myself.

"T.S. called over the weekend and said you're ready to move forward," Amy says.

I nod. "Yep."

"So what made you decide?" Amy asks.

I hesitate, wondering if this is a test I have to pass, if I have to answer correctly. Amy senses my nervousness and adds warmly, "Don't worry. I just like to ask."

"Well, you sort of know already, right?" I say, then take another bite. "I mean, you wouldn't have brought me homemade mac and cheese unless you knew."

Amy smiles; her light blue eyes have some kind of soothing quality, as if she can see into you and feel what you feel and know what you know.

"T.S. told you I don't go to the caf anymore, right?" I add.

Amy shakes her head, her ultrashort hair barely moving as she does. "Nope. But I never see you there. And you mentioned the comments his friend made at lunch that day so I put two and two together."

There she goes again, knowing stuff.

"I guess I'm getting kind of sick of feeling like I have to hide," I say. "The few times I've run into him, he seems to think I would want to be with him," I say, the vein in my forehead pulsing a little harder at the memory of his twisted expectations. "Which is totally sick and makes me sick. That he could do that and think I'd want to go out with him. To top if off, I get headaches sometimes and I never did before. And T.S. told me she was researching the effects of date rape and headaches are one of them. I think it's because some days it's all you can think about and your head feels as if it's going to explode."

"People suck," Amy says, agreeing. "That's why I have a job."

"Do you get a lot of cases each semester?" I ask.

"Enough," she says offhand, then takes another bite of her mac and cheese. That's all—*enough*. She finishes chewing, then asks, "And you're sure?"

"Of what happened?" I say, taken aback. Do I have to prove it again? Recite the story all over again?

"No, I believe it happened. I mean, are you sure you want to go through with this?"

"Are you saying I shouldn't?"

"Not at all. I believe in this, in what you're doing, in what we can do for you. It's just these things can consume you. That doesn't mean you shouldn't do them. Just know that they have a way of becoming bigger than everything else."

But it *already* is bigger than everything else. *It* already is the defining moment of my junior year. It lives in front of me, behind me, next to me, inside me every single day. My schedule is dictated by *it*, my habits by *it*, my music by *it*. This—the Mockingbirds—is how I deflate *it*.

"I get it," I say.

The receiver did this. The freshmen did this. I can do this. I can be bigger than me. I can take a stand. My sister started this group for that very reason.

"Good. I'm glad. And we're going to protect you. That's part of our mission," Amy says, putting her plate down on the floor and reaching into her canvas bag. She takes out

159

her notebook—the mockingbird on the cover looks like it's watching me—removes a sheet of paper, and hands it to me. She places the slightly worn notebook back in the bag. "Don't worry, this isn't like some binding contract. It's just you need to sign it for our records to say you want us to go forward and press charges against Carter."

"You want me to sign something?" I ask, holding back a laugh. It's not really funny, it's just—well, it's just the Mockingbirds take this so seriously. But it is serious, I remind myself as I take the sheet of paper and read. Just a few lines saying I approached the Mockingbirds on my own, I asked them to hear the case, and I authorize them to press charges against Carter Hutchinson for sexual assault on the evening of January tenth. There's another line too, and it reads: *If the accuser is found to have lied, he or she agrees to accept the standard punishment.*

I pause for a moment, astonished again by all the checks and balances in the Mockingbirds. The Mockingbirds exist to police and to protect, so they could be seen as favoring the people who seek their help. But then if you dare to think that, you learn that those who are judged innocent are vindicated with a leadership post, and you learn too that if an accuser has filed false charges, he or she gets the comeuppance. Even-steven, indeed.

I reach for a pen and sign the paper. I hand it back to Amy.

"It's just for our records anyway," she says, tucking the paper back into her notebook with a smile. *Records,* the

Mockingbirds have *records*. I bet they keep them stored in a secret vault somewhere, maybe in the basement, maybe even in the laundry room. I bet there's a dummy dryer—you open the door to it, reach your hand all the way to the false back, turn a hidden knob three times one way, three times the other way, then push open the safe. Inside are stacks of red flyers and white papers and rule books and case histories and guidelines for picking the New Nine and the board and a list of all the bad students ever.

"Where do you keep your records?" I ask.

Amy chuckles, amused by such a question. "In our files," she says, because of course she's not going to tell me where. She picks up her plate and continues eating. I take another bite of my food, then ask, "So who's on the council?"

"It rotates, as I said. But they're good kids. All nine of them. Sort of who you'd expect."

I don't really know who I'd expect. "Like Martin or Ilana?" I offer up, hoping for some kind of answer.

Amy's eyes go wide and she smiles like I got it right. "Exactly. Exactly like Martin and Ilana."

"Wait, I thought you said you three were just on the board and the council was separate?"

"They are separate. Absolutely. We have to keep the three branches separate, checks and balances and all," she says emphatically, and I assume by three branches she must mean the runners, the council, and the board. Amy goes on, "You just asked what the council members were *like*. And I was saying they are *like* Martin and Ilana. Students like that. Anyway, you should start thinking about who you want your student advocate to be. Kind of like your lawyer. They present your case to the council. But before that, we're going to serve him papers. Probably in a couple weeks," Amy continues. "There are just some preliminary things we need to do first."

"Preliminary things?" I ask. "Do you mean more attendance mistakes?"

Martin told me after physics one day this week that they've now shaved enough off Carter's attendance points that he's not going to be able to get off campus for quite a while—no lunch, no Friday Night Out.

"We have a few things in mind."

"But you're not going to tell me," I say.

"It's not that we're not going to. It's just we haven't decided yet. But Alex, don't worry, okay?"

"If you say so..."

"I do!" Amy says cheerfully, plunking her hand down on my leg. She leans her head to the side and looks directly at me. "Alex, we're going to take care of you, I promise. I wouldn't be doing this if I didn't believe in the Mockingbirds and you."

"Why do you believe in them so much?" I ask curiously.

"Because I know it works," she says.

"Why do *you* do this? Why are you involved?"

She looks away for a second, then back at me. "Because someone has to carry the torch."

"How do I repay you? You guys are doing so much for me."

"Don't worry about that now," she says, her eyes radiating that familiar warmth again. She gestures to the mac and cheese on my plate. "Just eat, eat!"

I take another bite of the food she made, finishing what's left on my plate. Seconds sound good so I reach for the spoon and scoop some more of Amy's family recipe. Maybe the Mockingbirds really will look out for me.

◆ ◆ ◆

"Shh..."

I look to Martin, who issued the shush. "But Mr. Waldman isn't here yet," I say.

We're waiting for physics class to start and Carter's talking to the guy sitting next to him. Martin leans close to hear what he's saying. I can hear too.

"I never got my cake," Carter whines.

"What's up with that?" the guy next to him says.

"I don't know. Everyone was waiting in the common room. Never showed up. Never came. It sucked. The birthday cake is the single greatest thing about this school."

I will agree with Carter on that point. Themis does a good job taking care of its students, including delivering a fresh sheet cake—of your choosing—to the common room of your dorm on your birthday. It's their way of making the school seem more like a home away from home. It also means there's pretty much birthday cake every night because it's always someone's birthday. It's a small perk of going to school here, but a perk nonetheless.

I tap Martin's wrist, then raise my eyebrow in question. He gives me a mischievous look. "You guys?" I mouth.

He nods proudly.

I lean in to whisper, "How'd you do that?"

He whispers back. "We have access to the birthday list."

They have access to everything. "What'd you do? Cross his name off it?"

"Something like that," he says, and I imagine the red-haired runner boy opening a drawer in the headmistress's secretary's office, discreetly pulling out a sheet of paper and quickly erasing Carter's name. The runner gently blows on the paper; the eraser remnants fall to the ground. He tucks the paper back in the drawer, leaves the attendance report on the desk, and slips back out. Quietly, of course.

Then Mr. Waldman enters and everyone stops talking. He does his normal attendance count, then hands the slip over to a runner. Martin gives the runner a curt nod. Poor Carter—no points and no cake.

◆ ◆ ◆

Two days later, Maia opens the door to calculus with such a spurt of energy I swear it's going to rocket through the wall and swing around again. She grabs a desk next to me, sits down, and tilts close to me, her sleek black ponytail swinging to hang over her right shoulder. "The water polo match against Choate was canceled," she whispers. "And, here's the kicker…Themis had to forfeit!"

"Are you serious?" I whisper back, even though our math teacher's not here yet. "Why?"

"The pool got the shock treatment."

"What's that?"

"They usually do it when a pool gets manky, you know *gross* manky. And you put this insane amount of chlorine into the water to break down the…well, you know," she says, then pauses, lowering her voice even more. "And evidently, the Themis pool got the shock treatment just now and I don't think it was because waste products were in the water."

"Then why?" I ask.

"It was to make it unusable for twenty-four hours. There's so much bloody chlorine in there right now— probably twenty times the normal amount—no one can swim in it today. So, what do you know—Themis just can't host the game against its biggest rival today. Choate. I'd feel bad for the rest of the team, but they all were kind of dicks for spreading his lies," Maia says, a satisfied glint flicking through her eyes. She knows exactly who did this and so do I. And they're making it clear you don't mess with the Mockingbirds. When they say show up, you show up.

I have to say, it feels kind of satisfying. It feels good, as if

I'm taking back the night or something. "Such a bummer that we're going to have to miss the water polo match," I say, masking a grin.

"Total shame," she says with a smirk as our math teacher enters. "I was really looking forward to it."

Chapter Seventeen

SHINING TREES

"Alex, come look."

"Hmm?" I half-mumble as I rub my eyes and look at the clock next to me. Five forty-five. Only athletes are up at this hour.

T.S. is perched on her bed, nose pressed to the window, dressed in soccer shorts and shirt already. "You have to see this. It's beautiful," she says.

She must be talking about snow. I picture freshly fallen flakes drifting down, blanketing the Themis quad. T.S. is from Santa Monica and is obsessed with snow. She still makes snow angels.

Maia must be thinking the same thing because she chides T.S. "Please tell me you didn't just wake us up to see snow yet again, because you know I love my sleep more than snow angels."

"It's better than snow," T.S. says as she waves us over. Maia and I grumble our way out of our respective beds and join T.S. at the window.

There is no snow.

Instead, shimmering, shining trees reflect back at us. It's as if each tree is sporting a tiny makeup mirror in the middle, a pinprick of light, a prism.

"Let's go see," T.S. commands.

I pull on clothes quickly and Maia does the same. The three of us head down the steps and out the door. Up close it's clear there are no mini mirrors on the trees, no reflective tape. Instead, every single tree in the quad has been marked—two pieces of gum in tinfoil wrappers tacked to each trunk.

"For the love of the queen, why is there chewing gum tacked to the trees?" Maia asks.

"You don't know?" T.S. asks.

Maia shakes her head adamantly. "No, I don't know, nor do I like guessing games at ungodly hours." Then she adds, "And besides, clearly you do know. So you can just tell us."

Before T.S. speaks an image races through my mind. Two kids. A tree. A knothole. "It's the first thing Boo Radley leaves for Jem and Scout," I say quietly. "He leaves them two pieces of chewing gum in shiny tinfoil wrappers inside the knothole of the oak tree."

Maia smacks her forehead, the details rushing back to her. "My God, I can't believe I forgot. Gum, soap figures, two Indian head pennies."

"So is this a message from the Mockingbirds?" I ask.

T.S. nods. "I think so."

"Did Casey tell you this was coming? What does it mean?" I ask.

T.S. shakes her head this time. "I have no idea."

Later that day I find out what it means. Only I don't hear it from Martin or Amy or Ilana. I hear it from some girls in my French class, then from some guys in my English class, then from Natalie.

Or *overhear*, I should say.

Because even though the maintenance guys removed the gum by nine a.m., that was more than enough time for word to zoom around Themis about the Juicy Fruit trees.

And double sticks of chewing gum means one thing only.

Notice of a case is coming.

◆ ◆ ◆

Two days later it comes.

Maia and I are back in calculus, ingesting another mind-numbing dose of indefinite integrals. When the bell rings at the end of class, we leave together, and the second we step out the door a runner walks by and presses a note into my hand. He doesn't even look at me, just keeps going. I watch him hurry down the hall, his red hair becoming a blur as he fades into the thick mass of students.

"What does it say?" Maia asks excitedly.

I unfold the note cautiously, my heart beating a little faster. For a moment, I think the Mockingbirds have turned against me. Maybe they're after me. My brain starts spinning as I open the note.

Go to the second floor of the library, to the reference room, and read Harper. Five minutes later, a notice will post in the usual spot.

A wave of uncertainty clutches me, like a hard grip. I breathe once, twice, then it releases and I say to Maia, "We have to go to the library, second floor, required reading. And we have to go fast."

"Let's go," she says.

She doesn't ask why and I wonder if she wants to be a part of this because she likes knowing things. She's getting all sorts of inside information now. My mind races and I start questioning if she has an agenda here. Then I feel bad for doubting her.

We reach Pryor Library and reflexively I survey the aisles, just in case Carter is nearby. But I don't see him and even if I did I'm with Maia, so it's like I have a shield. I tell her what the note said as we race up the stairwell to the second floor reference room, where the school keeps copies of the required-reading books. You can't check the copies out, so the library is their permanent home.

We scan the shelves quickly, looking for the ninth-grade list because that's when Themis teaches *To Kill a Mockingbird*. Maia spies it first, grabs it, and hands it to me. I open the first page, where someone's handwritten an inscription—*For Jen*. I wonder who Jen is, but now's not the time to figure it out. I flip through the book as if it were one of those cartoon flip books where each page contains a slightly different image. But there's nothing so far, just the actual chapters. I reach the back of the book, where there are ten or so blank pages. Only not all are blank. Some are filled in with writing and names and lists. The first one says *Bully Pulpit* and the names of several students listed in pen. I'm guessing they're the Honor Society bullies, the true Dishonorables. The next page says *If You're Queer Don't Buy Him a Beer* and Paul Oko's name is on it, also in pen. There are more pages, more names like one that says *Watch Your Back* and a name I don't recognize, *Ellery Robinson*, in pen as well.

Maia clasps her hand on her mouth. "Ellery Robinson," she says heavily.

"What? Who's she?"

"She graduated last year. Gorgeous girl. Lacrosse player, all-American beauty type. I heard rumors she did something horrible, though."

"What?" I ask, feeling a sudden chill.

"She wrote something on another student's back. With a blade."

"Oh my God, that's awful."

"It was right at the end of the year so details were very sketchy."

"Okay, let's move on," I say.

There's another page that says *Curtains Closed* and the names of two students, presumably the freshmen theater crew.

Then there's a new page and it simply says *No Sleepovers Allowed.*

It's underlined and beneath it there is one name.

Carter Hutchinson.

I touch his penciled-in name with my index finger to make sure I'm not seeing things. But it's there, in this book of lists, a book of names. I pull my finger back as if touching his name singed my skin. Now I know why the Mockingbirds are so confident Carter will show up at his hearing. Points, cake, pools, and now this. I'm reminded of that old movie line "We have ways of making you talk."

I turn to Maia, who's a little bit awestruck too. "Time to check out the notice" is all I can manage before I dash off down the stairs and across the quad to the big bulletin board outside McGregor Hall, just a few feet away from the music hall. There's a familiar red flyer pinned to it and flapping in the February breeze.

It's a notice, just like my note promised. The mockingbird is singing this time, the lyrics written in a bubble by its beak.

Hush, little students, we'll say the word,
Mama's gonna buy you a mockingbird.
And if that mockingbird won't sing,
Mama's gonna write down everything.
And so that book won't look the same,
Mama's gonna add a brand-new name.

Chapter Eighteen
HIGHER AUTHORITY

Look, it's not as if the Mockingbirds graffitied his name on the bathroom walls, slashing *Carter=date rapist* in black Sharpie or something. It's a code, just a code. Most students probably won't even give it a second glance. You don't really think about the Mockingbirds unless they're for you or against you.

Has Carter figured out they're against him? Does he know the lack of points, the lack of cake, the nasty pool, the Juicy Fruit trees means he's on their hit list? Has he seen this flyer? Has he found his name in the book? Will he know what it means? Will he know it was me? Because the book is just one more of the *preliminary things*, and this notice on the bulletin board isn't the official notice. They haven't even "served papers" yet.

I manage to pull myself away from the bulletin board and run into the music hall. I'm late, but Miss Damata's cool and we don't have attendance runners for our solo lessons. It's just her and me, like a private lesson a few times a week. Not because I need the extra help, but because I'm that good. I'm not trying to be cocky. It's just true. I hang up my coat by the door and take my seat at the piano next to her. "Sorry for being late," I say, and push my hair away from my face, swooping it into a quick ponytail.

"You're a busy junior," she says.

"Yeah," I say, because what am I supposed to say? Especially since I can't get the book and the flyer and the code and the list and Carter's name out of my head. I hit all the notes as we practice the Ninth Symphony for my performance, but there's no feeling behind my playing right now. I'm not connected to the keys, I'm merely pressing them. Miss Damata senses the difference.

"Are you okay today?" she asks. She's wearing her blond hair up again in a bun.

"Sure."

"You don't seem like yourself."

"I'm just distracted. I'm sorry. I'll do better."

"It's okay to be distracted. You don't have to be perfect." She lays a hand on mine. I don't pull my hand away. From her the gesture is genuine. "I can tell when your heart is in the music. And when it's not, it usually means your heart, or maybe your head, is elsewhere."

"Maybe it is," I say softly, and when I do I feel a little

better. I've told her nothing concrete, but just voicing the possibility that something is wrong is a relief.

"Do you want to talk about it? You know, off the record."

A teacher who says "off the record." A teacher who acknowledges there is even a need for off the record. She's not like the others, who're book smart but not street smart. Miss Damata's real; she sees through us. She sees through me. I look at her green eyes and consider confiding in her. Telling her about that night, about the cafeteria, about the comments Carter made, about the Mockingbirds, about the book.

"Just stuff going on," I say.

"Any kind of stuff in particular?"

I don't say anything for a few seconds. I don't know what to say or how to say it. I'm groping in the dark for a light switch, stumbling to find it, when I manage to say, "It's just...this semester is harder."

"I take it you don't mean academically," she says softly.

"Right, not academically," I say, "but more—"

Then I stop myself because it'd be like a dog chasing his tail—pointless. Teachers have no power. I know where the real power resides. I turn the conversation to Juilliard. "How hard is it to get into Juilliard?" I ask.

"Juilliard again?" she asks with a laugh.

"I'm dying to go there."

"It's not easy," she tells me.

"What are the other students like?"

"Driven, dedicated, competitive."

"Do you miss it?"

She shakes her head. It makes me wonder if I'd miss the school if I didn't go. But I push those thoughts out of my mind because I don't plan on not getting in.

"Alex," she starts.

"Yes?"

"You can always come to me if you want to talk. It'll stay between you and me. You can find me here or in the blue house with the purple door just a block off campus."

"Thanks," I say, knowing I should take her up on it, but I won't. "A purple door sounds cool."

When music is over I scan the quad. There's no sign of Carter so I race back to the bulletin board to see if anyone's there. I'm half-expecting a throng of students, like in those movie scenes when they post a cast list or something and everyone crowds around, peering over heads to see who's on it. But no one's looking, no one's stopping. So I go to my next class, then check again after that. A few students walk by, one or two glance, but that's all. I keep on like that the rest of the day, sneaking a peek at the bulletin board whenever I can.

I even slip back into the library, and like a shadow I flit up to the second floor to steal a look at the book. I notice a girl flipping through it, and just the presence of a person throws me off so much I scamper back down the steps, as if I just crank-called someone and hung up when they answered.

During my last class I even try to peer out the window,

eager for a view of the bulletin board from the second floor in McGregor Hall. But no one's there. No one's even in the quad—just bare trees and a few patches of hard, crunched-up snow from the week before. When class ends, I walk straight across the quad to make sure the notice is still there.

There's a tap on my shoulder as I read what I've already memorized. It's Ilana. "You like the note?" she asks.

"Very clever."

"I wrote it. I'm the writer in the group," she says proudly.

"Does everyone have a talent in the group?"

"Kind of," she says, but doesn't elaborate, just smoothes out a nonexistent wrinkle in her skirt, dark blue denim and calf-length. She wears brown slouchy boots with the skirt and a cowl-neck white sweater under her coat.

"But no one's been looking at it," I point out. "Hardly anyone's even seen it. Do they even know what it means?"

"Not everyone will know. Not everyone will care. But enough students pay attention when a Mockingbirds notice shows up. Any kind of notice. Could be a revision to the code, seeking the New Nine, or a notice of a trial. We had a sixty-five percent voter turnout for the revisions to the code. We always get more students than we need for the runners, the Nine, and so on. So students will look. And students will figure it out. Some have already."

"Really?"

She leans in close to whisper, "About a dozen students so far have seen the book."

"A dozen? How do you know?"

"We have people watching."

Of course. I should have known.

"Is a dozen good?"

"So far, yeah. And some will spread the word."

"Has Carter seen it?"

Ilana shakes her head. "Not yet. But he will soon. And he'll know Monday. That's when we serve the official papers. Amy wanted me to tell you."

"Monday morning," I repeat. "Five days from now."

She nods, her long dark braids moving up and down too. "Gives this time to sink in."

"Does he know you're responsible for the points and the cake and all?"

"He might have an inkling," Ilana says with a shrug. "We've done it before, with others. Well—points and cake. Everything else is tailored to the individual. So as soon as he gets wind of the book, he'll probably know he's due for a summons. But he'll definitely know it's all connected when he gets served. It's included in the notice. Our prior work, so to speak."

I nod, then ask quietly, "What do I do when I see him again? I mean, he's going to know it's me. That I'm the reason he's in the book."

Ilana shakes her head. "No, he's going to know he has to answer to a higher authority."

Chapter Nineteen
LOOK AWAY

No matter what Ilana says, there is no way I want to feel Carter's seamy eyes on me again. So the next day I'm doubly careful to avoid him. I put on sunglasses, tuck my hair into a Manchester United cap of Maia's, and pull on a short army camouflage jacket that's cool but I hardly ever wear, so no one knows it as "my coat."

I leave early for every class. I skirt around buildings to stay out of sight. When it's time for lunch, I head for my dorm, remembering there's a fresh bag of pretzels on my desk. Casey dropped it off the other night, along with apples, Diet Coke, M&M's, popcorn, and homemade blondie brownies. Oh, the choices—how will I ever pick?

But just as I'm about to pull open the heavy oak door to Taft-Hay Hall and escape the wintry air, I'm intercepted.

Amy hooks an arm around my right arm, Ilana around my left. They spin me around and walk me back down the steps.

"Lunchtime!" Ilana says cheerily. Her braids are gone today and her hair's been flattened into one long sheet of dark brown hair, practically draped over a caramel-colored wool coat.

"Are you taking me out to lunch?" I say.

Amy shakes her head, her cropped haircut a stark contrast to Ilana's. "Nope."

"More mac and cheese?" I ask, figuring maybe we're going to her room to dine.

"Not in the plans either."

I stop on the stone path. "I'm not going to the caf."

"Yes, you are," Amy says.

I shake my head and hold my ground, pressing my weight onto the heels of my boots.

"Alex, you can do this, and remember, you're safe with us," Amy says.

"How?" I ask.

"He knows who we are now. He knows we're the Mockingbirds."

"How does he know?"

"He just does," Amy says, looking at me.

"Do you send him notes from runners or something?" I press on.

"He knows the same way T.S. knew how to find us."

"Through Casey?"

Amy shakes her head. "That's not how T.S. found us."

"Did she put up a bat signal?"

Amy laughs and I can see her breath when she does. "Alex, it's not that complicated. T.S. left a note in our mailbox in the student activities office. Same place where you dropped off your vote on the code revisions."

"Did Carter leave a note? What did he write? *Call me and tell me who you are.*"

"Alex, we're not some supersecret organization. It's not like Clark Kent where he has to protect his real identity. My name is on the mailbox as the point person."

"Oh," I say, kind of surprised. I was expecting something more cloak and dagger. It's so pedestrian to have a mailbox for their fake singing group. Then again, it is kind of the perfect cover too.

"I *want* students to be able to get in touch with me if they need to," Amy adds.

I notice she uses the plural *students* and it hits me I might not be alone. I might not be the only one they're helping. "Are there other cases this semester?"

Amy nods.

"How many?"

"A couple?"

"You can't tell me?"

"They're not as far along as yours."

"You mean the names aren't in the book yet?"

"Right," Amy says.

"What are they about?" I press on.

"Would that be fair if I told you at this point?" Amy asks. "Let's focus on yours."

"Fine," I say. "So Carter went by your mailbox?"

"Last night," Amy says, and I realize the timing jibes with something Maia said when she returned from debate practice last night. She told me the swim team faction had been buzzing about the book at practice.

"So you're really taking me to the caf?" I ask.

Amy and Ilana nod.

"Won't it seem like you're favoring me, then? I mean, are people going to accuse you guys of being biased?"

"Remember, we don't decide the case," Amy says. "The board doesn't vote on guilt or innocence. The council does. Besides, this is part of what we do on the board. We *protect*."

"I take it Carter's not getting protection?"

"Carter doesn't need protection," Ilana says. "You do. And we don't give protection to everyone. Your case is different. It's a rape case. If you were pressing charges out there in the big old justice system, you'd get protection too. Your identity would be kept secret. They'd maybe even put a blue dot over your face if your trial was on TV. If you accused him of cheating or stealing, you wouldn't need company in the caf. You accused him of rape, so you get company in the caf."

Then Amy places a hand softly on my arm and even through my army coat it's like she has this weird super-power of touch because the second she lays a hand on me, it radiates calm. I suddenly feel as if I *can* do this. I'm with her, I'm with Ilana. They're the Mockingbirds; they're protecting others; they're protecting me; they're my bulletproof vest. "Nothing will happen. You'll see," Amy adds.

"Do you trust us?" Ilana asks.

I nod. "Of course."

"Then let's get some food into you, girl. Because you are getting thinner by the day," Ilana says, grabbing the waistband of my jeans, a little looser now than it was a month ago. "Oh, and you can lose the hat, sister," she says, pulling my cap off. She laughs, but it's a friendly laugh, and the next thing I know I'm walking back into the cafeteria for the first time in a month. I survey the huge room and find him quickly, the same place I saw him last, with Kevin and Henry and the other water polo boys. He doesn't see me, but still my heart catches in my throat; I swallow hard and steel myself as I make my way through the line.

"You have Mr. Christie for world affairs, right?" Ilana asks me as we grab trays.

"Yeah. Do you?" I ask. She's not in my class but I know he teaches a couple of different sessions.

"Nope, he doesn't teach seniors," she says.

"You're a senior?" I ask as I reach for some pasta. Cafeteria food never looked so good.

"What, the boobs didn't give it away?" Ilana teases, casting her brown eyes down at her big chest, then back up to me. "People always think I'm older because I have these monster boobs. I can't believe you didn't think I was a senior!"

"I just didn't think about it," I say.

"What year do you think I am?" Amy asks as we finish filling our trays. Slices of turkey for Ilana, mushroom soup for Amy.

"Um . . . ," I say, not wanting to get this wrong either.

"Go ahead. Guess. I won't be offended."

"Fine, senior," I say, going for the easy answer.

She shakes her head. "I'm a sophomore."

"Are you serious?" I say.

"I don't have monster boobs," she says, because she kind of has the body of a paper doll. I never thought about their ages though, especially Amy's, because it never occurred to me someone who had this much power could be anything but a senior. Except Amy's a sophomore, younger than I am. I guess this explains why I've never had a class with either one of them before.

I wonder what else I don't know about them; I wonder why Amy's a sophomore and she's leading the group and Ilana's a senior and she's Amy's right-hand man, Amy's muscle, along with Martin, whom I've kind of missed seeing lately. Whom I wouldn't mind doing French rhymes with again.

But then I stop thinking about them because we're leaving the food line now. I feel my muscles tighten. Amy senses the change and whispers, "You can do this."

We walk out into the cafeteria together, Amy on one side,

Ilana on the other. Out of the corner of my eye, I see Carter look up, then Kevin. It's all in slow motion, as if it's playing out on a movie reel, slowed down frame by frame. They see me, then Ilana, then Amy. The two Mockingbird girls stare at the two water polo boys. The boys look down instantly. They don't look up again, even when we sit down at our table, where T.S., Maia, Martin, and Sandeep are already parked.

Flanking me, Amy and Ilana pick seats so we're facing the water polo boys from across the room. That's how I know Carter and Kevin never look at me again for the whole meal. Even when I go to the salad bar, Amy by my side, they stay like that.

When I finish my pasta, a girl with broad shoulders and sandy blond hair tucked behind her ears, the ends curling back out under them, walks over to our table. She circles around my side and crouches down next to me. She places one hand on my back, the other on the back of Amy's chair.

"I'm Dana Golden," she says.

"Hi, Dana," I say tensely.

"I'm on the girls' water polo team."

Uh-oh. She's probably his girlfriend or his buddy, maybe even his henchwoman. She's probably going to give us a taste of our medicine. She's probably going to pin me down and swing at my face a couple of times.

"Was it you?" she asks me. "Because I know he was spreading rumors about you at the start of the term, and then when I heard he was in the book, I figured it was you. What a pig," she says.

"You know him?" I ask, but I don't answer her first question, even though I'm relieved she's not a friend of Carter's, or a fan.

"He's a douche," Dana answers. "I went out with him a couple times last year and all he wanted to do was get his hands on me. I literally had to slap him one time to stop him. He was pushing himself on me."

"Did you stop him?" I ask.

Dana nods proudly, her broad shoulders moving up and down as she does. Dana's got a swimmer's build and she looks tough. She fought him off. I didn't.

"Yeah, and he tried to start some rumors about me too, like he did to you. Last spring he started telling all the guys that I totally put out for him. So I just marched right up to him in front of his friends and asked if he had told them how I slapped him too. That shut him up."

"Wow...," I say.

"So listen. If you need a character witness, I will totally do it."

T.S. chimes in. "That's a great idea, don't you think, Alex?"

"Sure," I say, because it sounds like the sort of thing they'd do on *Law and Order*.

"Anyway, keep up the good work. See you around," Dana says, and heads out of the cafeteria.

187

"That was bloody brilliant," Maia says with a clap of approval. "Character witness. I love it!"

"Speaking of character witnesses, have you picked your student advocate yet to try your case?" Amy asks me.

Maia jumps in, waving her arms in the air. "Like a lawyer? Like a prosecutor?"

Amy nods and Maia turns to me. "You know there'd be no one better."

"Maia, are you trying to say you want to defend me?" I say playfully.

Maia bats her eyelashes, giving me a coquettish smile. Maia's been dreaming about attending Harvard Law School since she was three, so I'm not surprised she's salivating at the chance to play attorney here. Then I feel that same pang of doubt I felt yesterday. Is Maia interested for me or for herself?

I turn to T.S. "Did you want to do it?" I ask her.

Maia emits a huff. "C'mon. You know T.S. doesn't."

"Maia, would it kill you to let Alex decide?" T.S. asks.

Maia holds up her hands, like she did the night we first went to the Mockingbirds.

"Do *you* want to do it?" I ask T.S. again.

"I want you to decide," T.S. says.

There's no question. "Maia would be perfect," I say.

When we leave the cafeteria Ilana gives me my hat back. It looks like I won't need it again.

Chapter Twenty

ANOTHER POINT OF VIEW

That evening Jones meets me outside my dorm and we head over to the music hall. Mr. Christie and Ms. Peck—she's Jones's advisor, so it's like they doubled up on us—were so enamored of the Gershwin idea, they asked us to perform *Rhapsody in Blue* for their staff meeting. Not even the Faculty Club, just a regular weekly meeting. I know it's supposed to be an honor, like extra credit for extra-special students, but still it just feels so ridiculous. Wind us up, watch us go.

"What do you say we go wild tonight and screw the old masters?" Jones suggests.

"Ooh, that sounds vaguely dirty, Jones," I say as we cross the quad. Yellow light from the old-fashioned streetlamps lining the quad spills across the stone pathway, guiding our way. I use the light to avoid another run-in with an ice slick.

"I'm serious. Do you really want to practice frigging Gershwin again?"

"I like Gershwin," I say. "Even if we have to perform it at their stupid meeting."

"But what if we did it like we were rappers or something covering *Rhapsody in Blue*?"

"So just totally subvert things?" I ask as he opens the door, unlocked as always, to the music hall. We both pull off our fleece pullovers and toss them on the floor. No teacher, no need to use a coat rack.

"Yeah. What do you think?"

I roll my eyes. "I don't think so."

"C'mon, Alex. Don't you just want to shake things up a bit?"

I'm already shaking things up, I want to say. Instead I say, "Not that way," and sit down at the piano, then rub my hands together to warm them up.

He grabs his violin and pulls up a chair. "Saw you having lunch with Amy and Ilana. What's that all about?"

"What do you mean?" I ask, not looking at him.

"Alex, I'm not stupid."

"I never thought you were."

"They're in the Mockingbirds," he says firmly.

"How do you know?" I ask, trying to sound casual, but wondering if he went by the mailbox like T.S., like Carter.

"Because I pay attention. So are you in the Mocking-birds?" he asks point-blank.

I scoff. "No! Me? C'mon. Why would I be in the Mock-ingbirds?"

"Then why are you hanging out with them at lunch? You're not part of the cheating case."

"Cheating case? What are you talking about?" I ask him.

Jones shakes his head, kind of disapprovingly. "This dude in my dorm says his roommates are forcing him to do all their math and chem homework. He's this total math savant. I mean, he's actually taking math classes at William-son right now, applied math, not even intro level college math. He is already way beyond that. So his roommates are making him do all their math work. Guess they're telling him they'll tell everyone what he says in his sleep if he stops doing their homework. I don't know—sounds as if he's a major sleeptalker and maybe shares a little TMI while he's snoozing."

"That kind of sucks," I say.

"Yeah, and he's talking to the Mockingbirds about tak-ing on his case."

The math genius must be one of the other cases Amy alluded to before lunch, one of the ones she wouldn't tell me about. "How do you know?" I ask.

He gives me a look, then rolls his eyes. "Alex, he lives down the hall from me. I know what's going on. I keep my eyes and ears open. Besides, they've been by, talking to him, talking to the roommates too. I guess they're *investigating*," he says with a note of derision as he sketches air quotes with his fingers. "It's kind of lame, though," Jones adds.

"What do you mean? The cheating? Or the sleeptalking?"

He shrugs his shoulders. "The whole thing. Like he can't deal with it on his own?"

"Well, maybe he feels helpless," I say defensively.

"Anyway," Jones steers the conversation back. "So why are *you* hanging out with the Mockingbirds?"

"Why not hang out with them?"

"You're not answering the question."

"What's the question, Jones?"

"If you're not in the Mockingbirds, then what happened to you?"

He lays the violin gently across his thighs and leans toward me. His hair falls forward, but he makes no move to push it out of the way. He just waits for me.

I should tell him. The whole school is going to know any day now when Carter is served his summons. But when I try to speak, my throat closes, as if there's a hand on my neck, gripping tighter, choking the words into silence. I'm afraid to tell Jones for some reason. Maybe it was the way he said the math wiz was lame for going to the Mockingbirds, or the way he seems to disapprove of the Mockingbirds.

"What happened to you, Alex? If you don't tell me I'll go all Beastie Boys with Gershwin next week."

"Jones," I manage to get out before the hand clamps my throat again.

"Alex, I'm your friend. I've known you since we started here. You and me, we're the same. You're the only other person here who understands how I feel about music and I'm the only person who understands exactly how you feel too."

The hand loosens its grip, one finger after another slowly peeling off my throat. "Do you know Carter Hutchinson?" I ask quietly.

"Water polo dude?"

I nod. "Yes."

Jones sighs heavily. "I heard his name went into the book yesterday. Don't tell me he..."

I tell Jones the story. When I'm done, he lets out a long breath of air. "Man, I wish you came to me."

"Came to you?"

"I would have taken care of this."

"What do you mean?"

"I would have bashed his head in."

"Stop it, Jones."

"I'm serious. I can't believe he hurt you like this."

"I'm fine," I insist, and it's strangely true. I felt fine—good, really—when Maia told me about the pool. I felt better—strong, even—when I walked through the cafeteria with my protectors. "Besides, I don't want you resorting to violence, Jones. I don't want you getting in trouble."

"I know, and, look, I just meant this is crazy. There are other ways to deal with this."

"Oh, like you attacking him?"

"No, Alex. Forget that," he says, calming down a bit.

"You mean I should have dealt with it on my own like you think the math dude in your dorm should?"

"No! This is different, way different. That's small-time. This is a crime. Why didn't you go to the police?"

"Give me a break. This is not a police matter."

"He raped you!"

"It was date rape, okay? I was drunk. I was passed out. It's not like when someone rapes you in a dark alley with a knife to your throat."

"It's still a crime. And you should treat it like a crime. Why didn't you go to the cops?"

"I didn't want to. And you know as well as I do how these things turn out with the cops involved. It turns into a *he said, she said,* and they turn my life upside down."

"It's going to be *he said, she said* with the Mocking-birds."

"It's not the same."

"Fine, but what about your parents? Have you told them?"

I laugh. "My parents? I'm not telling my parents. My mom is a drama queen. She'd totally freak. My dad would enlist a few key contacts and secretly hunt him down."

"Maybe they *should* hunt him down."

"They'd pull me out of Themis. They'd send me to school in New Haven and make me live at home. You think I want that?"

"No."

"So that's why."

"I know; it's just this is so big. I think you should at least *tell* your parents."

I point a finger at him. "You don't even tell your parents you play the electric guitar. I'm not telling mine I was date-raped at boarding school."

He holds up his hands. "Fair enough." Then he adds, "So when is the hearing?"

"It hasn't been set yet. They're supposed to notify him Monday he's being charged. But I'm pretty sure he knows it's coming."

"Well, you know I'll do anything for you, okay? You know that, right?"

I nod.

"I mean it. Anything. If I can help in any way, I will."

"I know."

"You know I asked Amy out last year," he offers.

"You did? What'd she say?"

"Well, I'm not dating her, am I?"

"Why would she turn you down?"

"She said I wasn't her type."

"Her loss," I say.

"Anyway, should we practice?"

I raise an eyebrow playfully. "You want to practice? I'm shocked."

We settle in and play Gershwin—the normal way, not hip-hop. I'll take all the normal I can get right now.

Chapter Twenty-One
FOR THE LONGEST TIME

Carter's getting served tomorrow—Monday morning. I do my best to keep my mind in the present by working on my spring project. Alone in my room, I sift through the research I've compiled for my spring project—books and articles from musicologists, theorists, biographers, and others, some debating Beethoven's genius, others questioning whether the Ninth Symphony breaches the rules of classic composition, but none that acknowledge the central problem I've unearthed. The lack of a piano.

So it's up to me and Liszt.

Liszt, who adored Beethoven but didn't simply imitate the master. Liszt *reclaimed* Beethoven, made the piano-less work his very own. He didn't stand for things the way they were. He changed them. He stood up and made them better. I open a file to start the written portion of my spring project. As I write the first sentence, *At some point an artist must break with the past,* I feel a kinship with Liszt, knowing I am doing the same in my own way.

I write for another thirty minutes when there's a knock on my door. I get up and look through the keyhole. It's Martin. I tell myself there's no point in applying lip gloss this time, but I still run a brush through my hair before I let him in.

"Hey," he says. "I have dinner for you."

He hands me a napkin. I unwrap it and there's a sandwich inside, hummus and cheese on three-seed bread. T.S. was supposed to bring dinner back.

"Thanks."

"T.S. and Sandeep had a project to work on together," he says, explaining why he is the delivery boy.

"I didn't know they were working on a project."

He gives me an insider look.

"Oh," I say, nodding and understanding. "I guess that means you're out of a room for a couple hours."

"Yep," he says, patting his backpack. "I'm off to the library. Want to come?"

I remember last time, reading the book. I remember the time before, seeing Carter. I shake my head. "But do you want to study here instead?" I offer, gesturing to my room. I think back to when he visited a few weeks ago. I didn't let him stay in my room then. But I'm like Liszt now, I'm reclaiming me. I'm standing up for something tomorrow, so

I can do things differently tonight. "Is that allowed?" I add.

"Allowed?" he asks curiously.

"You know, *allowed*. Are you allowed to consort with me outside of the group?"

"Why wouldn't I be?"

"Because you're a Mockingbird and I'm a..." I pause, looking for the right word for what I am — but all I can think is I am under their wing. Is there a word for that?

"You think we have all these weird rules, don't you?"

"I don't know," I say. Then I add, "Yeah, I guess I do."

"Like you thought we were going to make you dry your clothes without washing them."

"Well, it's not as if I know much about how you work."

"Casey never told you?"

"She told me some stuff. Not details."

"Well, I'll tell you the details, and the details are I'm allowed to study in your room, just like I was allowed to work with you in the common room. If it's still okay with you?"

"It is," I say.

"Good," he says, then shrugs his shoulders happily. He comes in and sits down at T.S.'s desk. I return to mine and begin my sandwich.

"What are you working on tonight?" he asks.

I tell him about my spring project, then ask about his.

"Barn owls," he states.

"Interesting. How'd you get that idea?"

"I was driving this summer and I drove past this injured owl on the side of the road. I was about to call the Humane Society, but then he just died, so I took him home and I dissected him—"

I cut him off. "You dissected him?" I ask incredulously. "What, on the kitchen counter?"

"Uh, no," he tosses back at me. "In the garage."

"That's weird, Martin."

"What's weird about it?"

"You find a dead owl and take him home to slice him open. That's weird!" I cross my arms and lean back in my desk chair.

"He was already dead. It was a learning opportunity. It's no different than you going off to play the piano all the time even at night. This is how I *practice* what I want to do."

"Okay, fine. So tell me what you found when you dissected your roadside discovery."

"His stomach was full of rodents. Mice, chipmunks, even a gopher!" Martin grows more animated; his eyes sparkle as he talks about the contents of the owl's belly. I find myself both repulsed and curious.

"How could you tell?"

"I can just tell," he says. "Same way you can tell which chord is a C minor if someone blindfolded you. Anyway, you know why the owl had so much food in its stomach?"

I shake my head.

"Because the common barn owl has an insanely high

metabolic rate!" He says this as if he just discovered a lost city of Aztec gold or stumbled upon buried treasure. I picture Martin in his garage in upstate New York, an old rickety wood garage with a workbench full of tools and a dead owl. He grabs an X-Acto blade and delicately, but ever so precisely, slices open the owl. Dead mice spill out of the owl's belly, and Martin's brown eyes crackle with delight.

"So I'm going to do my project on how the barn owl's metabolism is the embodiment of survival of the fittest," he says.

"Who's your junior advisor? Mr. Christie is mine," I say, then stick my tongue out to indicate how I feel about that travesty.

"Yeah, he's mine too. So I know the horror."

Martin begins his patented impression, complete with the booming, baritone voice. "How many of you," he begins, then pauses heavily, portentously, "can write a seventeen-point-five-word essay on where our global economy is headed over the next one hundred years?"

I laugh.

Martin continues, back to his own voice now. "I can't figure out if the dude is lazy or just a freaking genius. Like he figured out it's so much easier to grade these essays that are the size of a molecule. Or if there actually is something to the whole idea of being succinct and being able to sum something up in ten words or less, or whatever."

"My dad always says you have to have your elevator pitch down," I say. "He's a succinct man. He says little, but it's always *high impact,* he says. He heads up fund-raising at Yale, so he's used to having to do the elevator pitch to hook people. He says that too."

"You do think Mr. Christie is a genius, then," Martin says, pointing his finger at me as if he's caught me in the act.

"Hey, you started it! You said he might be a genius," I fire back.

"And you agreed! I guess we're even."

"Even," I say, then take the last bite of the sandwich. "Thanks again for dinner."

"It's not Amy's homemade mac and cheese, but it's the best I can do," he says as he removes textbooks, mostly biology ones, from his backpack.

"So, were you assigned to me tonight?" I ask, because clearly the Mockingbirds share details and duties. Martin knew about Amy's visit, after all.

"Assigned to you?"

"By the Mockingbirds. Did Amy tell you to hang out with me or something because of tomorrow?"

"Are you nervous about tomorrow?" he asks, not answering my question.

"Should I be?" I ask, not answering his. "What will it be like?"

"I'll walk you to all your classes," he says.

"You don't have to."

"I want to."

"Were you assigned to me?" I ask again. Now I want

the answers I don't have, the things Amy won't tell me, the things Casey never told me. I don't have to be just the girl under their wing. I can speak up, like I'm doing tomorrow.

"I want to know," I say.

"No," he says, and shakes his head. "And I wasn't assigned to you tonight either. T.S. was going to bring the sandwich back; she had it all wrapped up, and I said I would. I offered. Amy didn't tell me to. Besides, it's not like that."

"What's it like?"

He laughs softly. "You think we're like a secret society or a fraternity. We're not. What you see is what you get. And you'll get me walking you to class."

I continue my line of questioning. "Do you guys assign people to all the cases you work on?"

"Like a bodyguard?" he asks.

"Sort of."

"I have my own reasons," he says, then he opens a book and says, "It's the least I can do."

I look at him quizzically. "What do you mean?"

He swallows hard, then looks back at me, the same look he'd give me in physics class sometimes, the same look he'd give me when he was about to say something but stopped. "I feel like it was my fault," he blurts out.

"What do you mean?"

"What happened with Carter."

I look at him as if he's crazy. "What are you talking about? Why would you say that?"

Martin runs his fingers through his hair. His hair's soft, I remember from that night. "Because I was talking to you at the concert and then when you came back from the bathroom you were talking to him."

"Oh."

"I'm really sorry, Alex."

"It's not your fault. Don't be crazy."

"I feel terrible. I should have kept you away from him. I should have done something."

"How could you have known, Martin?" I say softly. "No one could have known what he was going to do. He seemed just like any other guy at the concert and at the party."

"I shouldn't have talked to Cleo. I had no idea talking to her could turn into this."

"Martin, really. It's not a big deal."

His eyes widen with shock. "Not a big deal? He assaulted you."

"That's not what I meant. I meant it's not a big deal you talked to Cleo."

"I didn't even want to talk to her. I just talked to her because you walked away."

"I had to go to the bathroom," I say.

"It seemed as if you were looking for an excuse to get away."

"I had to pee! I told you that. And when I got back you were talking to Cleo. So I figured you were..." My voice trails off.

"Figured what?" he asks softly. "Figured I liked her?"

"Well, duh."

He shakes his head. "She's a cool girl. But I just…," he says, not finishing the thought.

"So is this why you're helping me? Because you think it was somehow your fault, which is totally ridiculous."

"No, that's not why I'm helping."

"How long have you been involved with the Mockingbirds?" I ask.

"Since start of sophomore year."

"A year and a half."

He nods.

"You were a runner sophomore year," I say.

"I was."

"And the runners become Mockingbirds, right?"

He nods.

"So you just go from runner to board?"

"Not exactly."

"Is there a step in between?"

"Yes."

"Well? What is the step in between?"

He leans closer to me, like he's about to tell a secret. "Well, you know the runners are the first level, almost like—"

"Like a pledge!" I say, because I'm starting to get how they work. Before he can answer, I continue, "So you go from runner to council to board."

Martin lightly taps his nose with his index finger, then points at me. "You're brilliant, Alex."

I jump up from my chair, the puzzle pieces fitting in. "So

I bet it goes like this. You have to prove yourself as a runner. Maybe some lose interest and drop out. Those who remain interested try out for the New Nine—the students who form the council. And you have tryouts for the council each semester, so you'll have a fresh batch of council members—judges—so they won't get corrupted, right?"

"You got it."

"And then who decides which council members become board members?"

"The board does and the leader."

I nod a few times, feeling as if I just cracked a code or something. I'm on fire tonight. I am writing a kick-ass spring project, I am giving notice to the asshole who assaulted me, and I am deciphering the inner workings of the school's very own underground judge, jury, and police.

"But if you were a runner last year, when were you on the council?"

"Last semester. The fall."

"You only did half a year? What, are you that good they just said, 'Wow, we have to have Martin on the board right now'?" I tease.

He laughs, then shakes his head. "Not exactly. One of the seniors on the board the first half went back to the grassroots side, so to speak."

"What do you mean?" I ask quizzically.

"He'd been through the system—runner to council to board, and he said he kind of missed the on-the-ground feel of being a runner. So he's a runner again."

"That's kind of funny."

"Yeah, he's going to be one of those community organizers, I bet. Sort of an of-the-people type of guy."

"So Mr. Grassroots steps down," I say, continuing my detective work, "and you step up. It's that simple?"

"Well, there's an interview process, a vetting process and all that."

"What do they ask you?"

"I can't tell you everything, Alex," he says playfully. "But point being, I had served on the council and Amy felt I was ready to move up and be a full-on board member."

"So when you said you heard the case with the freshmen theater students last semester, you really *heard* it, as in you were on the council?"

"Well, there are nine council members each semester, three get called for a trial, so there was a 33.33 percent chance of my hearing it."

I roll my eyes. "Okay, math geek. Were you in the 33.33 percent of the council that heard it?"

"Remember, the case was settled."

"If you didn't hear it, how do you know about it?"

"It all gets passed on."

Like the mac-and-cheese visit. "What made you want to be a Mockingbird?" I ask.

"My dad's a judge, my mom a prosecutor. I guess you can say justice is in my blood. I'm an idealist too, just like them. I guess I just believe we can do good. We can be the good the school can't be."

"You really believe that?"

He nods enthusiastically. "Look, it's not perfect. Nothing ever is. But I just think we have to exist, right? I mean, look at the teachers. They don't lock their offices, they leave the music hall open. They live in la-la land, like the little private Gershwin performance you have to give at their meeting," he says with a derisive snort. "Next thing you know they'll ask me to dissect a barn owl at the Faculty Club next month and everyone will stand around and ooh and ahh."

"Yeah, pretty silly," I say. "So would you ever be the leader, like Amy?"

He shakes his head. "I can't."

"You can't? Why not?"

He doesn't answer.

"Do you have to be a girl to be the leader?" I press.

"No, it's not like that."

"What's it like, then?"

"Can we talk about something else?" he asks.

"Like your own reasons?" I ask, bringing the conversation back to where it was before.

He smiles. "My reasons..."

"You feel guilty. That's why you're here."

"That's not why I'm here."

"Why are you here?"

"Because," he begins, and then it's silent. We're silent. We don't say anything. Our quietness fills up the room like a balloon expanding.

I decide to pop it. I am take-charge Alex tonight. "Do you want to skip studying and watch TV?"

He smiles, as if we just decided to do something terribly naughty. I grab my laptop from my desk and move over to my bed.

"You can sit on my bed too," I say. I pat my comforter with its purple, orange, and pink swirls and stripes and shapes. I sit with my back to the wall, knees up, feet on the bed. "Wait, is that allowed?" I ask, teasing him.

"Let me check the rule book," he says as he moves over to join me, the short way, like we're two buddies on a make-shift couch.

"Do you like *Law and Order*?" I ask.

"My favorite," Martin says, his long legs dangling off the bed. "And I'm pretty sure *Law and Order* is allowed," he adds, then looks at me, hoping I'll laugh. I do laugh, because I think he's funny, because I mean it, because I want him here watching television with me on my make-believe couch.

A half-hour later, some chick in a suit is discussing an arraignment, but I can barely follow what she's saying. Not because I'm bad at legalese—I'm good, I've been watching this show since I was thirteen—but because I have this overwhelming urge to kiss Martin. I can smell him near me and he smells good, he smells like a shower, like clean soap. And his hair, I felt it against my shoulder when he leaned over to turn the volume up, and it's making me crazy because I want to touch his hair so badly.

I wonder where this desire came from, how long it's been

in me, how long it's been dormant, waiting for me to remember it. To remember that *this is* what I wanted that night, and maybe what he wanted to, but he thought I wasn't into him, so he talked to Cleo, and I thought he wasn't into me, so I talked to... But I refuse to go there tonight. I am breaking with the past. I am reclaiming my present. Because what's happening now is something I want very much.

I want a kiss.

The only thing going through my brain is a kiss—all the permutations of a kiss—whether Martin wants to kiss me, whether I can kiss him, whether he's allowed to. I force myself to stare at the computer screen that rests on my legs, but I know my eyes keep darting his way. I'm trying to be cool, as if I'm just enjoying the show, but my mind is a pinball machine. The silver ball hits a bumper, a light goes off, the shiny orb swirls, another ball appears, then another, then flippers bang and crazy pinball sirens blare and suddenly the game is going into overdrive. Balls appear from nowhere, and everything is just so loud; the whole machine clangs in on itself.

And finally, everything is silent.

I hit the pause button on the computer screen and turn to him. "What are the other reasons?" I ask him again.

A half-grin lights up his face; the green flecks in his eyes sparkle as he smiles. "Other ones?"

"Yes," I say, insisting this time. I got the Mockingbirds info out of him. I want this info too. "What are the other reasons you're here?"

He doesn't say anything, just kind of holds my gaze with his eyes and my insides flip. I'm warm everywhere, my face, my chest, my hands, and he won't stop looking at me. I don't want him to stop looking at me.

"Martin," I whisper.

"Yes?"

"Are there rules against...?"

"Yes," he says immediately.

"You don't know what I was going to ask."

"I do know what you were going to ask, Alex."

"What was I going to ask?"

"Are there rules against someone in the group being involved with someone we're helping," he says.

I nod, slowly, my breath feeling heavier, filling up my whole chest, my whole body.

"Yes, there are rules against it," he repeats, and his breathing sounds heavy too.

"But you're only being nice to me because you feel you have to, right? Not for any other reason?"

"For other reasons, Alex. For other reasons."

"What are the other reasons, Martin?" I ask, and I'm aware of how we're saying each other's names with every sentence, it seems. As if saying our names brings us closer, even closer than this little bed and the twelve or so inches separating us. He looks away, swallows, runs a hand through his hair. God, how I wish that was my hand touching his hair. How I wish I knew if he wants me to be touching his hair.

He looks back to me. "You know what I'm talking about."

I shake my head.

"It would be easier for me if you knew what I was talking about."

"Why would it be easier?"

"When I told you I didn't want to be talking to Cleo. I'd rather have been..."

He waits for me to finish.

"Talking to me?"

He nods.

"Why is it easier if I knew that?" I ask.

"It would be easier for me if you started things," he says.

"If I started things, would you tell the Mockingbirds?"

He shakes his head.

"Would you tell anyone?" I ask.

He shakes his head again, then speaks. "Would you?"

"Not if I wasn't supposed to."

"It's not that I wouldn't want to tell everyone. I would. I would really want to. I really like you, Alex. I have for the longest time."

I'm speechless for a moment. The only thing I'm aware of is my body, how my face is tingling, how all I want is to be close to him, to this boy who has liked me for the longest time. I manage two words. "You have?" I ask.

"Yes, but you had a boyfriend and I had a girlfriend and

then finally we both were single at the same time," he says, then stops. "I'm not supposed to be doing this."

"You mean being here just as you?"

He nods. "So I kind of want you to go first."

I take the computer off my lap and put it next to me on the bed. "I want to kiss you right now," I say, feeling something a bit like bliss about getting a say in the matter.

He just smiles and reaches for me, putting a hand in my hair and pulling me close to his face. His lips are soft and sweet and they linger on mine and he takes his time and I take mine too and I touch his hair and it's soft just like it felt on my face that night. The kiss could last for ten minutes, ten hours. I lose track of time because with every touch, every taste of his warm lips, his cool breath, I'm reprogramming kissing, making it mine again, the way it should be.

Chapter Twenty-Two

THE UNTOUCHABLES

"How do they do it, Casey?" I ask, clutching my phone tight to my ear, pacing back and forth in my room. "Do they just go right up to his room and knock on the door like some private detective?"

"Pretty much," she says.

"Really?" I ask.

"Yes, really. It's pretty basic. Knock on the door. Hand him a summons."

My stomach twists in a gigantic knot. "Casey, this is the scariest and craziest thing I've ever done."

"You performed in front of hundreds of people. You played a Chopin solo at Yale when you were thirteen, remember?"

"That was nothing. It was just a young musicians' showcase. Everyone was thirteen."

"Who cares? Point is you did it. You are stronger than you think. You're a fighter. And you know me, Alex. I'm not a sentimental gusher. But I love you and I'm proud of you."

"I love you too," I say, and my other line rings. "It's probably Amy or someone. I better go."

We say goodbye and I click over.

"Alex?"

"Yes," I say.

"Alex Patrick." The voice drips with sarcasm as my entire body turns into ice.

"Alexandra Nicole Patrick," he says again. "Now I know your whole name. Your whole entire name. And it's Alexandra Nicole Patrick. The freak. Alex the freak who ran out that morning. Who ran away in the library."

"Leave me alone," I rasp. But I don't hang up. I should, but I don't, because I can't move, I'm paralyzed. My feet are blocks of ice concrete. My legs won't move, my arms won't move, my brain is frozen. Everything is happening to someone else right now. This is not my world, this is not me, I am *not not not* on the phone with the guy who screwed me while I was sleeping. It's not happening, because if it was I would slam the phone down.

But it is happening.

"I thought you were just a freak. Now I know you're fucking delusional."

"Not. I'm not." It's like I can't speak, can't form sentences. I'm just surrounded by thick sludge, quicksand, and it's pulling me under.

"You were begging for it," he says, oily and slick.

"Shut up!" I say, because I'm starting to thaw and the words are coming. "That's a lie."

He laughs harsh and cold into the phone. "Oh, it's not a lie, freak girl. You were all over me."

Hang up. Hang up. Hang up.

He keeps going, "And that's why I can't believe you would pull this shit and say I raped you and think you can get away with this."

I hate him I hate him I hate him.

He continues, "You can sic all your little Mockingbird friends after me, but I know you're wrong and there is no way I am settling this case. That's why I have no fucking problem showing up for this trial, you freak."

"You're the liar," I say. "You're the liar."

Then I hang up and just stare at the phone, bore holes in it with my eyes and I can feel my hands are hot and my cheeks are burning and my hair is on fire with rage and I have never hated anyone before but I hate him, I hate him so much for doing what he did that night and for doing this now. He deserves this, he deserves to be made an example of, he deserves to be punished. He was wrong then and he's wrong now. He's slippery, he's slimy, he's a water polo stereotype.

I want to throw the phone, I want to throw my

computer, I want to throw the chair, the desk, the bed. I want to smash the window. This is how it happens—this is how people go all postal. This is how you get so mad, so angry that you become not yourself.

I tell myself to breathe. One, two, three.

I take a deep, long, penetrating breath. I'm not going to be that person who loses it. No, I'm not and never will be. But I'm still angry, and when I turn to the mirror I see the vein in my forehead is throbbing. It's my own metronome pulsing in time, just like Carter's chest that morning.

I hear a ripping sound. It's loud, ridiculously loud. I cover my ears it's so loud. I open my eyes slowly, not wanting them to be open. Carter's on me, he's straddling me and he's naked. Something's wrong with this picture. He's got a leg on each side of me and there's this broad chest, a pale chest, a pale white chest, and I don't want to look down because if I do I'll see his penis and it'll be hard and I don't want to see his hard penis because he's trying to put a condom on it. Because that's what he just ripped open, the wrapper for the condom.

"What are you doing?" I mumble.

"Getting a dome out."

"A dome?"

I think he nods but I can't tell because he has two heads or something. Or his one head is blurry. I'm not sure, but it's spinning. His head is spinning, or maybe it's the bed, or maybe it's just me. Maybe I'm spinning. I close my eyes. It hurts too much to leave them open. But I spin more with them closed, so I open them again and Carter's still on me, this looming figure over me. I think he got the condom on because he's coming toward me now, his face is coming toward me, his body is coming toward me, and there's a hand, a left hand, a right hand, I'm not sure, pressed on the mattress right next to my arm. And his other hand, his other arm is between his legs. I think I know what he's doing. I think I know why his hand is between his legs. He's going to try to enter me. He's going to try to push himself into me. I look down at me, at my body, and I'm naked in this bed, and I don't know how I got naked in his bed. All I know is I don't want him inside me. I don't want it inside me. The spinning slows, then it halts, and the room's no longer turning, it's suddenly still and quiet and calm and I'm strong. I'm so strong I put my two hands on his big chest. I press my palms hard against him and push him. I shake my head; I say no. And I keep my hands on his chest like that, like a bodybuilder holding back a car, a strong man holding up a bridge.

My body is hollow, my insides a dark empty cave. Everything turns black for a moment as the filthy memory moves through me. There was no begging for it, only pleading to stop; I pushed him away and he pushed into me anyway.

I remember I'm nearly late for French class, so I grab my backpack and bolt. Martin's waiting right outside my dorm for me.

"Sorry, I'm going to make you late," I say.

"Us. Make *us* late. It's the same class for both of us.

French," he says, reminding me of the class we share. "But don't worry. It's no biggie."

"Right," I say, still distracted by the call and the memory.

"You okay?" he asks as we walk to Morgan-Young Hall, the regular way. I don't have to go the long way anymore.

"You okay?" he asks again.

Oh, I still haven't answered him.

"Yeah, I'm fine," I manage. Then, "Shit!"

"What?"

"We need to run," I say, grabbing the arm of his shirt. "Subjunctive, remember?"

If you're late for French you have to speak in the subjunctive mood for the entire class. *"Avis aux retardataires de mon cours, je vous imposerai l'utilisation exclusif du subjonctif,"* Ms. Dumas warned us the first day. It's a brutal but effective punishment because everyone who has ever studied French knows the subjunctive tense is the trickiest tense of all. Hence, no one is EVER late to Ms. Dumas's French class.

"We're not going to get in trouble," he says, running alongside me.

"What, are you omniscient?"

"No, I just took care of this already."

"Took care of it?"

"When I knew you were going to be late, I took care of it."

Before I can ask how, we push open the heavy door to

the building just as the bell rings. We're late. But right outside the French class there's Amy, immersed in an animated conversation with Ms. Dumas. Our teacher's back is to us, her brown curly hair pinned up on her head as she chatters away *en français* with Amy. Martin places a hand on my arm, slowing me down so we can tiptoe soundlessly down the hall. I mirror his stealth as Amy exclaims, *"Certainement! Il me fera un grand plaisir de rédiger un essai pour vous."*

"Formidable," Ms. Dumas says to Amy as Martin and I slip into class, undetected by our teacher. I take my seat; he takes his a few desks away. Literally two seconds later, Ms. Dumas marches into the class and issues an upbeat, *"Bonjour, mes amis!"*

She walks straight to the front of the class, to her lectern, and begins her lesson, without having noticed we were late. I breathe a quiet sigh of relief. I hate the subjunctive mood. But I feel strangely unsettled too. Where would I be without Amy and Martin and Ilana fighting all my battles, swooping in and saving me from teachers, from bad boys, from myself? I was Alex the music girl, the piano player, the Juilliard aspirant. Now I'm an untouchable.

When class ends, the girl who sits in front of me turns around to face me. I know her vaguely. Her name's Mel, short for Melissa, I'm sure. She's a tiny little thing; she must be under five feet tall. She has light brown hair she wears in a French braid every day (I know—I sit behind her in this class).

"Hi," she says quietly to me.

"Hi, Mel," I say.

Her eyes dart from one side of the room to the other, then she turns back around and says nothing more. Okay, whatever. I grab my bag and head out, Martin materializing by my side.

"So," he begins, then leans closer so only I can hear, "do you want to hang out again tonight?"

"Yes," I say. "But I don't know if Maia or T.S. will be there."

"We could sneak out somewhere," he says mischievously.

My eyes go wide. "You're a Mockingbird. You can't break the rules. We can't go out at night except for Fridays."

"You're such a good girl," he teases.

Chapter Twenty-Three

WORDS AND DEEDS

After calculus ends that day, Amy finds me.

"We've decided to hold the trial in about a month. Sometime in mid-March. We'll pick the exact date soon," she tells Maia and me, then adds with her calming smile, "I wanted to let you know myself so you'll have plenty of time to *prep*." She emphasizes the last word to Maia, who nods crisply, understanding the directive she just received.

"Of course. We'll be absolutely prepared," Maia chimes in.

"Does Carter know it's going to be in March?" I ask.

"He'll know shortly," Amy says, and heads off, maybe to deliver the message herself. I picture her tracking him down after his last class and telling him in person too, but the image doesn't compute. Maybe she has some other way—a safer way—of delivering messages to the accused.

"Let's start by reviewing your testimony first," Maia says as we return to Taft-Hay Hall.

I relive *that night* again for Maia as she writes notes in her black-and-white composition book. I tell her what I remembered this morning, how I tried to fight him off. "He is revolting," she says scathingly, then reaches to hug me. "I'm so sorry he did that to you." She continues like that— alternating between criticizing him and comforting me. I feel dirty just talking about it, so when she leaves for Debate I take a shower, washing off the latest coat of memories.

I get dressed, dry my hair, and pull on jeans, then a sweater I know Casey would give her Fashion Police thumbs up to.

Martin knocks at eight. I let him in.

"Hey," he says as the door closes behind him.

"Hey."

I sit down at my desk chair, he grabs T.S.'s. "So how was today? Was it hard?"

I shrug. The truth is I don't feel like talking about it much, even with him. Or maybe especially with him. I don't want this—*us,* if there is an us, or whatever we are—to be all about *him.*

"It was fine," I say, not telling him about the phone call earlier today.

He furrows his brow, giving me kind of a penetrating stare. "You sure?"

"Yes," I say emphatically.

"And Amy told you the trial will be—"

I cut him off. "Can we just talk about science or something?"

His eyes sparkle as I say that, then he starts in on the latest scientific findings about dogs, then dolphins, then pigs. I've never been a science person, but I'm strangely entertained by his tales, partly because his stories come alive the way he tells them. Then he reaches into his back pocket and takes out his cell phone. I tense for a second, thinking maybe the Mockingbirds have just paged him and he'll have to go. I don't want Amy to take him away from me.

"I promised I'd show you those Meissner effect pictures," he says, flipping his phone open.

"Right, I've been dying to see them," I tease.

"Hey! Sarcasm doesn't work on me. I'm showing them to you anyway," he says as he drags his chair across the room so he's right next to me. He leans in closer, and for a second I'm distracted by his nearness and how he smells clean and how much I like the way he smells. As he scrolls through some pictures of a magnet hovering, I bend into his neck, my lips brushing his skin, and he groans lightly. I like the sound of it.

"You really don't want to see my pictures, do you?" he teases.

"I do want to see them. I swear," I say softly as I graze his neck again.

"I have no idea where they are now," he says, and drops

his cell phone onto the chair. He makes the sound again, that groan, and it makes me feel powerful. It makes me feel in charge.

"No idea?" I ask as he closes his eyes and reaches his hands up into my hair.

"No idea at all," he says before he silences me with his lips. We twist around so we're closer to each other. His breathing grows heavier, his fingers play with my hair and a little zing rushes from my belly down to my toes and back up again.

I drift into the kiss, then another, then yet another.

Amazing.

Yes, this kiss is amazing.

Then another.

Heat.

I am warm all over.

Then a touch.

Weak in the knees.

This is the guy who makes me weak in the knees. The guy who makes me laugh. The kind of guy worth waiting for.

Worth waiting for.

Then like a kick in the gut, I'm doubled over. Because I'm *not* worth waiting for. I have no virginity to give up because mine was taken.

I pull away.

"Mmm. Come back," he says. His eyes are still closed; he's in the moment, still wanting me. His hand loops around my hair and he pulls me back, kisses me more, firmer, harder, trying to bring me back to now. But I'm not into it anymore. The connection's broken. I put my hands on his chest and push him away.

He opens his eyes. "You okay?"

"I'm fine," I say.

"You're not fine. One minute we were here. And the next minute you were somewhere else. Is this too soon? Are you okay with this? I don't want to push you."

Then another word appears in front of me. And it's a nasty word. It starts with an *R* and ends with a *D* and it's *rebound*.

I want Martin because he's not Carter. I want Martin because he's the reverse of Carter, the antidote to Carter. My eyes glass over with the realization that I'm using him to get over what happened.

"I should go," he says, and stands up.

I nod.

He gathers his backpack, stuffs his phone back into his jeans pocket.

"I'm sorry, Alex. I shouldn't have done this. I should have known it'd be too soon."

Too soon.

I let the words play, stretching them out letter by letter.

Too.

Soon.

Like they're the low notes on the piano. Warbling. ToooooooSooooon.

Then I snap out of it.

"Don't go," I say quickly.

He gives me a look. He doesn't believe me.

"I want you to stay. I *want* you to stay."

"You do?"

"I do."

I reach for his hand and lead him to my bed. "I'm not ready for more than kissing, but the bed is more comfortable."

"The bed it is," Martin says, stretching out next to me. Then he taps me on the nose lightly. "You're in charge. You know that, right?"

"I do. I do know that. So tell me about the freshmen theater students."

He gives me a grin. "You're only interested in me for access to information, aren't you?" he jokes.

"Yes, I want you to give up all your Mockingbird secrets," I toss back.

He smiles at me, brushes a strand of my hair behind my ear, and says, "Good thing I like you. It makes me want to tell you things."

"So the freshmen last semester, what did they do?"

Martin chuckles lightly, the memory amusing him. "It was really stupid and immature. That's why they confessed. They knew they had no defense."

"Tell me. What happened?"

He props himself up on an elbow and rests on his side. "You remember the musical last semester?"

"Wasn't it *Evita* but set fifty years in the future, and Eva was a princess warrior?" I say jokingly, because that's how Themis would do *Evita*.

"Something like that. Anyway, so the Theater Department cast a couple freshmen as understudies for the main roles. So there was a Che understudy and an Eva understudy, and they were also in the chorus. But these two freshmen thought they'd been robbed. They thought they should have been cast as the leads. They thought they were unfairly discriminated against because they were freshmen. So they..." Martin tries to suppress a laugh, but it doesn't work; he can't stop laughing. "It's so ridiculous what they did."

I start laughing too. "Tell me, tell me."

"They tried to make the leads sick so they could take over. Because apparently the leads had this ritual of drinking tea and honey before every rehearsal. Standard acting process, we learned. Anyway, so the freshmen started spiking the tea with cough syrup one day, Benadryl the next, Tylenol PM another time."

"Did it make them sick or just sleepy?"

"The latter," Martin says. "Dumb freshmen didn't have a clue."

"The seniors couldn't just deal with this themselves?" I ask. Because while spiking tea is petty and infantile, it also seems as if Che and Evita could have held their own.

"It wasn't the seniors who came to us," Martin said. "It was a couple other freshmen in the play. Freshmen who were in the chorus along with the understudies, but who were just chorus members. These *other* freshmen thought all the first-years were getting a bad rap because of what the two under-studies were doing, so they wanted to press charges."

"For what? Character defamation?"

Martin shrugs. "Kind of. I mean, it doesn't always have to be the wronged person, the victim, who comes to us. Sometimes other people do. People who hear about what's going on and who bring it to our attention, who want us to investigate. A lot of people are afraid or they think what's happening to them isn't a big enough deal. And sometimes when bad things happen, the impact goes beyond the people being wronged. Like in this case. The other kids saw it happening and wanted it stopped, so they came to us. The sleepy seniors didn't have to be the ones to initiate a case."

"When did the freshmen understudies confess?"

"Not long after we looked into it."

"So when you say *looked into it,* what does that mean?"

"It means we investigate the claim," he says, and I real-ize that must be what's happening with the math whiz who lives near Jones. The *investigation* phase.

"You're detectives too?"

"We look into what happened, talk to both sides if that makes sense, if that's what we've been asked to do."

"Asked? You mean sometimes when students come to you they don't want a trial, they just want an investigation? What's the point of an investigation?"

"Some cases can be settled before a trial."

"And the punishment is less, then, if it's settled?"

Martin nods. "Yeah, or reduced if the guilty party cops to it and is willing to make reparations."

"So why didn't we ask Carter to settle?"

"Your case is different, Alex. We're talking about a different level of offense. Plus, he had the option when he was served papers to discuss a settlement," Martin explains, and that jibes with what Carter seethed to me on the phone earlier today. There will be no settling in my case, no compromise, no coming to terms. My case will be black or white. But I've had enough of my case for the day, so I return to the thespians.

"And what happened when Che and Evita realized they were being drugged?"

"They laughed it off. They thought it was very *All About Eve* and said they used it as motivation for their roles."

"Actors," I say, and roll my eyes.

"Anyway, so now you know. What else do you want to pry out of me?" he says while tracing my arm with his fingertips. Suddenly I don't feel like talking anymore.

"I think that's all for now, Mr. Summers," I say, and relax into the feeling of his hand on my arm. Then I rest my head on his chest and before I know it I'm asleep.

When I wake up a couple of hours later, he's gone. But Maia is here changing into her pajamas. I blink a few times and look for signs of Martin. Maybe he went to the bathroom, but his backpack is gone; he's gone.

"What's up with you and Martin?" Maia asks casually.

Forget being a lawyer, she should be a detective. James Bond, indeed.

"Nothing," I say, wondering what she saw. Did she walk in while I was sleeping next to him?

Maia raises an eyebrow at me. "Nothing?"

"Yeah, nothing. He's a Mockingbird, Maia. He's helping," I say.

"I'm sure," she says.

"Why are you asking?"

"He was reading at your desk when I walked in," she says. "He said he came to check on you, then you fell asleep and he stayed here to read because it was quiet."

"Yeah, he stopped by to visit," I confirm.

"He's cute, don't you think?"

"Um..."

"Oh, come on, Alex. He's handsome. Why wouldn't you be into him?"

I scoff. "There's nothing going on," I say. Then I grab my history homework before my red cheeks give me away. "I need to study."

Maia plops down on her bed, reaching for a book too.

But the words aren't registering as I read. Because there's only one word on my mind right now and it's slinking on top of the textbook, slithering into my thoughts.

Liar. The word is *liar.*

Because I'm the liar now.

Chapter Twenty-Four

LIGHTNING ROD

A few days later Mel talks to me again in French class. She swivels around at the end of the lesson and says hi.

"Hey," I say.

Then she leaves again, quietly, like a mouse.

This keeps up for the next few classes. Each time she adds a sentence or two more. Something about homework or the weather, since it's still freezing cold here in late February. It's kind of weird, to tell the truth. But who am I to judge? We're all weird here in our own ways. Then it shifts one afternoon. She turns around, as usual, her hair braided, as usual, her voice low, as usual. But she says something meaty this time.

"It happened to me too," she whispers.

I know instantly what she's talking about. "It did?"

"Not with him. But someone else. When I was a first-year."

"I'm so sorry to hear that."

"I'm glad you're doing this," she whispers.

"Do you want to talk about it sometime?"

She nods and we agree to meet in my room at four.

When she shows up I have tea ready, like Casey did for me. I guess tea is what you give people when bad stuff has happened to them. So I offer tiny little Mel a cup of tea I've borrowed—taken, really—from Maia's never-ending stash. It's imported too. Her parents ship her a new batch every month so my English roommate is never out of her English tea.

Mel wraps her hands around the mug and blows on the contents.

"Thanks for meeting me," she says. "I've been trying to talk to you for a couple weeks now."

"I've noticed."

"Sorry to be so strange about it. I was just trying to get up the nerve."

"Hey, no worries. I understand."

"But ever since I saw his name in the book, I wanted to know who he did it to, and then when word got out about the charges, I knew I had to talk to you."

"You saw the book?"

She nods. "I check it every week just to see who to watch out for."

"You do?" I ask, quietly amazed at the reach of the Mockingbirds.

"Fear, I guess. But yeah, I do. Then I saw the flyer and knew there was a new name in the book, so I ran to the library and saw his name. And I kept waiting and waiting to find out when it would go official."

"You figured out pretty quickly it was me."

"Word travels fast," Mel says. "You're the first one, you know. To press date-rape charges."

"I know."

"I talked to them more than two years ago."

"You did? I don't think I would have had the guts to even approach them when I was a freshman."

She shakes her head. "I didn't have the guts. I didn't go through with it."

"Even talking to them took courage, Mel."

"He was a senior," she says, the words that have been stuck in her throat for the last few weeks suddenly spilling out in my room. "I was a freshman. I didn't stand a chance. So I did nothing. I just waited for him to graduate. I stopped going to the cafeteria, I took the long way to class, I stayed in my room all the time."

"I know the feeling," I say. "I was terrified to go anywhere. I don't think I was afraid he'd do it again. I think I was afraid of not knowing how I was supposed to react when I saw him. Does that make sense?"

"That's exactly how it was for me too. But now it's different?" she asks eagerly.

"Yeah, mostly. The Mockingbirds help me now. Some of them walk me to class and sometimes I have lunch with them. And he never says a thing, never even looks at me when I'm with them."

She shakes her head, kind of appreciatively.

"It's kind of wild, huh? How they can be so..." I pause, reaching for a word, the right word. "Effective," I say, though I'm not sure it's the word I was looking for.

"Yeah," she agrees. "I wish I had your courage."

"Don't say that, Mel. You do, or you wouldn't be talking to me."

"I'm glad I'm talking to you now," she says.

"Me too," I say. "And don't beat yourself up. You did what you could at the time."

"I'll be thinking of you the day of your trial. Will you let me know when it is?"

"Less than a month. I'll tell you when I know the date for sure."

She takes a sip of her tea, then adds, "Don't think this is crazy, but you're kind of doing this for all of us. That's how I see it, at least. You're doing it for all of us who didn't speak up, who were afraid. And I know you're going to make this place better for the girls who come after us. It'll be safer. Guys will think twice."

"I hope so," I say, thinking briefly of what that day later this month will bring and of how a girl who just wanted to play the piano came to be a lightning rod for an issue.

But it's clear that I am.

Chapter Twenty-Five

ACTING OUT

I give Maia a new nickname.

It's *lawyertrix*.

As March descends on us, trial prep is like a life force for her, the nightly reviews, prep sessions, and strategy pep talks she insists on are magical energy imps that make her want more, more, more.

For the first time in my high school life, I find homework a welcome relief. After the latest recounting of Circle of Death, I am grateful when Maia skips off to debate practice so I can put the finishing touches on my *Tempest* adaptation.

I turn it in the next day in English class. Ms. Peck nods and says "thank you." Then when everyone has taken a seat, she taps the stack of papers with the long red nail on her index finger and says, "Today we're going to perform scenes in your adaptations."

It's not drama class, I want to say.

"Ma'am," a voice begins from the back of the room, "I'm just curious why you want us to act out the adaptations."

Ms. Peck looks pointedly toward the back of the room. "Henry," she says slowly, a hint of her Texas accent coming through, "that is an excellent question." She taps her finger on the papers again, then holds it up in the air to make a point. "I have found that plays, because they are meant to be acted, need to be read aloud. Sometimes the dialogue can sound odd, even off, if we don't actually practice it. You can refine the dialogue, perfect the words, when you practice it."

I turn around to check out Henry, the same Henry who breathed my name to Maia at her Debate meeting at the start of term. He's big, has spiky blond hair, a strong nose, and reddish cheeks.

"Ms. Peck," Henry continues, "I understand and that makes sense. But are we going to be graded on our performance? This isn't an acting class."

There are chuckles all around the class.

Ms. Peck smiles, showing the cracks in her lips that her pink lipstick didn't reach this morning.

"You are correct, Henry. It's not an acting class. And you won't be graded. So I urge you all"—there she goes, dangerously close to slipping to *y'all*—"to view this as an exercise. This is an exercise in writing a better play, penning a stronger adaptation of the Bard. You will also find this skill will serve you later in life. I wouldn't be surprised if some of you turn out to be journalists, authors, speech-writers, even. Or," she says, this time standing up and walking around her desk, moving closer to us, "you could be public speakers. You'll find reading your written compositions aloud will only improve your writing, creative and other-wise. That's why each student will have a chance to revise his or her work after the readings. Now, let's begin. I'm going to randomly assign scene partners and scenes from your plays."

Random. Why do teachers always say that? Do they think we don't know it's not random, that nothing is random?

"Emily and Brent. You can do the fifth scene from Emily's version of *Romeo and Juliet* and the seventh scene from Brent's *Hamlet.*"

Random. Just so random.

"Julie and Jones. Second scene from *Othello*, third from *Antony and Cleopatra.*"

More randomness. We're awash in sheer random-ity!

"Alex and Henry," she begins, "let's have you do the eighth scene from *Troilus and Cressida* and the first from *The Tempest.*"

I stare at her, wide-eyed, waiting for the punch line. Because it's coming, right? This is Ms. Peck, after all. She thinks she's funny, wicked funny. This is her idea of a joke.

She keeps going, rattling off names of students, names of plays, numbers of scenes, but it all sounds muffled to me, like a Charlie Brown teacher. "Wah-wah-wah, wah-wah."

When she's done, she dispatches us into groups. I don't move. Henry's a big boy. He can find me. He lumbers to the front of the room, parks himself in the desk next to mine, then says my name. "Alex Patrick," he says like a character in a movie who has been tracking someone across mountains and rivers and valleys and then finally finds the hunted.

I don't like the way he says it, so I give it back to him. "Henry Rowland," I say tartly.

He places his big hands on the edge of his desk and pulls himself closer to me, his desk tilting forward on the front legs. "I know who you are," he whispers. "Carter told me all about you. I can't wait for you to get what you deserve at your stupid trial."

There's a chill in the room, a cold stillness. The sky's black, the room's dark, no one can move. I can't move.

"But your little bird friends aren't here in this class, are they?" he adds.

Then he tilts back, the four legs back on the ground. He slouches in his chair, looking all cool and casual as he reaches for the papers on his desk—my papers, my scene, my words. I want to rip them out of his big, meaty hands. I want to tear them up, shred them, toss them into the garbage can in tiny bits so no one can see what I wrote, least of all Henry.

I read his scene and it gets worse. Because the *Troilus and Cressida* scene is a love scene, and my *Tempest* scene is the attempted rape of Miranda by Caliban. I would do anything right now not to have do either scene. But there are no Mockingbirds to save me from what's coming next. Ms. Peck claps her hands. "Okay, let's do this. Let's just get up there and practice our scenes."

She looks at me pointedly, then gestures. "Alex, Henry. Let's start with you two."

God, please strike this room with lightning right now. Please, someone, sound a fire alarm. Earthquake, flood, I don't care. Something, anything to get me out of here.

Henry pops up out of his chair, holding the scene. To Ms. Peck he innocently says, "Alex's first, right?"

She nods, then shrugs a shoulder happily. "Sure."

I stand up, take a few steps, and turn to the class.

"'I've waited long enough for this,'" Henry begins.

The words I wrote sound foul in his mouth. So foul I could vomit. I could vomit on him, projectile-style, like in a horror movie.

"'And I don't see why I should wait any longer,'" he continues.

"'You're going to wait forever because this will never happen,'" I say, emotionless.

He creeps toward me, actually acting out my stage direction, looking just like that half-breed Caliban.

I know what's coming next. I wrote the Goddamn scene. We each toss off the next few lines until the part I know is coming, the part I know he wants to come, where he grabs Miranda's hair and pulls, one hand on her hair, one arm around her waist.

My back is to him, and Henry thinks he's freaking Laurence Olivier or something. He grabs my hair tight and hard in his fat hand and then reaches to my belly, gripping me, jamming his fist so hard into my stomach an organ jumps out of the way. Then he yanks my head back, practically snapping my neck. These moves are just for me, no one else can tell the force with which he follows stage directions.

But when he grabs my hair, I see Carter. Straddling me. Pinning me with his legs. Grappling with the condom—the *dome*; I hate him even more for being so slangy. Then Henry breathes into my ear; his breath is hot and smells like bitter coffee, his skin like chlorine. He whispers, not a stage whisper, but a personal whisper, just for me, "You little bitch."

That's not in the script. That's not in the scene. That's not what I wrote.

Even though I know Miranda is supposed to jam her heel—she wears leather boots with four-inch spikes in my version—into his shin, sending Caliban to the floor in a crippling mess, I don't do that.

Instead, like I'm some sort of primitive creature, an animal operating only on instinct, I whip around, lift my knee, and jam it into his balls.

Henry grabs his crotch and falls to the ground. He moans, the class gasps, and Ms. Peck stands motionless.

Chapter Twenty-Six

EUNUCHS

In retrospect, going off script isn't always a good idea.

But it felt good.

It *still* feels good even though I'm sitting in the headmistress's office and Headmistress Vartan is just so confused by my behavior. She doesn't get it, just doesn't understand what happened. Mr. Christie, here presumably because he's my advisor, is equally perplexed. Because Themis students don't hit other Themis students.

"Alex...," Ms. Vartan starts. She crosses her legs. She's understated, as you'd expect a headmistress to be. She wears beige slacks, navy blue shoes, and a crisp white button-down shirt. But she used to be radical; she used to think she was a rebel. I know this because her right earlobe is red and scarred. She once had a plug in her earlobe. I bet she was goth all the way, dyed her red hair black, wore thick leather bracelets and listened to Norwegian death metal all day. Then she went straight and narrow, became an educator, had the hole sealed up, the hair color restored, and started wearing proper blouses every day.

She purses her lips, furrows her brow, says my name again. "Alex, it sounds like we had quite an English class, didn't we?"

This is what she asks me? Be a real headmistress. Discipline me. Say it. Say I assaulted another student. But she can't. Because she can't even conceive that it could happen.

"And you and Henry must have had some kind of misunderstanding," she adds.

No, I want to say. There was absolutely no misunderstanding whatsoever.

Ms. Vartan takes a pause, another breath, and while she does I hear the clock ticking on the wall behind her, an old-fashioned cuckoo clock in a wooden house with a peaked roof.

"Alex, it seems on the surface," she says, then rolls her eyes in some sort of insider gesture that says she knows what she's going to say sounds far-fetched, "that you kicked another student in class?"

She's asking me, actually asking me, even though it's abundantly clear I *did* kick another student. But the idea of a student hitting another student is preposterous to her; it just doesn't compute.

"I'm sure you know, Alex, we're not supposed to hurt other students," Mr. Christie chimes in.

"I understand you kneed him between the legs, Alex," Ms. Vartan adds gently. "That can't have happened, can it?"

I look up at the ceiling, then the clock, then the *Excellence* poster on the other wall. A golfer swings his club, watches his shot, the sun setting majestically on the horizon. I wonder if Ms. Vartan plays golf now too. She probably does it to unwind from the terrible stress of Themis Academy. "It was in the script. It was in the scene. Ms. Peck made us act out a scene and the kick was in it," I say.

The two of them laugh, bright smiles beaming across their clueless faces. They lean back in their chairs, relieved.

"Well, that makes perfect sense now!" Ms. Vartan says, relieved her Candy Land school remains unblemished.

"We should probably bring Henry in here too," Mr. Christie says as he rubs his hand through his reddish beard. I half-expect him to pluck out food crumbs, little bits of blueberry muffin from breakfast or something. I bet he'd eat them again. "Just to make sure he's . . . fine."

"Fine?" I ask.

"Well, yes," Ms. Vartan says. "It *is* against the code of conduct to hit another student —"

I cut her off. "It was in the scene, I told you. It was in the scene."

"I understand," Ms. Vartan says. "And I don't suspect you'll get a write-up or suspension."

"Suspension? That's even an option here?"

"Like I said, the code of conduct does forbid hitting another student," Ms. Vartan says.

I scoff. "Code of conduct?" I ask, then I bite my tongue. I don't say what I really want to say—their code of conduct means nothing. There is only one code of conduct that matters here at Themis.

"I'm sure it will all be fine," Ms. Vartan reassures, but I'm not reassured because Henry's a pig and Henry will blame me because he hates me.

No, it won't be fine, I want to say. *A student date-raped me on your campus and it's not fine. It's not fine because you can't do anything about it, because you think we're fine, and you think this—my kneeing another student in the balls—is fine too. But it's not fine because there are no Mockingbirds around. So there is no way of knowing if I will be safe right now. Because you can't protect me and they're not here.*

I wait for them to swoop in, wait for Amy or Martin or Ilana to save me. They will, I know they will. They will save me from Henry. They will save me from myself, from my own emotions that swing daily like a pendulum—fine one minute, a total mess the next. I glance nervously at the door, waiting for the Mockingbirds. Mr. Christie leans in and asks gently, as if he's talking to a six-year-old, "What was the scene about?"

"It was a rape scene," I say coldly. But when I see the color drain from Ms. Vartan's face, as if I had just injected her with white dye, I keep going. Mr. Christie removes his glasses, presses his fingers against the bridge of his nose. "Ms. Peck picked the scenes she wanted us to act out. She read our early drafts. She knew my first scene was a rape scene. And she made me act it out. And she knew what was supposed to happen in the script. Henry grabbed my hair, he yanked my neck back, he slammed his fist into my stomach. It was in the script. I wrote it. It's an *attempted rape* scene. Caliban tries to rape Miranda. But she kicks him. She kicks him hard, twice. In the knees. So I slipped. So I kicked him in the balls. I meant to kick him in the knees, I meant to stick to the script, but I slipped. But the point is she stops him. Don't you get it? She. Stops. Him."

Ms. Vartan, her face still ashen, opens her mouth to speak, but then Henry walks in. Only he doesn't look like big, blond Henry. It's as if the edge has been stripped off him, as if he's been whitewashed. Ms. Peck follows him in, and I reason she must be his junior advisor. He hangs his head low, like a dog who has been caught eating his master's slippers.

"Hello, Henry," Ms. Vartan says kindly. "You two had such an interesting English class, didn't you?"

Euphemism.

Henry nods.

"And I guess you and Alex maybe are just better actors than we thought," she says a little too jovially for my taste.

He nods again.

"You really took the stage directions to heart," she remarks.

He nods once more.

"But you know, we do need to exercise better judgment. Because it is against the code of conduct to hit another student in the . . ." She trails off.

"Genitals," Mr. Christie says, finishing her sentence.

"Yes, there."

"Um, yeah. It wasn't Alex's fault," Henry offers up. "We were just trying to do the best we could. We both agreed beforehand that we really needed to give it our all in the scene, do the best we possibly could. That's the Themis way."

I don't dare look at him. I don't dare make eye contact because I can't believe he's lying to cover for me.

Ms. Vartan looks pleased. "See, that's what this school is about. Students who excel, even when the assignment is misguided," she says, then glares at Ms. Peck.

"We really shouldn't be asking students to act out rape scenes, Ms. Peck," Ms. Vartan says in a hard voice this time. "We don't want to create a climate where it seems we're condoning rape."

But you do and you have, I want to scream. You created this, you created this place, this perception, this environment.

Ms. Vartan turns to Henry and me. "I hope you can forgive us for putting you in this position."

Here we are, two students who attacked each other, not

because of a commitment to the assignment but because we hate each other. And they want us to forgive them. This is *The Twilight Zone,* this is *Pleasantville;* this is the world upside down.

"Uh, everything is fine," I say.

"Yes, fine," Henry echoes.

And we're dismissed.

Chapter Twenty-Seven
ROGUE

"Thanks for saving my ass today," I say to Amy at lunch.

She looks at me quizzically.

"You know, with the whole English class thing," I say.

"What are you talking about?" Amy asks.

I explain what happened and how Henry changed his tune. "I assume you guys got to him or something."

Amy shakes her head. "I had no idea that even happened," she says.

"Then why did Henry say everything was fine?" I ask.

I have my answer after lunch when Jones catches up with me on the quad. "I told you I'd look out for you," Jones says.

"What do you mean?"

"Henry the douche-pussy-scumbag."

"Right, but what do you mean?"

"Well, he backed off, right?"

I stop walking and place a hand on his arm. "What did you do, Jones?" I ask, and my heart plummets to the floor, then shoots back up again like a free-fall ride in an amusement park. Because if Jones violated the code—*our code*—then I hate to think about his being on the wrong side of the Mockingbirds. "Did you hit him, or beat him up or something?" I croak out.

He laughs. "No, that's so pedestrian and I might damage my hands. Besides, I'm more creative than that."

"What did you do?"

"After they pulled you out of class, I went up to him and told him I'd tell the entire school he came on to me last night in the common room of our dorm and that I rebuffed his advances."

"He did that?" I ask, shocked.

Jones shakes his head. "No. But I'd have no problem starting the rumor if it would help you."

"But it could have backfired, Jones. He could start rumors about you."

"One, I don't care. I like girls and there's no rumor anyone could start that'd change that. And second, I don't care; I just didn't want anything else bad to happen to you."

I don't know what else to say, so I say the simplest thing. "Thank you, Jones."

"Don't mention it."

♦ ♦ ♦

That afternoon, T.S. explodes into our room after soccer practice, all sweaty and muddy from playing in the rain, hair mussed up, dirt smeared on her thighs. "You are never going to believe what happened to Ms. Peck after today! She's on probation for the rest of the month!

She dances a little jig in the room, pumping her fists up and down as she turns in circles, sort of a half-tribal, half-hip-hop victory dance. I jump up from my desk, where I've been doing homework. "Get out of here! Are you serious, like totally serious?"

"I am so serious I am beyond serious. I am more serious than I have ever, ever been." T.S. punches the air with her fist. "Pro-ba-tion!" she sings, enjoying every single solitary syllable. "But it gets better. She's not allowed to see *The Merry Wives of Windsor* either. That's her punishment! Can you believe it? And she was devastated."

I laugh.

T.S. nods vigorously, then grabs my elbow and we dance in a circle together. "Isn't it great how the teachers get *all* the punishments, both the harsh discipline and the ridiculous kind?"

"Like probation paired with not being able to see a stupid play."

"Totally. And she was dying to see it. That's the thing. She wanted to see that production so badly because she's the"—T.S. stops to sketch air quotes—"*Shakespeare expert.* Anyway, so Ms. Vartan was all over her. She said 'Shame on you, Ms. Peck,' except Ms. Vartan doesn't call her Ms. Peck. She calls her 'Susan.' So she was saying, 'Shame on you, Susan!' I mean, that makes it even more demeaning because they're all into proper titles. But to say 'shame on you' to an adult? To a teacher? It's beautiful! She asked what she was thinking having students act out a rape scene, and a violent one at that, and what it might possibly do to us, what ideas it would put in our heads."

"As if that's where it came from."

But then T.S. stops laughing. "I do think it was wrong. No teacher should ask you to do that. You had every right to defend yourself. You said I'm not going to take it and then *wham*—right where it hurts."

"Too bad I didn't do that to Carter," I say dully.

"Alex, you couldn't. You can barely even remember what happened."

"T.S.," I whisper, "I remember more now."

She stares hard at me. "You do?"

I nod and sit down on the bed. "Yeah, sometimes when I play the piano or when I see someone who was at the party or even just hear a word, it comes back. I remember parts of it."

"Like what?"

"Just details, here and there."

"Like?"

"How I didn't want to go to his room. How on the way to his room I told him I wanted to go back. How when I was there I could barely stand up, I was so out of it. I just sank down to the floor and crashed. How when he started"—I pause and close my eyes when I say the next thing—"when he started with me, I tried to push him away. I put my hands on his chest. I shook my head. I said no."

"I'm so sorry, Alex. I'm so sorry it happened." T.S. moves over to me and places an arm around me. "But I'm glad you're remembering more. It's only going to help your case. It's going to help you at the trial. And I know you're going to win."

"Win" is such a strange word to use. Is this about winning? I can't even think about it that way, so I change the subject. "By the way, how did you know what Ms. Vartan said to Ms. Peck?"

She lowers her voice in some sort of conspiratorial whisper. "Ms. Vartan's secretary thinks I'm the bomb. I brought her truffles and she told me everything."

"You brownnoser."

"Whatever works," T.S. says, and hops up from the bed. "I guess the Mockingbirds are rubbing off on me, huh?" She rummages through her closet for a towel and her shower basket, kicks off her sneakers, and heads for the door. Before she opens it, she turns around. "Oh, I almost forgot. Amy called earlier. She said they set a date for your hearing. Day of your concert. The Saturday of your Liszt-Does-Beethoven performance in two weeks. Weird, huh?"

Quite the coincidence, indeed.

Chapter Twenty-Eight
SECRET BOYFRIEND

The trial countdown begins.

Maia, one-hundred-and-twenty-miles-an-hour Maia, kicks it up a notch. She now spends every spare second prepping, interviewing witnesses, and discussing strategies with T.S. and me in hushed tones in the caf, our room, in between classes.

One week before the trial, she sweeps into the room, opens her black-and-white composition notebook, and goes into prosecutorial mode. "Let's review potential witnesses."

"Again? Don't you think we're overpreparing?"

She gives me a hard stare. "There's no such thing," she says, and launches into the list of names, what they'll say, what Carter's team will try to rattle them on. After an hour,

I become convinced Maia could do this all night long and not lose a beat. But I need a break.

"I left something in the music hall," I tell her. She just nods and scribbles something in her notebook.

I walk down the hall and call Martin from my cell. "It's Friday night," I say. "Do you know what that means?"

"It means we have Friday Night Out privileges and you want to take me out on a secret date and have your way with me?"

"Something like that," I say.

"Where do you want to go?" he asks.

"The Brain Freeze," I say, referring to the ice-cream shop on Kentfield Street. "Meet me outside McGregor Hall in"—I look at the clock—"two minutes."

"Done," he says, and hangs up.

When I open the door to my dorm, I look furtively from side to side. But I'm not looking for Carter this time, and the realization thrills me. Instead, I'm checking to see if the coast is clear, and it is. I rush across the quad to McGregor Hall, where Martin's waiting. I'm like a normal girl, sneaking off campus with a boy, even though we're sneaking away from Mockingbirds, not teachers or campus cops. That's Themis for you, because the Mockingbirds are our police.

"You must have a fierce mint-chocolate-chip craving," Martin says as we slink past McGregor into the night.

"Best flavor ever," I say.

He moves closer to me. "You have no idea how much I want to hold your hand right now," he whispers in my ear.

My heart races ten thousand times faster. "How much?" I ask.

"I'm using all my powers of self-restraint," he says.

"You are powerful, indeed."

"The second we're far enough away, I'm holding your hand."

"I'll consider myself warned, then," I say. "Though don't you have spies all over?"

"Spies?" he asks.

"Yeah, isn't it possible Amy or Ilana could be hiding in the bushes down the street or something, waiting to bust you?"

He laughs. "There you go again, with your conspiracy theories."

"Well?"

"No," he says emphatically. "They trust me. That's why I'm in the group."

"Do *they* know your favorite flavor of ice cream?"

He shakes his head. "But I'll tell you," he says, and slips a hand into mine as we head farther away from Themis. His skin is warm, tingling against my hand. He leans in to whisper, his lips brushing against my ear. "I like mint chocolate chip too."

"Oh, stop it!"

"Oreo mint chocolate chip," he says playfully.

"Close enough. I guess it's a good thing we're hanging out," I tease as we turn onto the block with the Brain Freeze. "Or hiding out, I should say."

"Speaking of," he says, and I tense. *Speaking of* sound

like adult words, like breakup words, like *this isn't working out* words. But then he places a hand on my cheek, soft and warm. "I want you to be my girlfriend."

"Oh," I say. "Am I allowed? Are you allowed?"

"Allowed," he says, laughing. "You always want to know if we're allowed."

"You're the one who told me we weren't allowed to be together," I point out. "You wouldn't even hold my hand till we were a block off campus."

He sighs. "I know. I'm really not supposed to be doing this."

"So how can I be your girlfriend, then?"

"It'll be between you and me, okay? Then when the trial is over in a week and things settle down, we won't have to pretend."

"So I'm like your secret girlfriend?" I ask.

"Yes."

"And you're my secret boyfriend?"

He nods.

"Okay, I say yes."

Then, a recurring fear swoops down from the sky, black cape billowing behind it, like a dark superhero with a dark past. I tell myself to shut up, to keep quiet, to say nothing. But the fear, it's stronger than I am. "You're not doing this because you feel sorry for me?" I ask.

"C'mon. I thought we were past that."

"I know. I know you think I'm crazy. But just tell me.

You're not doing this because you feel like it was your fault?"

He pushes a hand through his floppy brown hair, shakes his head.

"But you said that night in my room bringing me a sandwich was the least you could do," I say.

"You're not a pity project, Alex. I wish you'd get that."

"I know. But I just want to know that this is just for this, not for any other reason. You know you can't change what happened."

"I'm not trying to change the past. The future, maybe. Like tomorrow night. Maybe we could hang out then too?"

I nod, but as we order ice cream a part of me worries we're both fooling ourselves in thinking this is real—being with me eases his guilt, being with him helps me heal. But for now, I'll have an ice-cream cone with my secret boyfriend. Who knows how long these secret boyfriends can last, anyway....

Chapter Twenty-Nine
ANY GIRL

I get raised eyebrows from both T.S. and Maia when I return two hours later.

"Late night at the music hall?" Maia asks, her brown eyes like a ray gun surveying the telltale sign of my true evening activities on the way home from the Brain Freeze— messed-up hair, extra-red lips, shirt freshly tucked in.

"Yes," I say, and change into my pajamas.

"And you got all your practicing done for your performance?" T.S. throws in, and I wonder if she's getting ready to cross-examine me too.

"Yes," I mutter, and then head to the bathroom to brush my teeth. When I open the toothpaste, I remember the cap that rolled onto the floor that morning in Carter's room, and I'm suddenly somewhere else.

"Uh."

There's a noise, a sound, like a cross between a bark and a whisper, like an "oomph." It's like someone just sat on my chest. It's dark and my mouth tastes like a sock, feels like wool. And there's Carter. On me. Over me. In me. He's pushing in me and I can feel him. I can feel his penis in me, even though I'm barely aware, half-asleep, half-awake, half-dreaming, half-dead. But I can feel him and he's breathing. He's breathing kind of heavy, hitting some sort of rhythm.

I realize the noise came from me. The "uh" came from me, from the feel of someone's weight on me, someone's body on me. And it's as if I just came to or something, the "uh" marking the line between sleep and awake, there and here. Now I'm here, still in his bed, still naked, still under him. Only now he's pressing into me and he's going faster and faster and I want to do something, say something, but all I feel is slower and slower and slower and all I can do is breathe, breathe, breathe....

I stand there, the toothpaste tube in one hand, the toothbrush in the other and the memory of my second time no longer dormant but vivid, alive and awful. I brush my teeth furiously as if I could erase the memory.

But I can't. It's here now, it's part of me.

I don't leave my dorm the rest of the weekend. I don't see Martin, I don't call him, I don't text him. Who was I kidding? I'm not the girl who sneaks off campus with her secret boyfriend. I'm the girl who got date-raped.

♦ ♦ ♦

"I've been meaning to tell you," Miss Damata says after I practice the Ninth Symphony one more time for her during my free period Monday morning. "One of my colleagues at Juilliard will be visiting with my family and me next weekend. The weekend of your performance. And he is an admissions officer at the university."

"Does he," I start, practically tingling with the possibility I think she is dangling before me, "want to come see my performance?"

She nods, a smile unfolding into a full-blown grin across her face.

I jump up and down, "This is amazing; this is too good to be true. Are you totally serious? You're not joking?"

"I think you know me well enough by now to know I'm not much of a joker."

"This would be…" I trail off, because the sheer and utter coolness of having scored a real, live Juilliard admissions officer at my performance is too awesome for words.

She adds, "You know this won't count toward your application next year. I just figured it couldn't hurt."

"It definitely can't hurt," I say, feeling like a bottle of Coca-Cola about to burst fun, frothy, fizzy bubbles everywhere. "I am so happy."

I lean in and give her a hug, she hugs back, then I leave for French, ducking into the classroom early, ten minutes before the bell. I'm the first student there, so I take my seat in the back. Ms. Dumas is writing on the board. "*Bonjour,* Alex."

"*Bonjour,* Madame Dumas."

I take out my French book as Martin walks by, tapping my desk as he does. I look away. I *should* feel guilty for not calling him, not seeing him on Saturday like I said I would. But I'm sick of feeling, sick of *should*s.

A few minutes later, Ms. Dumas asks us to hand in our essays chronicling our school day using the *on fait* construction. Then she tells us we will use *ça fait* for the remainder of the class.

When class ends I jam papers and books into my backpack. I can feel Martin near me, behind me, maybe waiting by the door. I zip my bag shut and stand up.

"Hey, you," he says.

"Hi," I say halfheartedly.

"You holding up okay? I know the trial's in less than a week."

"I don't want to talk about the trial," I say coldly.

Martin tenses, then starts to ask something else. But there's nothing I want to say about me or the trial or the Mockingbirds. So I deflect with a question. "What'd you do this weekend?"

"Wrote half of my paper on barn owls, watched hockey. My Buffalo Sabres lost. I know that breaks your heart too. So I took an epic three-hour afternoon nap, you know the kind where you're dead to the world?"

"God, I could use one right now."

"So ditch."

"Ditch and nap?"

"Ditch and nap. What's better than that?"

"Who would have thought you had such a lawless side to you," I say.

"Sometimes I like to break the rules," he says.

Then we lapse into silence, walk a few more feet to nowhere.

"So, I was hoping to see you Saturday like we talked about, but maybe you didn't want to," he says quietly.

I didn't want to see him. I didn't want to see anyone. I didn't want to do anything. Then I look at him, his brown eyes, the green flecks muted right now. And I see the slightest bit of hurt in them. Because he wanted to see me; he hoped to see me. He is *feeling,* feeling for me. He's not just Martin the Mockingbird, Martin the science geek, Martin the most excellent kisser. He's Martin, just a boy who likes a girl.

A girl the Juilliard admissions officer wants to see perform. A piano girl.

So I do something I'm not supposed to do. I reach for his hand and pull him into an empty classroom. I put my palms on his face, then push my fingers back through his hair, soft and feathery on my hands. I press my lips against his mouth, sweet and salty, warm and hungry for me. I take a few steps backward, holding on to him the whole time, until my back meets the blackboard, far out of view of other students, of any teachers. I lean against the blackboard and kiss him harder, draw his body closer to mine, his jeans against mine, his belt loops against mine. He's mine and I want him and I'm not letting him go. I pull him tighter and he responds, pushing up against me, his body pressed against mine, so there's no space between us and I can't stop kissing him and he can't stop kissing me and we're pressed together skin-tight and snug and I can't stand it—really, I *can't* stand it—how much I want him in every way right now.

Because I'm not *that girl* anymore. I'm just *any girl* now kissing her guy how she wants, where she wants, when she wants.

I am ready.

Chapter Thirty
A LOT OF LAUNDRY

I look at myself in the mirror and pull at my skirt. "This looks stupid," I say to Maia.

I'm wearing a cream-colored blouse and a long blue skirt. It's hideous. Maia selected it.

"It says *class*," Maia says.

"It says *no taste*," I say, picking at the dark blue cotton. "I mean, look at me, Maia!"

I stand in the middle of the room, planting myself in front of her, forcing her to eye my grotesque getup.

"It looks tasteful," Maia says.

"Tasteful?" I scoff.

"Alex," Maia snaps, "this isn't a bloody fashion show. Everyone has invested in this."

"Like I'm just a pet project," I say, finally revealing the tiny bit of doubt I've had about her.

Maia shakes her head. "You know that's not true."

"Seems that way," I say, knowing that I'm being a tad ungrateful.

Maia purses her lips, lets out an exhale, and pauses. "Alex, I know this is hard on you and I'm sorry. You're the one who went through this, not me. I'm sorry for jumping on you."

"I just think this outfit is stupid. I would never wear this. It's like you're trying to dress me up as some sort of virginal girl who would never even spread her legs for a guy. That's how this outfit feels. As if it's part of the show."

"Then change," Maia says softly. "I want you to be comfortable. I want you to be yourself." Then, even softer. "I'm doing this for you, Alex. Not for any other reason."

"I know," I say calmly, and my doubt leaves. I take off the skirt, toss it onto T.S.'s bed. "And I'm glad you're the one doing this."

I grab a pair of black slacks from my closet. I pull them on, model them. Maia smiles widely. She opens the door. "Ready?"

"Let's go," I say.

We leave, laundry-less this time. I guess we've graduated or something. But when we reach the basement it's clear someone brought laundry. Someone brought a lot of laundry. The machines rattle from all the way down the hallway, making background music. Martin and Ilana are stationed like sentries outside the laundry room doors. We walk past them and once we're inside, the doors close, as if by magic, but I'm sure Martin and Ilana pulled them shut. The dryers are running at full blast, the washers too. Loads and loads of sheets and towels fly around in them.

The couch and chair have been pushed aside and in their place are two long brown tables, one parked against the back wall, the other about ten feet in front. Next to the far table is a single chair, positioned at an angle.

Seated at the back table are the three students who form the council for this case. They're all dressed in button-down shirts and classic sweaters. Amy introduces them, and some I know, like Callie Regis from biology last year, and Parker Hume, whose dad is a senator. Then there's Lila Wong, a sophomore who's on the student council too, Amy says. That means she started early, a runner her freshman year. They each nod as they're introduced and smile quickly. Their smiles fade equally quickly. They look like judges. They are judges. They will judge me; they will judge Carter.

Amy motions for us to sit down, so I do at the far end of the unoccupied table. Maia sits next to me. There are three more empty chairs. Maia and I wait a few wordless minutes; only the noise of the washers and the dryers breaks the silence. Then Amy announces, "The defendant is entering now."

My heart catches in my chest. I decide to pretend this is just another performance, just another recital, a concert, like the one I'll give tonight, and Carter is just an audience member, just an average Joe here to see me perform. The ruse calms my skipping heart as Carter sits at the end of my table, the farthest seat away from me. Kevin Ward sits next to him. Kevin's his student advocate. The middle chair remains empty, a buffer between the sides.

Amy looks to the door, confirming it's shut. Martin and Ilana remain on the other side to stand guard for the rest of the morning. Amy introduces the council members to Carter this time. They do the same thing they did with me—nod, smile, stop smiling.

"Hello," Carter says.

"Pleasure to meet you," Kevin says with a slight bow.

Amy reaches for her notebook and clears her throat. "The function of the council is to listen to the evidence presented in the case against Carter Hutchinson for alleged violation of the students' code of conduct as it relates to sexual assault of another student. The council will listen to the evidence and determine the verdict. The punishment if Carter Hutchinson is found guilty will be voluntary withdrawal from the water polo team. He's signed the papers agreeing to these terms. If he's found not guilty, we will remove his name from the book and invite him to serve on the Mockingbirds."

Then Amy looks to Callie. "Callie Regis, I turn the proceedings over to you," she says, and moves toward the door, where she stands.

Callie peers through her thick black glasses and reads

the charges; her longish blond hair falls against her face as she starts reading, so she tucks it behind her ears. "Alexandra Nicole Patrick charges Carter Drake Hutchinson with sexual assault," she says, then reads from the recently revised code of conduct.

> **Sexual assault is against the standards to which Themis students hold themselves. Sexual assault is sexual contact (not just intercourse) where one of the parties has not given or cannot give active verbal consent, i.e., uttered a clear "yes" to the action. If a person does not say "no," that does not mean he or she said "yes." Silence does not equal consent. Silence could mean fear, confusion, inebriation. The only thing that means yes is yes. A lack of yes is a no.**

She looks to Carter and Kevin, then Maia and me, and explains. "As I'm sure you are aware, what we will do here today is hear your case. You each will tell us what happened, in your own words. You each can call witnesses. After each side is done presenting, we will deliberate and issue a verdict. The plaintiff may begin opening arguments."

Maia stands up and take a few steps closer to the council. "This is a simple case," she begins. She wears khaki pants, navy flats, and a navy blue sweater set. Her sleek black hair is clipped back in a brown tortoiseshell comb. "We intend to show that Carter Hutchinson had sex with Alexandra Patrick twice while she was sleeping. She had been drinking, and based on the number of drinks consumed—as witnessed by fellow Themis students—her blood alcohol content was point zero eight. Above the legal limit, as a matter of fact. The sex was not consensual. Alex was sleeping and therefore was not able to give consent. Just as there is no gray area in the revised code of conduct, there was no gray area in the events that transpired. A lack of a yes is a no, plain and simple. Thank you for your time."

Maia sits down and Kevin stands.

"I will agree with one thing my good friend Maia said— this is a simple case. This is a very simple case indeed," Kevin says in his slight New Hampshire accent. "And here's what's so simple about it," he adds, holding his arms wide open, his palms out, as if he's some genial Southern lawyer on a TV show. "Alex and Carter had sex. It's that simple. That's what high school students do, right?" He lets out a knowing laugh; I think he even winks at the council. "They were a couple of teenagers having a good time, having good old-fashioned consensual sex. And Alex is a girl who's been known to engage in consensual sexual conduct with the opposite sex, as we will learn here this morning."

Daniel. He's going to bring up Daniel. I dig my nails deep into my palms because Daniel has nothing to do with Carter. The two of them could not have less in common. I learned that way back at the lost-and-found bin the morning after. I stare hard at the brown brick wall in front of me, pretending it's a landscape painting of some serene mountain brook. Maia squeezes my wrist hard and I say nothing, do nothing, just like *that night*.

Sandeep is the first witness. He sits down on the lone chair, the one angled out near the council table. He's here to testify about how much I drank, to establish my state of mind. He talks about Circle of Death, about how many red cups of vodka and orange juice I consumed, how I stumbled when I walked, how I left with Carter.

I sound disgusting. I sound like a disgusting, dirty whore. I look at my hands most of the time while he talks.

Kevin asks him questions, tries to rattle him, but Sandeep holds his ground.

Next is Julie. She corroborates Sandeep's testimony, backs up what he's said. I make a mental note to follow through next time she asks me to help on a project.

Then she's dismissed. Amy announces Dana as the next witness. I turn around and watch as Amy opens the door for her. Dana walks in wearing jeans and a crisp button-down shirt. Her short hair looks freshly blow-dried. She walks toward us, all broad shoulders and wide hips and big muscles evident under her clothes. She's a big girl, but not fat. Just strong and sturdy and powerful. She parks herself in the chair Julie just occupied and Sandeep before her. Maia stands, smoothes an unseen wrinkle on her pant leg, and asks Dana how she knows Carter.

"I'm on the girls' water polo team. Sometimes we play scrimmages against the boys' team. And, you know, we just all know each other."

"And did you have a specific relationship with Carter beyond that last year?" Maia asks.

Dana nods. "We went on a couple dates. We went to pizza on Harris Street one night and then we went to a swim meet together another time."

"And was there anything unusual about those dates?"

"Besides the fact he's a total pig?"

Kevin bolts up from his seat. "Objection. Character defamation."

Maia interjects. "This is about character. This is about *his* character."

It's Callie's turn and she looks at Maia. "Perhaps you could ask the question another way."

"Can you tell us what happened on those dates besides the pizza and the swimming?" Maia asks.

"Sure," Dana says. "We had pizza together one night after practice. We went down to Ambrosia Pizza on Harris Street and he kept putting his hands on my legs while we were eating."

"What did you do when he did that?"

She shrugs. "I kind of just brushed him off. So we left and walked back to school and he walked me to my dorm and asked to come in. I said no. Then he leaned in to kiss me and I gave him a quick kiss on the lips and then he tried to push his tongue in my mouth. I shook my head and pulled away. I said, 'Not yet.'"

"And did anything happen after that?"

"Yeah, he put his hand on my ass," Dana says matter-of-factly. There are sniggers; some of the council members laugh briefly, then stop.

"And how did you respond?"

"I moved it." Dana demonstrates, putting her right hand on her own butt cheek and then quickly removing it with her left hand. "I've got pretty strong hands."

"Was that the end of the date?"

Dana nods.

"Did you go out with him again?"

"Unfortunately, yes, one more time."

"And that was to the swim meet?" Maia asks.

"Against Andover last spring. We were going to be playing them this year in water polo and some of the players are on both teams, so we thought it would be kind of a scouting opportunity. So went to the pool together and sat up in the bleachers, kind of the back row. And he did the same stuff. He kept putting his hands on me the whole time. Slipping them between my legs. At one point he tried to grab my boob."

"What did you do?" Maia asks.

Dana acts it out again, pantomiming removing Carter's hand from her breast. "And what happened next?" Maia asks.

"We left the meet and he walked me back to my dorm again and he tried to kiss me again. He kind of pushed himself against me, against the wall right next to the door of my dorm, and then he pressed his crotch against me. And then I slapped him," Dana says proudly. "I'd had enough of his routine at that point. Then I told him to keep his nasty paws to himself and never put them on me again."

"And did you go into your dorm at that point?"

Dana nods. "Yep, and a few days later he tried to start rumors about me, like he did to Alex at the start of the semester."

"What sort of rumors?" Maia asks.

"He told his friends I had put out for him. As soon as I heard what he was doing, I walked right up to him after practice, right in front of his friends—Kevin was there too, he knows what I said"—Dana points at Kevin with her right index finger—"and I asked them if he had told them too how I slapped him after what he did."

"How did they respond?"

"They laughed at him and he stopped talking smack about me."

"Thank you, Dana," Maia says, and sits back down next to me.

Then it's Kevin's turn. He ambles across the room, enjoys a pregnant pause, and asks slowly in a New Hampshire drawl, "So he put his hand on your, as you said in such a ladylike fashion, ass?"

Dana nods.

"And yet, you went out with him again."

"We went to a swim meet," Dana says defensively.

"A date," Kevin corrects. "You called it a date. You said you went on two dates with Carter. Isn't that what you said, Ms. Golden?"

Dana nods grimly.

"So you went on *two* dates, and the second date was after he touched your rear end, something you claim you didn't enjoy."

"I didn't enjoy it, Ward. That's why I took his hand off my ass."

"It seems as if you must have liked it if you went out with him again," Kevin muses.

"I didn't like it," Dana says through gritted teeth.

"So you removed his hand from your fanny and went out with him again. Perhaps you were teasing him? Or perhaps you didn't really remove his hand, and you're just claiming you did?"

Dana's eyes burn holes through Kevin, and I have no doubt somehow, some way, Kevin is going to pay for this.

"HE PUT HIS HAND ON MY ASS AND I REMOVED IT."

"Or so you say," Kevin remarks.

"I do say. Because that's what happened."

Maia stands up tall this time. "Objection. He's badgering the witness. She already said what happened."

"See? Even the plaintiff's own advocate admits it's a *he said, she said* situation," Kevin says righteously, seizing on Maia's words.

Callie raises a hand and everyone stops talking. "I think we're clear on the point you're trying to make, Kevin," Callie says, peering at him over her glasses. "You can finish with this witness."

"I'm pretty sure I'm through with this witness," he says, casually strolling back to his seat.

Then it's my turn.

I tell the council step-by-step how the night unfolded. As I hear myself talk about drinking, meeting Carter, playing Circle of Death, drinking more, kissing Carter, more, more, more, I sound like a pig. They're going to think I'm a pig. Worse, a slut. A pig-slut, slut-pig. I pretend I'm a reporter, talking about someone she's covering, about this girl, about that night, about how she was sleeping.

And then she's done. That girl is done.

Chapter Thirty-One
THE OTHER GIRL

It's Carter's turn to call witnesses.

Kevin calls Natalie, as we expected. She walks in, towering above me, her quads practically rippling through her jeans, her crazily toned arms evident through her red knit sweater. Even her cheekbones are cut.

The picture of poise, precision, with her black hair pulled back tightly at her neck, she casts her cold brown eyes hard at me, then sits in the witness chair.

"Natalie Moretti, thank you for joining us this morning. You've been called here to testify because you were at Salem Jim's the night in question, correct?"

"I was there," she says crisply, then pauses. "With you."

He nods politely. "But of course," he says, then looks to

the council. "Let the record reflect Natalie Moretti and I have been dating for six months."

"Six months, one week, three days," Natalie adds, giving Kevin a just-for-you look that makes me want to gag.

He smiles back at her, then continues. "And you and I were dancing together when Alex and Carter began their date?"

"Objection," Maia says harshly. "It wasn't a date."

"Natalie, since you were there, what did it look like to you?" Kevin asks.

"They were having a great time together," Natalie says.

"Can you elaborate?"

I lower my eyes, because I'm betting she can and she will.

"They were dancing together and she was kind of rubbing up against him," she says, like I was some kind of animal in heat.

"That is so not true!" I shout before Maia can even raise an objection.

"You were kind of all over him, Alex," Natalie says quietly, judgmentally, talking just to me. I clench my fists, digging my fingers into my palms and fantasizing about her spontaneously combusting right now.

Callie intervenes. "Let's get back to the questions, please."

"Natalie, can you describe how Carter and Alex interacted?"

"She grabbed his hand, led him to the stage, and started dancing with him. It was so cute," she says with a perfectly calibrated mixture of sweet yet cool in her account. "And I have to say, I had been hoping Carter was going to find a nice girl to go out with because he is such a sweetheart and totally deserves a great girl. And they seemed to be having such a good time at the club. So I was excited to see if they were going to become an item."

Yeah, so we could all double-date.

"Was there anything you saw between them indicating Alex didn't want to be with Carter?"

Natalie shakes her head. She's rehearsed, she's hitting all her marks, but when she looks at me, ice in her eyes, we both know we were never going to be girlfriends gabbing about their guys. "Not at all. What I saw was two people having fun. There was something starting, something sweet. I can tell these things because *I* don't drink. *I* was sober," she says, her voice slicing through me.

"Thank you, Natalie," Kevin says, and sits down.

Maia hops up. "Natalie, it's interesting to see your astute relationship observations. Perhaps a column is in your future. But for now, let's clarify a few things. Were you at the party afterward in the common room?"

"No."

"Were you in Carter's room with Carter and Alex afterward?"

Natalie almost laughs. "Of course not."

"So you weren't actually present when this *blossoming relationship* between Carter and Alex went from dancing at a concert to rape?"

"Objection. Carter hasn't been convicted of any crime, especially not rape," Kevin calls out coolly from his seat, barely moving a muscle. He's still sitting cross-legged, leaning casually back in the chair next to Carter.

Callie looks at Maia. "Please rephrase the question."

Maia begins again. "Were you there, Natalie, in Carter's room when the incident in question occurred?"

Natalie presses her lips together hard, then seethes at Maia, "I said I wasn't there later on."

"So then, you actually know nothing. And you have nothing meaningful to contribute about anything of consequence that night."

Maia's good; she's halfway to mowing her down. But Natalie Moretti doesn't go down without a fight.

"I know Alex was all over him at Salem Jim's," Natalie starts, digging a knife into my chest as I picture rushing the stage with him. "I know Alex *wanted* it," she adds, and it's like I'm being gutted as I remember kissing him in the common room. "I know she got herself drunk, and now she's just using that as an excuse," Natalie spits out, yanking the knife out of me with a rough final tug that dredges up my own memories of the room spinning, the bed spinning, my crashing into a dark, dreamless sleep.

"Thank you, Natalie, for corroborating that Alex wasn't in a position to be giving consent to this so-called *relationship* that was never a relationship but rather a crime. That's all."

Maia sits down and squeezes my hand. I barely have the energy to squeeze back because I've just been wrung dry.

Chapter Thirty-Two
SURPRISE WITNESS

The second person Kevin calls is Martin.

Maia jerks her head toward Kevin, then back down at the stack of papers in front of her on the table. She flips through a few pages. Martin's name isn't on the witness list. We submitted the names of the witnesses we planned to call, and so did Carter. He listed Natalie, that was it. Not Martin; he didn't list Martin.

Wait...Maybe he's calling Martin because I had been talking to Martin right before I met Carter. That must be it. Except...if that were the case, then Martin would have been on the witness list. I press my thumb and forefinger against the bridge of my nose and close my eyes. I know why he's calling Martin.

Maia whispers to me, her voice worried but strong. "Why is he calling Martin?"

But before I can answer, and I don't even know what I'd say, Callie speaks up.

"That name's not on the witness list. Amy?"

Amy marches forward, her Mockingbirds notebook in hand. She flips through a few pages, then says, "I have no record of the defendant requesting to call Martin Summers as a witness."

Kevin stands up, a self-satisfied grin on his face. "He's a last-minute request. We just received intelligence he has information pertinent to our case."

"Pertinent?" Amy asks, raising an eyebrow.

Kevin nods. "Yes, pertinent. Very pertinent. And in the interest of justice we should be allowed to call any witnesses who could have useful information. Should we not?"

Callie speaks. "If Martin has information relevant to the case, the defendant should be allowed to call him to the stand. It's only fair."

Amy breathes hard, the checks and balances between the three branches of the Mockingbirds clearly in force right now, then says crisply, "We believe in fairness. I'll get the witness."

As Amy walks to the door, Maia turns to me. "Why is he calling Martin?" she whispers.

I need to tell her, but the words are lodged in another galaxy. Because everything is exposed. Everything about me is now public property.

"Why. Is. He. Calling. Martin?" Maia asks again, her voice cold and clear this time.

I'm too embarrassed to look at her. She leans down next to me. "Tell me now," she instructs.

"I'm kind of involved with him," I say under my breath.

Maia breathes in through her nose, pursing her lips together. "As I suspected." She pauses, then says, also in a low voice, "But it doesn't change anything. It's not a big deal. This changes nothing. We'll be fine."

I wonder if she's talking to me or giving herself—as the lawyer hit with a surprise witness—a pep talk. But there's no more time to wonder, because when I lift my head Martin is sitting down in the witness chair. I sneak a brief glimpse at him, at his slightly shaggy hair, hanging soft as always. At his brown eyes, their multicolors flickering in the morning light.

"Martin Summers," Kevin begins, striding tauntingly, like he's got a super-slippery secret up his sleeve.

Martin looks straight at Kevin, refusing to be unnerved.

"Martin, I'm wondering if you could tell us what you were doing the morning of March thirteenth?"

Martin chuckles. "I don't really remember."

"It was a Monday. Five days ago to be precise. I believe it would have been right after your French class in Morgan-Young Hall."

The empty dark classroom where no one was supposed to see us.

Kevin continues, "Why don't I ask the question another way?"

"Yes, because we're curious to hear how this relates to the case," Callie says coolly.

But Kevin seems to like playing with his food, so he keeps toying with Martin. "You spend a lot of time in Alex's room, don't you?"

Carter has spies too.

Carter has friends in Taft-Hay Hall reporting back to him, spies in the classrooms too, following me, tracking me. No wonder Carter was so cocky, so confident, so willing to come to the hearing. It's not just because the Mockingbirds are powerful, but because he's created his own power as well.

"It's my job," Martin replies.

"It's your job?" Kevin asks.

"Yes. It's not a secret Alex came to the Mockingbirds and asked for help. That's why we're all here today."

"So you *help*"—Kevin pauses to sketch air quotes with his fingers—"by visiting her in her room?" he asks suspiciously. "What kind of help exactly do you give her *in her room?*" he says, adding his own knowing little laugh at the end.

Martin stays calm and for once I'm glad he's acting as if I'm a pity project. "Many of us visit her. Amy did, Ilana did. Plus, Alex and I are friends and have been since last year."

"That's true. You are awfully close to this whole thing and I'm sure she needed your friendly support to get through a tough time."

Martin says nothing because Kevin has asked nothing. Kevin cocks his forehead up, staring at the ceiling, stroking his chin. He takes a breath, exhales, walks back and forth down the tables.

"And that support would extend to, how shall we say?" He stops in the middle of the room. "I know!" He holds up his index finger, like he's just discovered something. "Shall we call it heavy petting?"

"Objection!" Maia calls out.

"On what grounds?" Callie asks.

"He's not asking the witness a relevant question."

"Kevin, please ask a relevant question," Callie says exasperatedly.

"But of course. My apologies," Kevin says, then turns back to Martin. "Martin, did you engage in a heavy make-out session with Alex Patrick on March thirteenth in an empty classroom in Morgan-Young Hall after your French class and during which the two of you kissed, groped, pressed your bodies against each other, and felt underneath the other one's shirt?"

Martin's eyes stay fixed on Kevin. "Yes."

"And do you regularly engage in physical contact with Alex, like holding hands on the way to the Brain Freeze?"

How could I have been so stupid?

"Yes, we hold hands when we go out for ice cream," Martin answers, his voice strong and unwavering.

"That's so sweet. What's her favorite flavor?"

"Objection!" Maia calls out.

Callie gives Kevin a hard look as he resumes. "So let's go back to these visits to Alex's room that are part of *your job* with the Mockingbirds. Is part of your job when you're there to make out as well?"

"It's not part of my job," Martin says.

"So you lied when you said it was your job to visit her?"

"No, I didn't lie. It was my job. I visited her. We also kissed. That was not part of the job. But I did it anyway."

"Is it against the rules of the Mockingbirds? Getting involved with a plaintiff? I don't know. I'm just curious."

"It is."

"And you did it anyway."

"We did it anyway."

"And was Alex aware it is against the rules?"

"Yes."

"So you regularly engage in sexual conduct with Alex?"

Martin nods. "Yes, and it's completely mutual. Completely *consensual*," Martin says, slowly sounding out the last word, making sure the impact is clear.

"Oh, I'm sure it is," Kevin says brightly. "Just like with Carter. Because Alex has a pattern of engaging in sexual activity with boys where she wants, when she wants, whenever the mood strikes, regardless of the consequences. And you're part of that pattern."

Kevin practically sails over to his seat, ridiculously pleased with himself. He and Carter exchange a mini high-five under the table. Everthing about what Kevin said stings, especially since Martin and I haven't slept together.

Maia pops up, paces to the center of the room. "Martin," she begins, "you're not the one being tried here. So I don't think we need to get into the ins and out of your relationship with Alex. Your *consensual* relationship. But a few brief questions just to clarify the differences. Was Alex ever drinking when you were with her?"

"No."

"Was she ever sleeping when you kissed her?"

"No."

"Passed out?"

"No."

Maia looks to the council. "I don't really think there is any need to ask this witness any further questions because to do so would be offensive. Not to him. But to everyone. To you, Callie. And you, Lila. And you, Parker. In fact, it would be offensive to every man and woman on this campus, at this school, in this country, and in the UK as well. To bring up a relationship Alex has that is mutual and consensual, to discuss what she and her boyfriend do—what they both *choose* to do, *choose* being the operative word, *choose* being the only word that matters—when they are together in her room or in a classroom or at an ice-cream shop is despicable. It is distasteful. And it has no place here.

"It undermines all of the progress we as women and men who believe in right and wrong, who believe *no means no,* who believe every act of sex and intimacy should be consensual from both sides, have made. To bring up Alex's very real and ongoing and *mutual* relationship with Martin and somehow suggest it has any relation whatsoever to what happened in January in Carter Hutchinson's room against her wishes, against her will, is inappropriate and completely irrelevant. Being with Martin is a choice Alex made willingly and actively. Being with Carter was not a choice. She had no choice. I urge you to disregard this as it has absolutely zero bearing on what happened the night Carter date-raped Alex."

Chapter Thirty-Three
BREATHE IN, BREATHE OUT

Martin is excused. Whether he returns to his post as sentry or whether Amy banishes him—to what? To Mockingbird jail?—I don't know.

Kevin calls his third and final witness. Carter rises from the end of the table. He's wearing a white-and-blue-striped oxford cloth shirt, a green tie, and dress pants. His white hair is slicked back.

"Let's set the scene a bit," Kevin begins. "How did that evening in January begin, Carter? The one when you met Alex?"

As if there were another night we were discussing.

"Um, well it started in the library...."

I cough-laugh quietly. Give me a break.

"I was studying for Spanish class."

I tap Maia on the leg, then whisper in her ear. "He's lying—"

She shushes me before I can continue, before I can say he told me the *next* morning he hadn't even started studying for any classes yet. He was at water polo practice before we met.

"Then I went back to my room and, uh, called my mom to tell her about my classes. And to check in and see how she was feeling. She'd been sick during the break."

Don't they realize he's lying? Can't they see through him like I can?

"So after I talked to Mom, I went with some friends to the club. And while I was there I ordered a club soda, because of course you can't drink there. I can't drink anywhere. I'm only seventeen."

Kevin nods, all thoughtful and paternal, as if Carter is the model student, the exemplar of virtue.

"No, you can't drink when you're seventeen," Kevin states.

Thanks for the clarification, asshole.

I tap Maia again, shrug my shoulders as if to ask her *what do we do next?* She shakes her head, signaling me not to talk. I resist the impulse to cover my eyes with my hands, because if I did, I'd just watch through my fingers like it was a horror movie, because it is.

Carter, the white knight he's pretending to be, continues, "And then I met Alex. And I just remember thinking how very pretty she was," he says, painting a shy, almost

289

lovestruck puppy-dog look on his face. "So I walked up to her and introduced myself, and she shook my hand and smiled. She was very sharp and witty and we talked about how much we liked the band."

Right, let's pretend I was straight up and sober the whole night. Because he forgot to mention how I practically stepped on him I was so buzzed. He continues in this vein as he details leaving the club, going to Sandeep's dorm, playing Circle of Death—claiming he drank only orange juice when it was his turn. Then he describes our kiss there in the common room, like he's some blushing Southern gentleman overcome by my beauty.

"And then you left to go back to your dorm?" Kevin asks.

"Yes, Alex said she wanted to go to my dorm."

I snap my head toward Maia. *Do something* I say with my eyes.

"Objection!" she calls out, standing up.

Callie looks to Maia. "Yes?"

"His side is wrong," Maia argues. "You already heard Alex say it was his idea."

"You may sit down, Maia," Callie tells her. "We're listening to *his* side of the story."

"Can you tell us what happened when you were back at your room?" Kevin asks Carter.

"We kissed some more and then..." Carter pauses, blushing a bit.

"Yes?" Kevin asks gently.

"Then we moved to the bed and we undressed each other."

My forehead pounds; the vein I despise is angry too, filling with fire.

"And she lay down on my bed and pulled me closer to her, and I got a condom on so we could make love—"

I cough loudly this time; I don't bother to cover it up. Carter stops and looks at me for the first time—they all look at me—coughing. "We didn't make love," I spit out at him. I don't care if it's not my turn.

"We did," Carter says, gazing—actually gazing—right at me. "At least, it felt that way to me," he says, then puts a hand on his chest and sighs.

The flames lick higher in me; they coat my body and my skin and I'm boiling inside and out.

"Then we fell asleep. She fell asleep in my arms."

I close my eyes so I can't see the lies; I only have to hear them.

"And I fell asleep too, for a couple hours, maybe three," he continues. "Because when I woke up I looked at the clock and it was around three thirty in the morning then. And she was kissing me."

"I wasn't kissing you!" I shout, my eyes wide open now.

He gives me his look again, his demure look. "You were, Alex," he says softly. He's not the Carter he was on the phone, all brash and ready for war, or in the library, slick and ready for action. Now he's a new Carter, the worst one of all. He's sweet, sensitive Carter, dousing himself in syrup and honey. I want to peel every last inch of his sugar-coated lies off of him.

"So I reached for a condom again and put it on and we started having sex—I mean, *making love*," he says, quickly correcting himself, and it's so clear to me he's playing a part, so clear to me he missed his rehearsed line. I look to the council next to see if they noticed his mistake. But their faces are stone.

"She didn't push you away?" Kevin asks.

"She did not."

"She didn't say no?"

"She didn't say no."

"She didn't shake her head?"

"She didn't shake her head."

"Thank you, Carter," Kevin says, and sits down.

Maia leaps up, grabbing her chance to ask questions.

"You claim she didn't say no. But not saying no isn't enough. The code of conduct says, and I quote: 'Sexual assault is sexual contact (not just intercourse) where one of the parties has not given or cannot give active verbal consent, i.e., uttered a clear "yes" to the action. If a person does not say "no," that does not mean he or she said "yes." Silence does not equal consent. Silence could mean fear, confusion, inebriation. The only thing that means yes is yes. A lack of yes is a no.'"

Maia pauses, letting the weight of the words fill the room. Then directly to Carter, her brown eyes boring into his blue ones, she asks, "Did she say yes?"

"She didn't say no," he says.

"Did she say yes?" she asks again. "Did she say yes either time? Did she say she wanted to have sex with you?"

"She didn't say no," he says again, stealing a *help me* look at Kevin, but Kevin's got the same lost look on his face as the boy in the witness chair.

The dryers are still rattling, but it's as if the laundry room went dead silent, and this is one of those moments when everything is shockingly clear. There's practically a collective holding of breath at the realization of Carter's fatal error. He never prepped for this question. They never planned the next lie he would tell, because to Carter my not saying no *was* consent. He didn't devise a lie this time. He didn't think he had to. It's as if he never read the revised code or—more likely—that he didn't care what it said. Because he thinks what he did was okay simply because I didn't utter a *no*.

When it's not okay for so very many reasons.

"Did she say yes?" Maia asks for a third time, and each time she asks the question the room grows quieter, waiting for his answer.

"She was breathing."

"She was *breathing*?" Maia repeats. "She was breathing?"

Carter nods, latching on to this idea. "Yes, she was breathing."

"That was her consent in your view? Breathing?"

Carter doesn't know what to say; he's Bambi without his mom. "Um, yeah."

"She was breathing," Maia says, incredulously, then looks at the three students on the council. "A lack of no is not a yes. The absence of a no doesn't mean consent. Nor does breathing equal consent. Breathing is breathing. Breathing is sleeping. Breathing is not saying yes. Breathing simply means you're alive."

She reaches for my hand, squeezes it. I squeeze her hand back, feeling neither fire nor ice, just calm, because for all of Carter's lies, for his puppy-dog routine, for his faux-gentle demeanor, I'm pretty sure Maia just nailed it right there, when he finally told the truth.

Maia finishes with a quick closing argument. Then Kevin gives his, stumbling a bit on his words, still smarting from Carter's slipup that neither one of them saw coming.

Callie says "thank you" to Carter, to Maia, to Kevin, to me. "We'll reconvene tomorrow at noon with a decision."

Chapter Thirty-Four
THE WHOLE STORY

"He as good as admitted it!" Maia shouts for maybe the ten thousandth time. We've just told T.S. every detail after returning to our dorm ten minutes ago.

"I know," I say, shaking my head in amazement at how all Carter could come up with was the breathing defense. "Weird, isn't it?"

"Breathing!" she declares again.

"Breathing," I repeat. "That's it. That's all he could say."

"And while we're at it, it would have been helpful if you told me about Martin," Maia says. "But now that the cat's out of the bag, do you really like him a lot?"

"Yes, do you?" T.S. asks eagerly.

"I do."

"I want to know how it started with him. Tell us how it started," T.S. says. "Tell us every little detail you've been keeping all to yourself for the last month, you little secret keeper!"

I flash back to the morning after Carter, when I didn't want to tell her anything. Now, with Martin, I want to tell her everything.

There's a knock on the door. "I'll get it," T.S. says, and she opens the door to Martin. "Well, hello there!"

"Hey," Martin says, not nearly as festive as T.S. or Maia.

"I'm betting you want a few minutes alone with Alex," T.S. says.

Martin just nods, and Maia and T.S. exit quickly.

"I'm so sorry," I say.

"Don't apologize," he says. He nods to my bed. "Can I sit down?"

I say yes and he is careful to sit a few feet away from me. The air suddenly feels heavy and I know why he's here. To break it off. I swallow sharply and wait. He turns to me. "I should have just told Amy from the start."

"What did she say?"

He pauses, then says, "She said it's not how she would have liked to have found out."

"Oh."

"She said my actions could have seriously undermined the Mockingbirds' credibility."

"Amy doesn't mince words."

"And then she said it was a good thing Maia's quick on her feet and delivered her brilliant speech."

"It was brilliant," I agree.

"Brilliant and true," Martin adds. "And then Amy said in the end it didn't hurt the case and may have helped it, but still she said she'd deal with me later."

"What do you think she means?" I ask, wondering if the Mockingbirds will use their very own Mockingbird-ian ways to punish Martin.

He shrugs. "I don't know."

"I'm sorry, Martin," I say.

"Don't be."

"But I feel terrible."

"Don't. I made my choice. I knew what I was doing," he says firmly as he looks straight at me, his eyes still deadly serious, all brown, no flecks right now. His hands are holding the edge of my bed tight, like he's not letting go, he's angry or something. Angry at me. "It was worth it," he says.

The only word I hear is the one in the past tense. *Was.*

"It *is* worth it," he quickly adds, correcting himself. "It *is* worth it. You are worth it. And I hope they nail him," he says, releasing his hands and balling his right hand into a fist. "He deserves it, that asshole."

He slides close to me. "To do that to you," he says, anger still lacing his voice as he lays his right hand on my hair, sweeping it off my face. "To do that to someone I'm so crazy about." Then softly, letting go of his fury, he says, "Someone I'm falling for."

He closes his eyes, leans into my neck, nuzzling me, his hand on my cheek now, warm on my face. I relax into the feeling of his hand on me, knowing I am close to falling too.

◆ ◆ ◆

I have to admit I feel a twinge of victory in the air about the verdict tomorrow, not to mention the fact that someone—someone I really and truly like—is *falling* for me. So as I pace backstage, waiting for the quartet to finish their rendition of *A Little Night Music,* I tell myself not to be cocky, not to assume the game is in the bag. Then the last note of the Mozart serenade ends and there are cheers and clapping. The foursome bows and leaves the stage, and the spotlight is on me, just me. I walk straight to the piano, ready to perform the most awesome piece of music ever written in front of my friends, my boyfriend—no longer my secret boyfriend, now my *boyfriend* boyfriend—my teachers, Miss Damata, and a freaking Juilliard admissions officer.

The instant my fingers hit the keys, I soar. I fly. I glide back into the music, only music, and Beethoven is mine again; we're reunited, we're not mad anymore. We're on the same side. And on and on we go through the first movement, then the second, into the third, and now the fourth, and I feel as if it's righting all wrongs, stitching up wounds, rewriting history. And it's beautiful and it's loud, but loud-good, loud like sweep-through-your-body-and-carry-you-away loud. Loud like the whole audience is enrapt. Loud like it's epic because it is and we all are just bathed in music and light and sound and magic and art and perfect perfection. We're not just in the concert hall; we're in Carnegie Hall, we're on the world's greatest stage, and all I can feel is music, sweet music, pouring over me.

And then we come to "Ode to Joy," the most perfect piece of music tucked near the end of the most perfect symphony by the most perfect composer. And it's just me and the piano crashing through space and time. I'm me again, restored. I'm me, who I was, who I'm supposed to be, who I've always been.

And I'm nearing the end, I'm just a few bars away; I wrap the music around myself and I'm so unbelievably far away from *that night*. I strike my last triumphant chords, the sound reverberating.

But then I'm back....

He has the condom on and he's coming toward me now, his face is coming toward me, his body is coming toward me, and there's a hand pressed on the mattress right next to my arm. His other hand is between his legs. I think I know what he's doing. I think I know why his hand is between his legs. He's going to try to enter me. He's going to try to push himself into me.

I look down at me, at my body, and I'm naked in this

bed, and I don't know how I got naked in his bed. All I know is I don't want him inside me. I don't want his penis inside me. The spinning slows, then it halts, and the room's no longer turning; it's suddenly still and quiet and calm and I'm strong. I'm so strong I put my two hands on his big chest. I press my palms hard against him and push him. I shake my head; I say no. And I keep my hands on his chest like that.

And then I'm somewhere else. My brain goes someplace else, it wanders off because it doesn't want to be here, but now it's back, and a boy I don't want to be with is on top of me and it makes no sense, so I turn to my side and fall asleep.

When I wake up again, there's a noise, a sound, like a cross between a bark and a whisper, like an "oomph." It's like someone just sat on my chest. It's dark and my mouth tastes like a sock, feels like wool. And there's Carter. On me. Over me. In me. He's pushing in me and I can feel him. I can feel his penis in me, even though I'm barely aware, half-asleep, half-awake, half-dreaming, half-dead. But I can feel him and he's breathing. He's breathing kind of heavy, hitting some sort of rhythm.

I realize the noise came from me. The "uh" came from me, from the feel of someone's weight on me, someone's body on me. And it's like I just came to or something, the "uh" marking the line between sleep and awake, there and here. Now I'm here, still in his bed, still naked, still under him. Only now he's pressing into me and he's going faster and faster and I want to do something, say something, but all I feel is slower and slower and slower and all I can do is breathe, breathe, breathe....

And there's nothing I can do to stop this, nothing I can do to move. My eyes are closed, and I'm just going to pretend I'm not here.

I will pretend, I will pretend, I will pretend I am enjoying it. It's the only way to get through it. The only way is to pretend.

I'm enjoying it, I'm enjoying it, I'm enjoying it.

Then I open my eyes and I see my hands are on his back. My arms are around him. They're around him and my hands are on his back, almost as if I want this, but I don't want this, I don't want this at all, I'm just pretending, so I don't know why my hands are on his back.

Because this is not how it's supposed to be. I'm not supposed to be enjoying it. My hands are not supposed to be on his back.

Chapter Thirty-Five

FIX IT

Somehow I finish the last few bars of the Ninth Symphony and this must be what they say about adrenaline, about lifting a car when your kid's stuck under it. Sometimes you just do it. I do it, I play through it and I don't know how. I make it through my world completely crashing in on me, and now I'm standing up, taking a bow, walking offstage.

Miss Damata finds me. She says she was blown away. She introduces me to the admissions officer. He says I have mad talent. He will arrange for an early audition in New York in the fall. How does October sound? I nod. Walk away. I see T.S. and Maia and Mel and Dana and Amy and Ilana and Sandeep and Martin. They all want to hug me, touch me.

But *my hands were on his back,* I want to say. My hands

were on his back and I pretended to enjoy it. And then I did enjoy it. I didn't have a choice. I made myself enjoy it. And now I feel sick, horribly, awfully sick, because there can be no other explanation for my hands being on his back other than my enjoying it. My hands should have been pushing him, fighting him, or at least limp at my sides. But they were on his back. Forget the first time when I was practically asleep. Because the second time I let it happen with my hands.

I try to grab T.S.'s wrist, pull her aside, whisper in her ear, "T.S., I think I made a mistake. I think I messed up. I think I was wrong." I try hard, so hard, to lift my hand to grab hers. I put my left hand under my right hand and try to push my hand closer to T.S., try to make it move, but it's lead and my mouth is cotton and I can't speak. Because if I did I would scream or I would whimper, "My hands were on his back."

Somehow, like I did when I was onstage, I find the will to say something. "I have to go to the bathroom. I'll be right back."

I walk away, like a robot, a sleepwalker, heavy anti-gravity boots on. They wait for me, thinking I'll be right back. But I slip out the back door of the music hall and they don't even see me. I walk across the quad; the cold March air nips at me, but I don't care because I don't feel anything anymore. I'm in a cocoon with only one thing to keep me company—a memory that's now come careening back at full speed.

I walk past my dorm, past McGregor Hall to the edge of campus. I walk and I don't have a clue where I'm going or if my friends will figure out and follow me or if I have points, but I don't care because I have to get away from here, away from me, away from the awful truth of my own hands that betrayed me.

My hands that are everything to me. My hands, the map that led me back to *that night*. These are the hands I play the piano with; like a surgeon's hands, they make everything I do possible. They are the agents, the instruments that revealed me—who I really am.

Someone who got it wrong. Someone who liked it.

Thick shame fills my head and I keep walking down the hill, down the street, away from Themis, away from people, away from music, from Beethoven, who did it again, who deceived me again.

I walk and I walk and soon I'm on Kentfield Street and then I'm crossing it and then I'm walking up another street and up the porch and I'm at my sister's house and I pray she's here on a Saturday night. I knock on the door and her roommate Mandy answers.

"Is Casey here?"

"She's spending the evening with *Vogue*," Mandy says drily.

I walk past Mandy, up the stairs, down the hall, and into my sister's bedroom. She tosses her fashion magazine to the ground and says, "What's going on?"

I say nothing.

"Today must have been really hard. The trial, then your performance. You went one hundred eighty degrees the other way. Come sit," she says, patting her bed.

I sit next to her on her bed, as I did when we were little. "Casey, why did you start the Mockingbirds?"

"I told you, Alex."

"No. I mean why did you really start it? Who was that girl to you?"

"Her name was Jen."

For Jen. The book—*To Kill a Mockingbird*—was inscribed to Jen. My sister started the Mockingbirds for Jen.

"She lived next door to me senior year," Casey continues. "We weren't good friends. I mean, I had nothing against her. But she was..." her voice trails off.

"She was what?" I ask.

"She was really heavy," Casey says quickly.

"Okay?" I say, not sure where she's going.

"And some of the students called her names. They called her Beluga Whale and Goodyear Blimp, and it just kept going on. Sometimes when I heard them say things, I'd tell them to stop, but it didn't make a difference. They kept doing it."

"So that's why you started the Mockingbirds? Because you couldn't get them to stop calling her names?"

"There's more to it than that. She knew I'd defended her, so she came to visit me one night to say thanks. And I said it was no big deal. And then she said, 'I want you to tell me the truth, Casey. You're the only one who will. So I'm going

305

to ask you something, and I want you to promise to tell the truth.' And I agreed to. Then she said, 'Is it true what they say? Am I really that fat?' And I said, 'No, of course not.' And she laughed at me. She said, 'I know you're lying. I want the truth. I'm not afraid of it. Am I that fat?' So I said, 'The truth? It probably wouldn't hurt if you lost a few pounds.' She nodded her head and said, 'Thanks.'"

My heart sinks because I know what happened next. But I ask anyway. "And then?"

"The next day she was dead. Overdose of pills."

"It wasn't your fault," I say immediately.

Casey nods. "I know that now."

"But you didn't at the time?"

"I felt horrible. I felt as if it was my fault. So I started the Mockingbirds—to help other girls like Jen. Well, to keep other girls from becoming like her."

"That's why you stopped playing soccer," I say suddenly, because it just dawned on me. Casey gave herself the very punishment she built into the Mockingbirds system—she took away the thing she loved most.

She nods. "That's why I stopped."

"But you started again."

"I finally forgave myself."

"It took you this long?"

She shrugs. "I guess I wanted to see that it could work, see that the Mockingbirds could do what I couldn't do. That a group committed to good could do good. I wanted to see if they could solve the problems the school couldn't solve and I couldn't solve alone. I wanted there to be other options."

Other options.

That's what I need right now. *Other options.*

I need to do what my sister did when she thought she had done something wrong. She fixed it. I have to fix this.

"I have to go," I say.

"I'll take you back," Casey says.

And I let her. Because I need this day to be over.

Chapter Thirty-Six
TIME OF YOUR LIFE

T.S. gets up first and leaves for a run. I say nothing to her.

Then Maia wakes up and cracks open a book. I say nothing to her either.

They're not the ones I want to talk to right now. They're not the ones I need to tell. They're my friends. They'll get my back. They always do. But right now, I need the truth, the cold, hard truth.

I take a shower, where I try to practice saying the words I need to say. Only I barely know what those words are. I barely know what happened anymore. *I was pretending. Then I wasn't?*

Pretending, that's what I do. That's who I am, the pretender.

I turn the water off; wrap a towel around myself; return to my room; put on jeans, a sweatshirt, and my Vans. I dry my hair, twist it up in a clip, and leave.

Because I know where to go.

I have to find the purple door. I have to find Miss Damata. She will know what to do. She will tell the truth. She's the only adult, the only teacher, who has a clue and now I need her. It's Sunday morning and she won't be in the music hall, she won't be in her office. But she lives a block off campus, in the blue house with the purple door, she told me.

There is little else I know about her. I don't even know why she's a *Miss*. I don't know if she was once a Mrs. and is now a Miss again or if she's simply never been married. She's mentioned *family* once or twice but has never said more, and I haven't asked. Maybe she has kids. Maybe she's raising them alone. We students pride ourselves on knowing everything about teachers' private lives. But she's managed to defy the natural order of students and teachers. She's maintained her privacy, and this only bolsters my decision to seek her out.

I walk through the quad and out to the street that wraps around campus, looking for a house with a purple door.

I don't see it on the first block.

There are no homes on the second block with purple doors. Their absence makes my forehead hurt. By the time I reach the third street, the vein in my forehead is beating so hard I'm sure it's about to have its own personal heart attack right now.

I try the final block, my last hope. No purple, no purple, no purple.

But then when I near the end of the street, I see it. There's a faded purple door on a light blue house and I want to run to it and away from it and through it all at once. I want to be on the other side and have said what I need to say without going through the saying of it.

Instead, I walk up the stone steps, across the crickety porch, and knock lightly on the purple door. I pray Miss Damata answers, not her boyfriend, if she has one, not her kids, if she has them, and certainly not the Juilliard admissions officer who thinks I have mad talent. I don't want him to see my hands.

Someone pulls open the door, and I hold my breath. It's Miss Damata, already dressed in jeans and a long-sleeve brown polka-dot blouse. She smiles. "You were amazing last night, but I have a feeling that's not why you're here."

I shake my head. "That's not why I'm here."

"There's a park a few blocks down. It's always quiet there on Sunday mornings, quieter than my house."

I nod and she tells me she'll be right back. Five seconds later she has boots on and a sweatshirt. She shuts the door behind her. We start walking and we reach the park, a tiny little thing with just a wooden bench and some gardens that are bare but aching to bloom soon.

"I'm guessing this has to do with *stuff*," she begins as we sit down, using my word when I almost told her everything.

"Yes," I say.

"Do you want to tell me this *stuff*?"

I turn to look at her. "I think I made a mistake," I blurt out.

She nods. "Which makes you human."

I shake my head. "This isn't an ordinary one."

"So tell me what happened and we'll figure it out."

"We will?"

She smiles briefly. "Yes, we will."

I feel calmer already, like I can manage this, like I can say this, like I can do this. She said we can figure it out. If she said so, it must be true; this must be figure-out-able.

I look down at my shoes, then at the ground, then at Miss Damata. "One night at the beginning of the semester, I got really drunk and I was date-raped that night. I mean, it seemed that way. And I told some other students." I pause, considering my words. "Some students and some friends," I add. I don't mention the Mockingbirds. That's a secret just for students. "And together we sort of accused this other student. Everything seemed so clear at first. Certain, you know? I didn't remember much because I'd been drinking. And I don't usually drink. I haven't even had anything since then.

"And I didn't remember a lot of what had happened at first, but then I'd remember more and everything I remembered seemed so certain. Like I'd remember saying no and putting my hands on his chest and I'd remember everything feeling kind of fuzzy and it all made sense as date rape. And then it stopped making sense."

"Why did it stop making sense?" she asks.

311

"Because last night I remembered something," I say stiffly, fighting back tears of shame, tears of embarrassment. I am not going to cry. I am absolutely not going to cry.

"What did you remember?" she asks gently.

I tell her how all I wanted was just to get through it, so I told myself to pretend. But then before it was over I had my hands on his back. And isn't that the proof, the evidence, I was wrong, I enjoyed it, and I made a mistake in accusing him?

I say this all and the words taste horrible in my mouth, like fire, like bleach.

"What do I do?" I ask.

"Alex," she begins, "you were drunk."

"I won't drink again. I'm sorry."

"You're not in trouble for drinking. Of course, I'm glad you know it's not a good idea to drink like that, or frankly at all. My point about the drinking is a simple one. You couldn't give consent. You were drunk."

"But…"

"But *everything,*" she declares, her voice rising firm and steady, her hands cutting through the air for emphasis. "*Everything* that happened to you, everything this boy did after that point, after you were drinking too much to give consent, was wrong. *Everything.*"

I give her a look as if she's from another planet. "Miss Damata, don't you understand what I'm saying? I stopped resisting! I stopped pushing him away! I gave in. I gave in and let him do it and then it was like—" I stop, then choke out the rest. "It was like I was enjoying it."

"Were you enjoying it?"

"No," I say adamantly, shaking my head.

"You don't have to have been fighting him off the whole time for it to be date rape. You don't have to have been saying no the entire time either. In fact, it doesn't even matter if you were having the time of your life, Alex," she says, her words precise, like individual slices of certainty. "What he did to you was nonconsensual, and it doesn't suddenly become consensual because for one moment you put your hands on his back. That one moment doesn't wipe the slate clean and make you sober. You were drunk. And you said no. That's why it's date rape."

I press my fingertips to the vein in my forehead and strangely enough, it's not hammering like mad. It's not going crazy under my skin. It's quiet and calm. And my head is starting to clear.

"So you're saying...," I begin.

"I'm saying it's unfortunately very normal to doubt, to think it was your fault, that you let it happen. And it's also completely awful to feel that way, because you're the one who got hurt. You're the one whose rights were taken away. And you're the one—I'm getting the sense—trying to stand up for yourself now."

I tense for a second, thinking she knows about the Mockingbirds. But if she does, she doesn't let on.

"Standing up for what's right is a huge burden to bear. It's normal to have some doubt."

"But that doesn't mean I made a mistake?" I ask.

She shakes her head. "Alex, there's a boy you like, right?"

"Yes, there is," I say, and for a second my mood lightens just thinking of Martin.

"When you remember the *other* boy, even the tiny sliver where you think you were enjoying it, did it feel like it does with the boy you like?"

"No. Not at all. Not even close," I say, because being with Martin *only* feels right.

Miss Damata nods and places her hand on mine. "Nobody said this was easy. Nobody said you were going to get over it right away. But I think inside"—she points at my heart—"you know what happened was wrong. That's why you're taking a stand." She gives my hand a squeeze. "Do you want to go to the police?" she asks gently.

I shake my head.

"I can take you if you want to go."

"I don't. But thank you."

She simply nods, accepting my decision. "When you're ready, there are people you can talk to, people who can help you feel like your old self again. I will help you find someone to talk to."

♦ ♦ ♦

At noon I file back into the laundry room. Martin's still standing guard, waiting for Amy to deal with him later. Maia sits down; I sit down. A minute later Carter enters. He sits down, then Kevin. I look at the three students in front of us who form the council, the three students who will decide the fate of Carter Drake Hutchinson, the junior-year student at Themis Academy who has been charged with a crime he committed against Alexandra Nicole Patrick, a fellow junior-year student.

Callie clears her throat. "We have reached a decision in the sexual assault case against Carter Hutchinson."

I wait, and in the interminable moment before Callie says the next words—words only the students will hear, decisions teachers won't be privy to, verdicts parents won't learn—I know I did the right thing. I know in the way Amy was sure when she took on my case; in the way T.S. understood from the start; in the way Maia, Sandeep, Martin, Casey, Jones, Amy, Ilana, and now Miss Damata all saw the truth that I now know too.

And then she says it.

"Guilty of sexual assault. The punishment begins immediately."

Chapter Thirty-Seven

JUST ANOTHER AVERAGE SCHOOL NIGHT

We eat cake later that night.

Casey picked up a chocolate cake from a bakery on Kentfield Street and dropped it off. I'm sure we could have pilfered a school birthday cake, but somehow it tastes better since we bought it.

T.S. hands Maia a large knife and says, "As the most kick-ass lawyer this school has ever seen, you should have the honor."

Maia bows, then curtsies—for the queen, she says—and doles out slices of chocolate layer cake to T.S., Sandeep, Martin, and me. Dana even stops by and has a piece too. Amy's not here; Ilana's not here. It's not a Mockingbirds celebration, just a friends one.

Everyone is still a little high from the victory, a little thrilled the trial is behind us now because they all invested their time, their effort. I watch them laughing again, loose again, reliving certain moments, like Maia's imitations of Carter's Southern gentleman routine. The rest of them didn't see him being questioned, so Maia's reenacting parts of it.

"'And then we made love, at least it felt that way to me,'" Maia says, imitating him. She gags afterward for effect, letting her audience know what she thinks of Carter's words.

But I don't want to hear them again.

"I'll be right back," I say, and slip out of the common room. I head outside, where I sit on the steps outside my dorm. I don't feel like eating cake or celebrating or conducting a play-by-play as if we just won the basketball tournament or something. Justice doesn't work like that. It doesn't erase what happened. It doesn't make you who you were before. I'm becoming someone else—someone else I'm figuring out how to be.

I wonder briefly why I went through it, why it was worth it. Because in some ways, nothing changed. This is just how it goes, this is how it feels to take a stand. It feels like life, like chocolate cake, like just another average school night; it feels like wanting to be alone. You don't parade in the streets, you don't dance on the grave. You sit on the steps and you watch the school go by and the moon rise higher in the sky and it feels like...

Like normal, actually. It feels like normal.

I want normal. I like normal. I did this for normal.

So I stand up and walk across the quad. Alone. I don't need a bodyguard and I don't need to hide and I can choose—*I* can make a choice—to look up at the trees and around at the dorms and down at the path and whichever way I want because I'm not going to be afraid anymore.

I walk to the dorm all the way across on the other side of the quad. I go up to the second floor. I knock on a door. Mel answers.

"Hey," I say.

"Hey," she says, and her eyes ask the question.

I nod.

"Good," she says quietly.

"Yeah, I think it is. I mean, I think it will be."

"I think it will be too," Mel says. "When will his punishment be announced?"

"Tomorrow. Lunchtime in the cafeteria."

"Are you going?" she asks.

I hadn't thought about it before. But something about it feels like attending an execution, and that's not the kind of thing I'd do. So I decide to be me again and to do what I do.

"I don't think so."

Chapter Thirty-Eight
HOW TO PLAY GERSHWIN

"Do you want to skip lunch?"

Jones looks at me, raising his eyebrows at the question I ask when English class ends. "You want to skip lunch today, of all days?" he asks suspiciously.

I nod.

He knows what happened. We haven't talked about it, but he knows.

He shakes his head, kind of in fascination. "Isn't this the moment you've been waiting for?"

"No, this isn't why I did this," I say, but I don't add anything more because I don't have to keep explaining why I did it, even to Jones, even to my friend who doesn't believe in the Mockingbirds, who believes in something else, in his own sense of right and wrong. Maybe, ultimately, that's what we're all aspiring to—to have our own sense of right and wrong and to act on it.

"Where are we going when we skip lunch?"

I roll my eyes. "You don't actually know?"

"No."

"Think, Jones. It's not hard."

"Music hall?"

I nod.

When it's time for lunch, they're waiting for me on the steps of the cafeteria. Martin and Maia and T.S. and Sandeep and Amy and Ilana. They expect me to join them for this moment.

"I'm not going in," I tell them.

"Not again?" T.S. asks woefully. "I thought you were cool going to lunch now?"

"I thought that's why we did this," Ilana asks, a touch of indignation in her voice, as if I'm not grateful. But that's not what this is about.

Martin says nothing and his eyes are quiet too. The green flecks aren't sparkling; they aren't moving today. I know why. He's thinking I disappeared last night. He's thinking I'm disappearing now.

"I'm cool going to the caf. But I don't want to. I don't need to," I say. "I'll see you guys later."

I leave and walk across the quad, knowing that shortly Carter will do his requisite Paul Oko routine, announcing he's voluntarily withdrawing from the water polo team and if anyone wants to know why, the answer is in the book. In a few minutes there could even be a schoolwide dash to the second floor of Pryor after that. His entry will have shifted to ink then. Permanent.

I push open the door to the music hall, and Jones is there with his violin. He doesn't ask questions. He doesn't ask how I feel. He doesn't need to.

"I would have thought you'd bring your guitar," I sass as I sit down at the piano.

"I didn't know you were that kind of girl," he says.

"Guess we'll have to see if you can keep up on your violin."

"Oh, I can keep up with anything you throw my way."

I give him a smirk, say nothing, and let the music do the talking. The second Jones hears what I am up to, a knowing grin breaks across his face.

Because he's finally playing Gershwin how he wants. The hip-hop way.

We play through the whole lunch period, blasting *Rhapsody in Blue* as if we're a couple of rappers, jamming fast and to the beat and with a new kind of rhythm Gershwin never intended but probably wouldn't have minded. And I don't need to be in the cafeteria; I don't need to be anyplace else, because the music takes me to the only place I want to be right now. To the place where I am and have always been wholly me, the only church I've ever belonged to, the only place I've ever prayed.

And we're all good, everything is forgiven between Beethoven and me because this is the part of me that hasn't changed. In this moment I'm not defined by the other things, the things that happened to me, the things I didn't choose. This is the part of me that defines me for all time, for always. The thing I choose completely.

Chapter Thirty-Nine
PAY IT FORWARD

After French class that afternoon, Martin taps me on the shoulder. "Hey, you," he says.

"Hi."

"How're you doing?"

"Good," I say.

I know he wants to say more but doesn't know what to say. I don't know what to say either. Because now it's just us, no trial, no case, no protection.

"Amy wants to see you tonight," he says.

"She does?"

"Yeah, we'll all be there. Well, the board, at least. Laundry room. Eight o'clock?"

I nod. "Do I have to bring quarters this time?"

"I'll get your back," he says.

I think I should start getting my own back now, so I say, "It's okay, I'll bring them."

Later that night I stuff four quarters into my jeans pocket. But I don't bring laundry. The dryers work the same with or without clothes in them.

I run into T.S. on the stairs. She's bounding in, wearing soccer clothes. "I just had the best idea! I'm going to be a runner next year. Well, I'll try out, at least."

"For the Mockingbirds? Really?"

She nods excitedly. "Yes. I've been practicing my poker face for when the board gives me the sign-off to mark someone absent." Then she demonstrates with her best stony look.

"You're a shoo-in," I say.

"Besides, I'd kind of be defying the stereotype of freshmen and sophomores as runners. I'd be the senior, getting in there on the ground floor, mixing it up. A runner of the people," she says, and dashes up the stairs.

When I reach the laundry room, it's like I went back in time. Amy on the couch, Martin and Ilana on the floor. Trivial Pursuit spread out. I walk back to them. Amy's wearing a dark green V-neck T-shirt and jeans.

"Hey there," Amy says, a big smile on her face. I wonder if she is mad about my missing today's main event. If she is, I can handle it.

"Hi," I say.

"How are you?"

"Fine," I say.

"How was not going to lunch?" Ilana asks.

"I didn't want to be there," I say defensively. "I didn't think I needed to."

"You didn't," Amy says. "It's fine you weren't there. Do you want to hear how it went, though?"

I shake my head. "No interest."

Amy nods sagely. "Good for you."

Good for me? I guess it is.

"Are we playing?" I ask, gesturing to the game.

"Sure," Amy says, and rolls the die. A two. She moves her piece to the music category. "Alex, music! Your favorite."

She whips out a card but doesn't ask a question. Instead, she says, "First of all, I want to thank you for your courage. You held up well and you're really a great example. Actually, you're a rock star."

She continues, her blue eyes lighting up as she speaks. "Even though we had a few surprises"—she looks pointedly at Martin when she says this—"all in all I think our tradition of justice continued." Then she lightens, laughs a bit, and says, "Man, what a douche bag Carter is!"

Ilana laughs too. Martin doesn't.

"And I think you did every woman at this school a service by speaking up," Amy adds. Then she leans back on the couch, crosses her legs, one black Converse–clad foot kicking up and down absentmindedly as she speaks. "Back when we started, you asked me why I did this. Why I was in the Mockingbirds."

I nod, remembering the night she brought mac and cheese to my room.

"And I told you it worked," Amy adds. "Do you know how I knew that?"

"No," I say.

Amy twists around on the couch, her back to me. She turns her head back though, her eyes on mine as she pulls her ·shirt up. Right above her black bra strap is the word *Queer*, marked on her skin like a patchwork quilt. The first two letters are a scar, barely fading, still more pink than white. The last three are tattooed on. I shudder, feeling a phantom pain in my back too. But her back had a real blade on it, one that dug into her skin for two long letters. She pulls her shirt down and turns back to me. "Do you know Ellery Robinson?"

I shake my head, but the name sounds terribly familiar.

"She was a senior last year," Amy says. "She did this. Well, the first two letters. I finished what she started with a tattoo last summer."

Then it hits me, like a bullet. Ellery's name was in *To Kill a Mockingbird*. Under "Watch Your Back." The name I didn't know, the crime I didn't recognize.

"It happened in May after I'd asked her out on a date. I thought she liked girls. I was wrong. Or maybe she's just still in the closet. Either way, she didn't like it because I asked her in front of some of her friends. So she did this to me. She left her mark. So I sought out the Mockingbirds."

"But," I jump in, "you could have gone to the police with that!"

"You didn't go to the police," Ilana says matter-of-factly. "You came to us."

"But you have evidence there," I argue. "On your body! You could have gone to Ms. Vartan."

"And what good would it have done?" Amy asks, then gives me a kind sort of shrug. "The receiver didn't. The kids who weren't in the Honor Society didn't," she says, reminding us of the first cases the Mockingbirds tried. "And you didn't either. You know what the school's like. I came to the Mockingbirds and they helped."

"What happened to Ellery?" I ask.

Amy waves a hand in the air dismissively. "It was the end of the school year and the hearing was in late May, just a couple days before she graduated. Nothing happened to her, but it didn't matter. I did it to make a point. What she did was wrong."

"Obviously." I look to Ilana and Martin, wondering where their scars are. "So are you guys in the Mockingbirds because something happened to you?"

They both shake their heads, then Ilana says, "After I heard what Paul Oko did my freshman year I got involved. I've been involved the last three years. I'll miss this most when I go to Columbia next year."

Then it's Martin's turn. "You know my story. Besides, this is the only extracurricular group that really matters in the long run."

I look to Amy. "So you're the only one on the board who's been through a case yourself?"

Amy nods. "Yes. Because that's how we keep going."

"What do you mean?"

"We pay it forward."

"Meaning?" I ask slowly.

Amy smiles, that same sort of mesmerizing smile she's been flashing all semester. "It's not bad, Alex. It's just we have to ensure the group can keep going. And we do that by asking"—she pauses after the last word, giving it space—"those we help to take over. That's how we sustain the group's survival to keep doing good. And now," she continues, "it's my honor and privilege in the great tradition of the Mockingbirds, because we believe in justice and goodness and fairness, to ask you, Alex, to take over for me as the head of the Mockingbirds next year."

"Why not Martin? He loves the Mockingbirds."

"I can't," Martin says. "Remember when I told you I could never be the leader? This is why. You have to have been helped to be the leader."

From victim to ruler, powerless to powerful, that's how the Mockingbirds work.

"You never told me this. Casey...Casey never told me this," I stammer, because I kind of just want to go back to being me again.

Except life doesn't work that way. I have to go forward.

"Some things are on a need-to-know basis," Amy says in a reassuring tone.

"What about the others you helped? The junior whose roommates were cheating off him? Or the freshmen theater students who brought the others to you?" I ask. "And it's only March. Aren't there other cases? There could be other cases the rest of the year."

"Yes, but you're the one I want to carry the torch," Amy says proudly, as if she's asked me to be the godmother of a child or something. "I was hoping you'd want to."

Do I want to? It's never occurred to my uninvolved, apathetic heart to lead, to *want* to lead. But that girl is making room for this new one.

"Yes, I want to," I say, and the words don't feel foreign. They feel like a new beginning.

Amy claps happily. "Great, I'll teach you everything. You can observe for the next two months and learn how we work. As for next year, I'll be like an informal advisor to you. Ilana's off to college but Martin is eligible for one more term if you want to keep him on next year. However, there is one thing you'll have to do first.

"As you know," Amy continues, "Martin violated the rules by being involved with you. Members of the Mockingbirds can date one another, but we forbid involvement with people we're helping. It's a conflict of interest. It could hurt our credibility. Anyway, now that you're the leader-*elect,* I'm going to leave it up to you to decide whether he can stay on for another term or not."

I laugh. Like I'd say no, like I'd forbid him, like I'd be that kind of a person? He's Martin. I want him to have what he wants. He loves the Mockingbirds.

I look to Martin and my lips curl up in a smile, like we

have a secret, only now everyone knows it. "Do you want to stay on?" I ask curiously.

"Of course," he says, the sparkle in his eyes returning.

"Of course you can, then," I echo back.

"That's settled, then," Amy says with a knowing look. "I figured you'd say that and I was hoping he'd stay on too. That's why I had you decide, so he could."

Even black-and-white Amy has a shade of gray. Even Amy can bend the rules in her own way.

"If you want to get up to speed, you can read everything you need to know in here," Amy says, and taps her notebook, the one with the mockingbird on the cover. "I'll need it back in a few days. But when the school year ends it'll be all yours." She hands it to me. "Guard it with your life. It has all our rules and information on where records are kept."

I hold the slightly worn notebook as an archaeologist would a newly found treasure, one that has great and forbidding powers.

"Well, kids. I have to study," Amy says, and skips up.

"I don't," Ilana says smugly.

"You still have classes, Miss Early Admission to Columbia," Amy points out.

"Yeah, but they don't really matter."

Then they walk out of the laundry room and it's just Martin and me and the notebook. I rub my thumb on the edge of the pages, not ready to open it yet, not ready for it to spill its secrets for me. But I will be. Soon I will be.

"You're going to be a hard-ass ruler, aren't you?" he says playfully.

"Oh yeah. Just like I was back there."

"Thanks for letting me stay."

"Did you really think I was going to kick you out?"

Martin shrugs. "Honestly?"

"Well, yeah. Honestly."

"I didn't know what you were going to do."

"Why do you say that?"

"Because now that this is over, I feel like you don't need me anymore," he says.

I shake my head in answer, because Martin might once have been about need, but now he is about want. "Do you want to go to your room?" I suggest.

He shrugs his shoulders happily. "Sure. Sandeep's in the library anyway. But we don't have to if you don't want to."

"I *want* to. I don't want to be here in this laundry room anymore. I want to be in your room."

He holds out a hand and we head to his dorm. I keep the notebook tucked tightly under my arm the whole way. I walk into his room and it's the first time I've been alone in a boy's room since *that night*. But this boy's room I want to be in. So I close the door behind us. I place the notebook gently on a chair, knowing it's safe for now. I pull him to the bed, wrap my arms around his neck, and place my hands on his back.

Then I look at my hands on his back.

And it's different. It's completely different.

Because here with my hands on his back, there's no pretending, there's no getting through it, there's no getting past it. My hands are supposed to be here. They look right; they look good, like Beethoven, Mozart, Gershwin kind of good. Come to think of it, Liszt and Schumann too.

I close my eyes, but not before I catch one last glimpse of the mockingbird on my new notebook watching me.

Author's Note

Though *The Mockingbirds* is entirely fictional, I feel close to Alex. Like her, I was date-raped when I was a teenager.

It happened in the fall of 1990, just a few months into my freshman year at Brown University. Even now, I can still picture that night with a harsh kind of clarity. I can still remember how it felt to walk the long way to class and avoid the cafeteria at all costs so I wouldn't run into him. My entire schedule was dictated by staying far away from one boy.

I didn't want to spend the next four years of college living in fear, so I decided to do something about it. I pressed charges through the University Disciplinary Committee.

It wasn't an easy choice or an easy road. In fact, my case was one of the first heard at Brown after a very contentious time when it seemed to many that the school had looked the other way. Back then, many universities were largely ignoring women who were date-raped. Most schools didn't have systems in place to hear cases. Awareness programs didn't even register on their radar screens.

Naturally, many students at colleges all around the country were angry. Some women refused to stay silent. At Brown, women who had been date-raped started writing down the names of the perpetrators on a bathroom wall in the university library. But they didn't stop there. They went to the administration and demanded that the university step up. The *New York Times* even wrote about their efforts. It's amazing what a group of vocal students, the image of a long list of names of rapists on a bathroom wall, and a national newspaper article can do!

Brown began changing its own processes and procedures for handling date-rape cases, and I was able to file charges in this newly revised system, which operated a lot like a traditional court. Both students called witnesses and presented their sides to the disciplinary council through an "advocate," who acted as a lawyer. The system was similar to the one in *The Mockingbirds* except for one big difference: The administration knew of and supported the process. Cases were heard in one of the university buildings, rather than in a basement laundry room.

My case was tried one winter evening, and I testified in front of the council and in front of the boy.

The committee ruled in my favor, and he was suspended for a semester. I felt safe again.

So did other women who went on to press charges. I know because I heard from them. One night during my junior year, I got a phone call from a girl who'd been through the same thing. We met in her room and sat on the carpet while she told me what happened the night she was date-raped — the chilling effect it had on her studies, and what was said during the trial itself. It was as if we could finish each other's sentences.

I decided to keep speaking up. I wrote about my experiences for the school newspaper, and I heard from even more women who'd been date-raped and from others who hadn't but who were glad the school was finally listening *and* acting. Other universities took notice of what happened at Brown and also started changing their policies and systems for handling date rape. Things are different now, and schools are doing a better job of protecting women.

Looking back nearly twenty years later, I know my experience speaking up and listening to others was critical to my own healing and, eventually, forgiveness.

As you can probably tell, I'm a big believer in speaking up, but I am also keenly aware of how it can feel to believe you have no options—to have to resort to writing on the walls. *The Mockingbirds* is inspired by one of my favorite books, *To Kill a Mockingbird*, and born of that feeling of powerlessness I once felt. What if no one can protect us? What if the school can't help us? Can we help ourselves? Can we do the right thing?

I'd like to think the answer is yes.

Acknowledgments

I am fortunate to have the support of so very many incredible people. First and foremost, none of this would be possible without the guidance, dedication, and insane business savvy of Andy McNicol at William Morris Endeavor. Andy, you are a fierce matchmaker. Also at WME, a big thanks to Caroline D'Onofrio, an early champion, and to Anais Borja, who got to place "the call."

I have a thoroughly amazing and brilliant editor at Little, Brown in Nancy Conescu, who fought for this story. Nancy, you wanted the best for these characters, and under your direction *The Mockingbirds* became a much better book. I adore your commitment to excellence. Many thanks to everyone at Little, Brown who has supported this book from the start, including Jennifer Hunt, Megan Tingley, Lauren Hodge, and Melanie Chang.

I am deeply grateful for Amy Tipton, the first professional to see my potential, who is both a friend and a colleague.

I have learned so much about writing from Danelle McCafferty, whose early coaching and editorial insight left an imprint. Danelle, I still hear your voice in my head when I write.

My parents, Michael and Polly Whitney, instilled in me a love of learning, a persistent spirit, and the need to create. Thank you for teaching me to be relentless and expecting my best. My entire family has been endlessly supportive of my writing. Barbara, Kathy, and Jill, you buoyed me when I needed support and you read, read, read.

Classical music plays a big part in *The Mockingbirds*. Mark Owen at www.classicalreview.co.uk, as well as Brian Reinhart, Crystal Manich, and Petronel Malan, answered my very rudimentary piano questions and also introduced me to Franz Liszt's transcription of Beethoven's Ninth Symphony. Petronel especially made herself available as an ongoing resource on all matters of music, small and large. Any inaccuracies regarding music are solely mine. The website Beabondgrrl.com was useful for the Bond Girl scene.

Josyan McGregor checked and corrected the French in this novel. Greg Baumann taught me not to be married to my words.

When it comes to writing friends, I count myself lucky to have Suzanne Young, Amanda Morgan, Courtney Summers, Victoria Schwab, Bill Tancer, Gary Morgenstein, and my long-time friend Theresa Shaw in my camp. Amanda, you get a medal for reading pretty much every single draft of this book. Suz, you were my cheerleader. Courtney, there has never been a better line editor and brainstormer.

There to weather the tough times and celebrate the successes were Michelle Hay, DeeDee Taft, Ilene Braff, Cammi Bell, Wadooah Wali, Jim Maiella, Kristin Morelli, Jennifer Mai, Jerilyn Bliss, Bob Christie, Kika Kane, David Bloom, Clint Stinchcomb, Len Ostroff, and Jill Ciambriello.

Thanks to my friends at This Week in Media, Beet.TV, iMedia, Twitter, Facebook, and all the other places I hang out during my day job for letting me share this journey with you.

To those who stood by me when I stood up at age eighteen—Geoff, Gigi, Jamin, Shari, Josh, Elaine—I remain grateful.

My dogs have been my daily companions, logging countless hours by my side while I wrote. Lucy and Violet—best dogs ever!

My children deserve so many more thanks than I will ever be able to give, for letting me slip away to my stories and for wanting this just as much as I did. I love you both so much and am glad you take karate and gymnastics, so I can "sneak write" while you run, kick, and flip.

Most of all, I thank my husband, Jeff. You never once stopped believing, and I hope you know how very much that means to me. And if you don't, just check the dedication. (I couldn't help myself—the dog insisted on playing a role in it!)

Finally, this book would not be possible without its inspiration, Harper Lee's *To Kill a Mockingbird*. She said it best—it's about a code of honor and conduct.

Resources

Note: *The information below is current as of the date of publication.*

NATIONAL RESOURCES
The National Domestic Violence Hotline can be reached twenty-four hours a day, seven days a week, at 1-800-799-SAFE (7233). Find out more at www.ndvh.org.

The National Sexual Assault Hotline can be reached twenty-four hours a day, seven days a week, at 1-800-656-HOPE (4673). Find out more at www.rainn .org.

The National Center for Victims of Crime Helpline can be reached Monday through Friday, 8:30 AM to 8:30 PM Eastern time, at 1-800-FYI-CALL (394-2255). Find out more at www.ncvc.org.

For a list of state resources, visit www.womenshealth.gov/violence/state.

RESOURCES FOR EMPOWERING YOUNG WOMEN
Girls For A Change (GFC) is a national organization that empowers thousands of teen girls to create and lead social change. GFC provides girls with professional female role models, leadership training, and the inspiration to work together in teams to solve persistent societal problems in their communities. Visit GFC online at **www.girlsforachange.org**.

Girls Inc. is a national nonprofit youth organization dedicated to inspiring all girls to be strong, smart, and bold. Innovative programs help girls confront subtle societal messages about their value and potential, and prepare them to lead successful, independent, and fulfilling lives. Visit Girls Inc. online at **www.girlsinc.org**.

Girls International Forum (GIF) is a nonprofit organization created to empower girls to take action on issues affecting girls everywhere now and in their future. Visit GIF online at **www.girlsforum.org**.

WriteGirl is a nonprofit organization for high school girls that is centered on the craft of creative writing and empowerment through self-expression. Visit Write-Girl online at **www.writegirl.org**.